DIRTY FILTHY RICH LOVE

LAURELIN PAIGE

PAIGE PRESS LLC

© 2017 by Laurelin Paige

Cover: Tom Barnes and Laurelin Paige

ISBN: 978-1-942835-27-1

PROLOGUE

I BROUGHT the tumbler of scotch to my lips, taking another sip as the Frou Frou song playing from the Spotify app on my phone started up again. How many times could a song be listened to on repeat? If there was a limit, I was approaching mine.

I pressed my cheek against my bedroom window and watched the lonely street below. The glass was cold against my skin, a stark contrast to the liquor burning in my chest. Winter had set in just in time for the Thanksgiving holiday. The few people still out this late were well bundled in gloves and scarves, and hats pulled down over their ears.

I still didn't have enough winter wear. There'd been no need for warm gloves in L.A., and I'd only been in New York since September. My sister had already given me a hard time about it when she'd arrived earlier in the evening, and a shopping trip was on the agenda for the next day.

My wardrobe would soon be remedied. Audrey would make sure of that. In one night, she'd already rearranged my living room furniture and put up the rest of the framed photographs and knickknacks I hadn't bothered to unpack.

If only she could fix the inside of me as easily as she addressed the outside.

No, I had to be the one to fix this mess.

I thought back to the conversation I'd had with Audrey before she'd slipped off to bed in my guest room.

"Will you press charges?" she'd asked.

"I don't want to press charges." I wanted explanations. I wanted theories confirmed. I didn't want more distance between us.

I didn't want any distance at all.

She'd smiled as though she got it, and because she was my sister, maybe she did, even without me explaining. "So you'll go to France, then. Make him tell you what's up."

"He doesn't deserve that either. He can run all he wants. I'm not chasing. I have more respect for myself than that."

"Good. I respect you too." She'd laughed then. "Probably not the best idea to chase someone who's obviously been stalking you for ten years anyway."

"Probably not." Though I wasn't really worried about him. He was dangerous, yes. Dangerous *to me*. But he wouldn't hurt me. Not like that. Not the kind of hurt that anyone else could see.

"You'll figure it out," she'd said in the end. "You always do."

I knew what I had to do already. Just...being bold enough to do it.

Another sip of scotch. Another full listen to the old song on repeat.

This time when the silent pause came at the end, I put down my glass and reached over for the phone instead. I turned off the music, pulled up my contacts and only shivered slightly when I found his name.

Two weeks had passed. I didn't have to do this now.

But it might as well be now.

I hit the CALL button and waited.

It rang once. Twice. It was after midnight here. He'd just be waking up. Another ring. Was he alone? One more ring.

Then his voice.

His voicemail, actually. I hadn't exactly expected him to answer, and it was easier leaving a message.

Still, somehow it was disappointing. As though a small part of me had hoped he'd see my name and rush to hear my voice. Wouldn't I rush to answer if he'd been the one to call?

Maybe not.

Probably not.

The beep sounded and caught me off guard. But I was ready with what I wanted to say.

"Donovan. It's me. I know about the file you have on me. We should talk."

ONE

"THERE'S NOBODY HERE," Audrey said as we stepped out of my office.

It was Monday evening and wrapping things up after a hectic afternoon had taken longer than planned. It was hard enough getting everything done in a short holiday week. On top of that, I'd lost my weekend to visiting with my sister—time I would have usually spent behind my desk.

It had been three days now since Audrey had arrived.

Three days since I'd left the message for Donovan.

Three days and no return call.

But I wasn't thinking about that. Or rather, I was trying as hard as possible not to think about that. Trying as hard as possible not to let on how much it hurt.

Work was a good distraction. Audrey was an even better distraction.

"When you got here it was almost five," I said, locking my office door behind me. Thankfully, there was plenty to occupy her in the city while I worked. It would be a miracle if she got even a quarter of her agenda crossed off before she had to go back to school on Sunday. But even with the many other exciting items on her list, I'd convinced her to stop by my office so I could show her around.

More like so I could show off.

I glanced at the clock on the wall. "That was an hour ago. Most everyone's gone home now."

"Do you always work this late?" The question was accusatory.

"I usually work later." I didn't mention that part of the reason we'd stayed late tonight was because she'd had to tell me all about the bus tour she'd taken earlier in the day.

Crossing her arms over her chest, she glared in my direction. "Workaholic."

I rolled my eyes. "You're a workaholic too. Your work is just more artsy so you can more easily disguise it as a hobby. Come on." I threw my keys in my bag and hitched the strap on my shoulder. "Let me show you around."

She followed me to the main hallway. Out of habit, I glanced down the dark corridor leading to Donovan's office, feeling a pang in my chest before leading her in the opposite direction to the large open section of the executive floor. Usually, the floor-to-ceiling windows there would be a feature worth pointing out, but the sun had already set and the cleaning crew had turned on the lights so the glass just looked black.

Another light shone farther down the hall, and I steered us in that direction.

"Roxie," I exclaimed, when we came upon my boss's assistant gathering her things at her desk. "You're here late!"

"Just leaving. You caught me." Eyeing Audrey, she set her purse down and thrust her hand out, introducing herself before I had a chance. "I've heard wonderful stories about you. Sabrina is very proud of her sister."

"Thank you. Great to meet you," Audrey said, trying not to appear stunned by Roxie's brusque hospitality.

"You look alike," the Hungarian native said after studying us for a beat. "Light and dark versions."

Audrey and I laughed as we exchanged glances. She wasn't just a lighter version of me in coloring with her chestnut hair and almond eyes, but also in temperament. She was bubbly and romantic. I was serious and practical. She liked men who adored her and were into public displays of affection. I liked a man who enjoyed rape play and apparently had a serious problem with stalking.

It was something we joked about often.

"Night and day," I said.

"Chocolate and vanilla," Audrey agreed. "That's us."

"Is Weston in there?" I asked nodding to the office behind Roxie. The door was still open and the lights were on, but I didn't see him at his desk.

"No, but he be back any minute. You can wait inside for him." Roxie buttoned her coat and picked up her purse. "He in a good mood today. He won't mind."

We said our goodbyes and after Roxie went her way, I ushered Audrey into Weston's spacious corner office, switching off the light as we walked in.

The effect was immediate. "Holy bananas!" Audrey exclaimed. "This is insane!" She ran to the closest wall of glass and gazed out at the city. "It's an endless sea of lights! I bet you can see everything in the daytime."

"Not everything. But a lot." I stood back, watching her with a smile. My reaction to the view had been quite similar. It had been exhilarating, not just because of how much I could see, but because I finally felt like I was on top of it all.

And then Donovan had walked in, putting my new world in a spin. Reminding me it had been his world first.

Whatever. It was my world now. He wasn't here, and I was. I wasn't going anywhere.

Audrey craned to look farther out the window. "If this isn't everything then you're too greedy. Hey! It's the empire! Why isn't this your office?"

"It will be soon enough," Weston's baritone sounded behind me. "With the work she's producing."

I rolled my eyes while he came to stand next to me. "Oh, hush."

He frowned as though I'd offended him. "I'm serious. You're the first name on a short list to replace me if I ever leave."

Weston was a sweet talker. All the smart women knew it. Still, I was warmed by the compliment, even though it wasn't one that mattered. "You'll never leave," I said dismissively. "I hope you don't mind we were in here. I was showing my sister the view. This is Audrey."

The lighter, younger version of me had already abandoned the windows and was prowling toward us, her hands behind her back. "Let me guess—you're Weston."

Weston stuck his hands in his pockets and lifted his chin proudly. "You've told her about me."

"We're close." I watched apprehensively as Audrey circled my boss, sizing him up. I knew full well she wasn't evaluating him as my superior, which would have been embarrassing enough. No, she wanted to figure out what it was about him that had lured me into his bed for an entire weekend earlier in the year.

Not that it wasn't obvious—blue eyes, blond hair, built like he was a personal trainer rather than a CEO. He was eye candy for sure. Add the charm and a smart head on top of that?

Yeah, my panties dropped.

"Nice," she said appraisingly. "Whoa. Real nice," she said when she got to his backside. "Good job, sis."

Weston's eyes widened as he interpreted her comments. "Ah,

you've really told her about me." He turned his attention to my sister. "Maybe Sabrina didn't get a chance to tell you I'm involved with someone else now. I'm engaged."

"*Fake* engagement," Audrey corrected.

His head spun around to glare in my direction. "*Everything* about me. Wow."

"Audrey!" My face flushed. "She won't tell anyone. I promise." I shifted to scold her again. "That was supposed to be top secret."

Weston's engagement and impending marriage to Elizabeth Dyson was all an arrangement to get Elizabeth her trust fund money and to get Reach, Inc.—our company—access to an advertising firm in France she owned. Once married, Elizabeth would get her inheritance, sell the firm to the men, and the two would divorce.

At least that had been the plan.

That was supposedly why Donovan was in France—to pave the way for an easy merger. Only Weston and I knew it was really just an excuse to get away from me.

Very few people knew about the fake marriage—only Elizabeth, the five guys who owned Reach, Inc., me, and now, my sister.

Weston chuckled. "It's fine. I mean, you're not a secret spy for the Dyson's, are you?"

Audrey lifted a brow. "No."

"Then we're cool. Besides, it's not a fake engagement anymore. Or, it's not a fake relationship anyway."

She raised both brows now and looked at me accusingly. "Now I didn't hear this."

"Weston and Elizabeth like each other for real now. There. Are you happy?" I didn't give her time to respond. "It didn't have to do with me so I didn't fill you in," I added, unapologetically.

Also it wasn't really fun to talk about someone else being lucky in love when my own heart was hurting like it was.

She clapped her hands. "Of course I'm happy. I adore a good coupling! Tell us more, Weston."

"She left today to go to her grandmother's for Turkey Day," he said, directing this to me despite Audrey's eagerness. "I'm joining her Wednesday night, and we're supposed to do the whole pretend, pretend thing, but all I keep thinking is *I'm going to meet her grandmother*. This is the single most important person in her life. Which shouldn't matter because this is all temporary. But maybe it's not temporary. Maybe it's something more."

The last Weston had talked to me about his relationship with Elizabeth, they'd slept together. He hadn't said anything about *more*. "Then things are still going well?"

He sighed, running a hand through his hair. "Honestly, I don't know what things are. It's a mess. I want to wring her neck most of the time and she doesn't really seem to like me much either, but I kind of can't stand to be away from her for more than a day. Whatever that is, it's that."

"That's love," my sister said, her voice all swoony.

I groaned. "Audrey's a hopeless romantic. It's her only flaw."

But she made me think, too. Things between Donovan and I were a mess too. I wanted to wring his neck, and I was aching inside with him so far away. Was I so far in that I was in love with him?

Well, wasn't that going to be a bitch if it was the case? Because next time I saw him, I was planning on killing him.

"Weston, I can call my driver anytime you're ready to—" The man who'd walked in stopped when he saw us. "Oh, excuse me. I didn't realize you had company."

I stood up straighter, immediately on guard. I didn't know the man. His suit was expensive and he had brown wavy hair and a British accent. He appeared older than us by at least a dozen years, but was quite attractive and distinguished. What was odd was that a stranger was wandering the office halls after hours.

"I can go anytime," Weston said in reply. "But this is perfect. You haven't met Sabrina yet, have you?"

The man frowned. "Can't say that I have."

Weston shifted to me. "Sabrina, this is Dylan Locke. He's in the States this week to visit his son."

That explained things. Dylan Locke ran Reach's London office. He was one of the founders of the company. There were five of them in total—Nate Sinclair, Weston, Donovan, Dylan, and Cade Warren, who ran the Tokyo office.

"It's a real pleasure to meet you," I said, shaking his hand. "I'm the director of marketing strategy here."

"Ah, you took Robbie Wise's place when he came over to our office in London," Dylan said. "Robbie's fine at his job but he isn't as lovely as you. And he smells." He turned to Weston. "Is it entirely sexist if I say I think you got the better end of the deal?"

"Donovan got the better end of the deal actually." His subtext suggested he'd mentioned me to Dylan before. That this was his way of saying, *This is her. The one that Donovan was involved with.*

Which was fine. But I didn't want to talk about Donovan right now. "Weston, please..."

"He called earlier," he said soberly. Simply. As though he knew the words would knock the wind out of me, and still he'd thought the best way to present them was plainly and without a fuss.

"He called you?" I hoped no one noticed the hitch in my voice.

"He told me not to say anything."

"To anyone? Or to *me*?" Fuck, I shouldn't have asked. I didn't want to know. I *already* knew. If he'd wanted to talk to me he would have called *me*.

Weston lowered his head, confirming my suspicions. "I'm sorry."

It was sweet that he cared how I felt. And nice, I supposed, that he'd bothered to tell me about it at all. Though Weston and I had formed a friendship over the last several weeks, he was Donovan's friend before mine. He didn't owe me any loyalty.

I couldn't bring myself to thank him at that moment.

"I don't care," I said, when he took a step forward to comfort me. "He can do what he wants. I don't care anymore." Lies. But maybe if I kept saying it, someone would start believing it. Maybe even me.

And now things had gotten awkward.

"Hi! I'm Audrey. Sabrina's sister."

I wanted to shoot her a thank you glance for breaking the weird mood, but her attention was completely on Dylan. The way she flipped her hair and threw her shoulders back told me she wanted his attention on her too.

"I see the resemblance." Fortunately for Dylan, he kept his gaze on her eyes, the place any decent man in his forties should keep them when he meets a girl half his age.

If he'd looked anywhere else, we may have had to have some words, owner of my company or not.

"Do you work here as well?" he asked.

"Nope. Just getting the tour. It's my first time in the city. It's exciting."

Dylan seemed to be taken by surprise by her enthusiasm, though not exactly put off. "Yes. I'm sure it is exciting the first time."

"Been too long since your first time, Locke? Have you forgotten what it's like to get your cherry popped?" Weston teased.

"Apparently I've forgotten what it's like to spend an evening with you and your innuendos." The look he gave his partner made me think he'd appreciate those innuendos more if he weren't in mixed company. Spending time with Weston would be a lot more fun for the older man if he wasn't worrying about offending his young female employee and her even younger sister.

Which was why I didn't expect it when he next said, "We were just going to dinner. We'd love it if the two of you would join us."

TWO

"ART CONVERSATION?" Weston asked, an hour later, his fork paused mid-air.

Of course we'd accepted the invitation to dinner. Audrey seemed so smitten with Dylan's British dialect that she likely would have killed me if I'd suggested we do anything else. And I wouldn't have anyway. When your employers invite you somewhere, you try to go.

Though if I'd known the destination planned was Gaston's, I might have considered my options, for no other reason than I didn't want to be at a restaurant that Donovan owned.

Perhaps that was the reason I'd gotten so tipsy. I didn't know why the others had.

"Art *conservation*," Audrey repeated, over-enunciating in that way that told me she was also not quite sober. She was only a little more than a semester away from completing her master's at the University of Delaware in their art conservation program, and Dylan had just asked about her degree.

Weston swallowed his bite of foie de veau and nodded. "That

makes a lot more sense. Is that like the people who work in museums to preserve the paintings?"

"That's some of it. It's a little chemistry, a little archeology, a lot of art, a whole lot of art history. Not nearly as exciting as your jobs." She was way too modest, in my opinion.

"I'm not sure what Weston does day-to-day, but it sounds a hell of a lot more exciting than my job," Dylan said.

While Weston had gotten louder as the wine had poured, Dylan's lips had gotten looser. It was a great way to learn about the new man, actually. Though I'd only gleaned surface details—born in Southampton, lived in the US for a number of years, back to London, secretly loved Metallica, played electric bass in a local pub band—he was turning out to be quite fascinating.

"That's because you handle finance. There is nothing creative about finance," said Weston, obviously quite smug about the fact that he handled marketing.

"I think your father finds finance to be quite creative," Dylan retorted.

"Rumors. No one can prove anything." Weston took a swallow of wine. "But also why I don't work for him."

Donovan and Weston's fathers dominated the financial industry. I'd never gotten a straight story on why the guys had decided to go into advertising instead of following them in the family business.

This breadcrumb was one I ate up eagerly.

"Corruption at King-Kincaid?" I scooted my chair a little closer to him. "Am I allowed to ask?"

Laughing, he shooed me away with a soft pat of the back of his hand. "No. You are not allowed to ask."

I continued to stare at him. Apparently drinking made me shameless.

He let out a sigh. "It's nothing that hasn't already been suspected by someone at one point or another. Your guess is as good as mine. It was definitely one of the reasons that D and I wanted to do our own thing, though. So we can genuinely say we don't know."

While I doubted that Donovan ever preferred being in the dark, Weston probably truly did. "Well, that was smart, I suppose. And boring. Who's going to give me gossip now?"

I turned to my other employer. "What about you, Dylan? How did you end up part of Reach with these bozos?"

He smiled and wiped his mouth with his napkin. "I'd had previous experience managing operations at another advertising firm. Donovan wisely saw the need for another rational man to balance out the unruly ones."

"*Another* rational man? Who are you counting as the first?" I regretted the question immediately because I knew the answer was Donovan. He was the man who formed Reach. The one who brought everyone together. The impetus behind all of it.

So I didn't bother waiting for an answer. He was the one I really wanted to know about anyway whether I wanted to admit it or not. Might as well just go there. "How did you know Donovan? I don't really picture you running around in the same circles."

"Ha. No. We don't exactly," Dylan admitted. "We met years ago. I used to be married to the mother of his fiancé."

My skin went cold despite the alcohol warm in my blood. I hadn't been expecting that. "Amanda?"

"You know about her."

"Yeah. Donovan's told me." The bare bones anyway—that he had loved her, that he'd been obsessed with her, that he blamed himself for her death. He'd told me that she'd been trying to outrun the private investigator that he'd hired when she got in the accident that killed her. I'd been searching for more information on *her* when I'd found his file on *me*.

"He did?" Dylan was openly surprised. "That's good he's

talking about her. He tends to not mention her at all. He took her death very hard. As we all did. Sweet girl. So young."

I glanced at Weston, ready to let him jump in. But he seemed to be happy to let me be Donovan's spokesperson.

"I think he still takes it pretty hard," I said. Besides blaming himself, Donovan had told me he couldn't love anyone after her. Because of whatever it was he'd done to her. Which, if I had to guess without any real proof, looked a lot like what he'd done to me.

"Not surprising," Dylan said, disappointment in his tone. "Tortured son of a bitch. That relationship was doomed from the start."

"Why do you say that?" I tried not to sound too curious, not the easiest of tasks considering how desperate I was to know everything. Anything.

"He was too in love with her." He set his fork down and began pouring the last of the bottle of wine around the table.

Audrey frowned. "*Too* in love?" She said each word deliberately. "How can someone be *too* in love?"

"He obsessed over her." Dylan filled my glass, and I took a swallow. Okay, a gulp. "Knew everything about her. Cared everything about her. He hung the moon for her."

It was ten years ago and the woman was dead and still I ached with jealousy.

I shouldn't ask any more.

I couldn't stop myself. "Like, what did he do?"

God, I was so pathetic.

"Dylan," Weston leaned over to his partner. "She's. You know. With him." As if I wasn't sitting right there. As if I couldn't hear him talking.

"I'm not with him," I snapped a little too defensively. "He's in France. And I'm here. By no definition am I *with* Donovan." I pressed Dylan. "What did his too much love look like? Was it obvious?" *Did it look like what he does to me?*

Or, what he *did* to me. I had no reason to believe he was still having me followed and watched. No reason to believe he still cared about me at all.

Dylan seemed to consider Weston, but answered me anyway. "Not flagrantly, no. I'm sure most people didn't notice. It was subtle. The way he was always in control. Always a step ahead where she was concerned. I remember once she'd wanted this specific Tiffany bracelet. It was a piece the company didn't make anymore but she'd seen one up for a charity auction and had convinced her mother to try to bid for it. She failed. Her mother didn't try very hard, to be honest, and someone else bought it. Donovan found out and tracked down the person who'd bought it or something. A week later, Amanda had the bracelet."

Audrey sighed next to me. "That's actually quite romantic."

I concentrated on Dylan's eyes so that I didn't shoot daggers with mine at my sister for her obvious betrayal.

"Another time," he continued, almost as eager to share as I was to learn, "she'd gotten in an argument with her advisor at Harvard. A class she'd taken didn't count like she'd thought it would. It wasn't too long before her advisor was dismissed from the school on allegations of credit fraud."

Weston scoffed. "Are you saying that was Donovan too? Because I heard about that and there was nothing tying him to it."

Dylan shrugged. "King-Kincaid Financial couldn't alter credit reports? All I know is that Donovan didn't seem a bit surprised when it happened and Amanda's next advisor had no problem accepting her course credits. He also drove a brand new Jaguar. What do you want to bet his loan had been approved through a King-Kincaid bank?"

Weston shook his head, unconvinced.

But he hadn't seen the file on me. I had, and there were many things Donovan had done for me that had been just as extreme. And I wasn't his fiancée.

"And you think those were signs that he loved her?" I asked Dylan, desperate for those acts to mean something.

"Those are definitely signs that he loved her," Audrey said dreamily. She looked pointedly at me. "Anyone who did those things for someone else is obviously in love."

I ignored her. I already knew her opinion on the matter. Already knew what she hoped would happen between Donovan and I.

"Loved her too much," Dylan repeated. "If she'd lived, it wouldn't have worked out."

"You don't think so?" Weston asked. He'd always said that Amanda and Donovan had been the real deal.

"Because he'd eventually smother her?" I asked, making my own guesses.

"Because it's not real," Dylan said matter-of-factly.

"What isn't?" I asked, confused.

"The whole thing. Love. Marriage. It's an outdated arrangement. Amanda seemed to know what was what and had reasonable expectations. But Donovan bought into the pitch. He bought into the *feelings*."

"You don't believe love is real." Audrey's statement was a mix of shock and disbelief.

Weston waved his hand in the air. "Don't listen to him, Audrey. He's a bitter divorced old man."

"Bitter, yes. Divorced, thank God. Old..." Dylan scanned the faces of his companions. "Well, maybe that's true in the present company. It doesn't mean I'm wrong. In fact, by default, I'm the wisest one here, experience points and all, and I'm telling you: love's not real. It's a card trick. It's a marketing ploy. It's a term we use to pretty up a rather dull and worn out social system built entirely on the tradition of coupling off. Weston's fake relationship is probably the smartest arrangement I've seen in a long time. That's about as true as it gets, kid. Enjoy it for what it is and stop trying to figure out the mess. There's nothing to figure out. It's messy because it's fiction. And for some insane reason, modern western civilization has decided that the messier the story, the better the tale."

Audrey finished off her wine and set down her glass. "That was really sad."

Sad but probably wise, I thought. I was already twenty-seven years old and had never come close to finding a relationship that I would have called the real deal. Donovan had been the closest I'd come, and that was only because he'd been the first man to force me to be honest sexually. We hadn't had a chance to get any further than that. Maybe there wasn't any further to go.

"Wow Dylan," Weston said, setting down his napkin. "That was a major downer. You're not getting enough pussy, man. Should we talk about your Tinder options across the pond?"

Dylan glared at Weston. "Perhaps this isn't the most polite conversation for our dinner guests."

Weston glared right on back. "And trampling all over America's number one reason for living is?"

"You know what?" I turned to Weston. "You're whipped." He wouldn't have defended romantic relationships a month before. Elizabeth Dyson had gotten under his skin.

He shook his head. "You're on his side. Of course."

I wanted to disagree, for Audrey's sake. Say I still believed in the happily ever after. Our parents were dead. I was her example of what adulthood should be. I didn't want her to grow up to be a cynic.

But after everything tonight and the last few weeks, I didn't know if I believed in happily ever after anymore.

And she was already grown up.

"I'm not on anyone's side," I said. "I'm on my own side."

Dylan raised his wine glass toward me in a toast. "Thatta girl."

We'd finished our meal by then. Weston charged the bill to a company account, then stood and helped me with my chair.

"Go on ahead," I said to the men. "I need to use the restroom before we leave. Audrey?"

"I'm good." More like she didn't want to miss a single second with Dylan. I wanted to attribute her fun and flirty nature to her age, but I had never been that easy with people. It made me jealous sometimes.

But also, good for her.

"We'll meet you by the elevators?" Weston asked. "We'll get your coat."

"Be right there."

On my way back from the restrooms, I took a different pathway through the restaurant than I had on the way there. I hadn't planned it. I'd just gotten my directions mixed up and suddenly I was walking past the table that Donovan always used when he ate at the restaurant. It was a total accident.

At least, I told myself it was an accident.

It was definitely an accident that I happened to catch the eye of the woman dining there as I passed by.

"Sun?" I'd only met her once, but her face was unforgettable. She was a model who Donovan used to sleep with. "What a surprise."

She smiled in greeting, her eyes darting from me to the companion across from her.

I turned to follow her gaze and found myself face-to-face with Donovan Kincaid.

THREE

THE GROUND beneath me suddenly felt unsteady, as though the floor had been yanked away. My mouth gaped, but nothing came out. No words. No sounds.

He was here.

With fucking Sun, the most gorgeous woman on the planet.

All I could do was stare.

"This isn't what it looks like," Donovan said quickly. The long blink of his eyes afterward and the quiet curse under his breath told me he understood how trite and canned he sounded.

At least he was ruffled too.

It made it possible for me to speak. "It doesn't matter what it looks like. It doesn't matter what it actually is. I don't even care." And then, just to prove how catty I was, I said, "*Weston*'s waiting for me. So if you'll excuse me. Nice to see you again, Sun."

I left before he could say anything else. Before he could touch me. Before he could look at me another second with those fucking green-brown eyes that saw everything inside me. Those eyes made me confess secrets I never wanted to share. Those eyes made me *be* and feel and try, and how the fuck could he see all that he'd seen and still be able to look away so goddamn easily?

"Sabrina!"

My legs almost gave out when he called after me. Even now, even after this, there was a part of me that wanted to go to him. Just to talk. To show him that running wasn't the way to handle conflict.

But I didn't look back.

Because I didn't want to do this here.

And I'd turned around too many times for him before.

I realized a second later that walking away was going to be a short-lived victory. As soon as I got to the front of the restaurant, I'd have to wait for the elevator. He'd catch me there.

He'd also catch Weston and Dylan, though. Maybe they could distract him. Or keep me from causing a scene.

But somehow I got lucky.

The elevator opened as I approached. Weston caught my eye, and I nodded for him to go ahead and hold it. Then I slipped in and turned around in time to see Donovan's face just as the doors were closing.

"Was that...?" Weston asked when the car started to move.

"Yep." I was shaking so bad, even that one word sounded tremulous.

"That was Donovan?" Apparently Dylan had seen him too. "I thought I was seeing things."

"Donovan was here? *Your* Donovan?"

I glared at Audrey. "He's not *my* Donovan." Especially not now. "He was with someone else."

"I'm sorry," she said quietly, helping me on with my coat. "That must have been a shock."

"I didn't even know he was in the States." I looked down at my trembling hands. I hugged myself to still them.

"Uh," Weston said, already sounding guilty. "I probably should have told you..."

My head snapped up. "You knew he was here?"

"When he called earlier he said he'd just landed. I told him your sister was visiting. I didn't know he was going to be at Gaston's. Hell, at that point, I didn't even know we were going to be at Gaston's."

I stared at him incredulously. "Why didn't you say he was here?"

"He told me not to. Remember?" A simple reminder that he'd betrayed Donovan to tell me about the phone call at all.

The sting of that snub returned on top of the newer pain. "Right. Probably because he didn't want me to know he was in town seeing his lover, Sun." My voice cracked. "That was sure polite of him."

He shook his head. "Sun is *not* his lover."

Yeah well, Weston also didn't want to believe his father was corrupt or that Donovan had framed a college advisor.

I wasn't going to argue about it. "Whatever she is, he's with her tonight." *And not me.*

Well, I didn't want to see him either.

The elevator stopped. The doors opened, and I hustled out, half expecting to see that Donovan had run down the stairs to meet us. But the lobby was empty.

"I've texted my driver," Dylan said. "We can try to make a speedy getaway, if that helps."

"That does. Thank you."

Outside, I pulled my coat tighter around me and paced the sidewalk, keeping one eye out for Dylan's limo and the other eye on the doors to the building in case Donovan showed up. The cold temperature sobered me up and left me with a throbbing headache.

"Here's the car," Dylan said as the limo drove toward us a few short minutes later.

This was it. We'd done it. Escaped. He hadn't even come after me. If I was disappointed about that, I wasn't admitting it to anyone.

But no sooner had the car parked then I heard my name again.

"Sabrina, wait!"

All of us turned together to see Donovan rushing toward us from the building. Rushing toward *me*.

"Oh, Christ," I mumbled. Though inside I felt a little relieved.

And also a whole lot pissed off. And hurt. So hurt.

Dylan spoke first, greeting the man who had no business looking as outrageously handsome as he did. "Donovan!"

It took Donovan a second to pull his eyes from me to the man at my side. "Dylan?" He seemed almost unable to process his friend's presence. "I didn't realize you were in town."

"I'm visiting Aaron. He has the holiday weekend. I'll be in the office tomorrow, though." He snuck a glance at me, and I realized this banal small talk was meant to diffuse the situation.

Thank you, I mouthed silently.

Not that Donovan was deterred for long. "We can catch up tomorrow, then. If you don't mind, though, I need to just borrow Sabrina for the rest of the evening. Don't worry. I'll drive her home."

Before I knew what was happening, he had his hand on my back and was pivoting me away from everyone else.

"Hold on," Audrey ordered. "She's not going anywhere with you unless she says that's what she wants."

Donovan dropped his hand and turned to her. "You're protective of your sister. That's very sweet. We haven't met, Audrey, but I work with everyone here."

She lifted her chin and took a step forward. "I know who you are too, Donovan. Don't try to bulldoze me."

I bit back a proud giggle.

Donovan took a beat, and I could tell he was trying to remain calm. "Then if you know who I am, you likely also understand that I need to talk to her."

"I don't want to talk to you," I barked. Which wasn't true. I wanted to talk to him so bad I'd called him all the way in France.

"Then you'll listen." He shifted his focus back to my sister. "I promise to have her back to you in one piece."

I didn't understand why he was so insistent to talk now. Why did he care? He was already dating other women. Defending himself was needless. It wasn't like we had a relationship to save.

But we would need to talk at some point, and before Audrey agreed it was a good idea, she'd have to approve of Donovan's motives.

"You need to talk to her as her *boss*?" she asked, obviously poking at his choice to introduce himself as one of my coworkers.

"I need to talk to her as her boyfriend," Donovan corrected.

"Whoa," Weston said, echoing my thoughts. Audrey grinned, the traitor.

"You are *not* my boyfriend," I growled, though deep down inside of me I already knew I was going to replay those words over and over again later on. Analyze them. Dissect them. Cut them up and see if there was any possible meaning to them besides as a tactic to grab my attention.

Donovan let out an impatient huff of air. "Then I need to talk to you as the guy you've been fucking."

Dylan cringed visibly.

I fumed. "Not anymore. You made sure that was over when—"

"Sabrina," Donovan interrupted, his low authoritative tone impossible to ignore. "Give Audrey the keys to your apartment and tell her you'll meet her at home in an hour. I'm sure that you trust both Weston and Dylan to make sure she gets there safely."

God, I hated everything about him right then. The way he'd inserted himself into my evening plans. The way he made my skin prickle and buzz. The way he made me think I might actually be someone who mattered to him.

It was too cold to continue standing on the curb arguing, and it wasn't fair to keep everyone. I was giving in.

I met Audrey's eyes. I didn't have to say anything for her to know what I was asking.

"I'm fine," she said confidently. "You should go."

"I'll be less than an hour," I said, handing her my apartment key. I wasn't sure I could keep that promise, but I made it anyway.

She shook her head, nonverbally telling me not to worry. "You have the History channel. That's enough entertainment to last me quite a while."

I waited until the three of them were in the back of the limo, and the door was shut. Then I took a deep breath, turned away from the curb, and stepped toward Donovan.

Donovan. Fucking Donovan in his tailored suit and five o'clock shadow.

Walking toward him was like deciding to walk through fire when I was already covered with first-degree burns. It hurt like I couldn't describe.

But I was a girl who lived in darkness. His fire sure looked bright.

He took my arm. It was a polite gesture, and the pressure of his hand felt comforting through my coat, but I pulled away immediately.

"Don't touch me. We can talk, but you don't get to touch me."

I know I didn't imagine the flicker of pain I saw in his eyes even if he refused to acknowledge it.

"We'll just talk then." He gestured to his Jag, which had pulled up along the sidewalk ahead while we'd argued. "After you."

FOUR

HALFWAY TO DONOVAN'S CAR, I realized we were leaving without Sun.

Not that I minded. But I sure as hell was going to make a point to mention it.

"You just abandoned your date?" I didn't want to seem like I cared about his response, but I glanced over at him from the corner of my eye.

His mouth tightened. "It was a business dinner. Not a date. We came separately. She'll get her own ride home."

That did make me fairly gleeful. Whatever happened tonight, at least I wouldn't have to wonder if Sun would be dropping her panties for Donovan in the backseat like she had the last time he'd driven her home from one of their dates.

I knew because he'd later told me about it in detail. It was months ago, and I still writhed with jealousy when I thought about it.

At the car, Donovan reached down to open the back door, and then held it so I could get in.

I paused at the curb and met his eyes, the door a barrier

between us. "So no going down on Sun in the car tonight then. What a pity."

He didn't flinch. "You're the one I'm putting in a car, Sabrina. If that's how you want to spend the drive, I'm more than happy to oblige."

A shiver ran down my spine that I hoped he didn't see.

"I'm getting in the car to talk." But maybe I didn't mean that.

Did I? How strong could I be in Donovan's presence? Could I be as strong as I needed to be?

"Get in the car then."

I guessed we'd find out.

I slid across the backseat until I got to the other side and buckled myself in. It was a sad excuse for a barricade, but I pretended it would keep me safe. As long as I stayed on my side, and he stayed on his side, everything would be fine.

But then he got in next to me, his long legs taking so much more space, his very being taking up even more space. He *filled* the car. There was no escaping him. He was everywhere—beside me, in my skin, on my tongue. I couldn't breathe without inhaling him.

I needed to do or say something to remind myself what the situation was.

"Just because I'm leaving with you doesn't change the fact that you came with her," I said, bitterly as the car pulled away from the curb.

He studied me a moment. "I came here for you."

"Because you just happened to know I'd be at Gaston's tonight? That makes perfect sense. Bring along your girlfriend. That will show Sabrina what's what."

"I came *to the States* for you."

My heart tripped.

It had to be bullshit. "And you proved it by going out with Sun the minute you got here. I completely believe you."

"I didn't go out with her romantically," he said tersely. "I called Weston when I landed. He said your sister was in town. I didn't want to interrupt your evening. I planned to see you tomorrow. Meanwhile, I needed to negotiate some terms with Sun. We've hired her to be the face of the campaign for the merger in Europe, and she's playing hardball with some additional requests."

"So you thought you could wine, dine, sixty—"

He cut me off sharply. "It was dinner, and I'm in the goddamn car with *you*. I came back *for you*."

I looked over at him. The car was dark, but there was enough light from the street to see his face. His crushingly handsome face. He seemed tired. Jet-lagged, probably. His scruff was maybe older than a day. His jaw was also tight, like it got when he was frustrated. I wanted to reach out and run my hand along the muscle. Wanted to feel the warmth of his skin burn my fingers.

I didn't really have any reason not to believe him.

He'd called her first, but his reason made sense. If he'd really wanted to be with Sun instead of me, wouldn't he be with her now? If he said he'd come back to the States for me...

I'd been so wrapped up with Sun I'd forgotten about the rest. This was the first time we'd been together without the veil. I knew about the file. And he knew that I knew. There were so many bigger things than Sun between us, and if he'd come back for me, was it to...explain? To try to make up a lie? To convince me not to press charges for invasion of privacy?

"Why?" I asked outright. "Why did you come back for me?"

"Don't play dumb, Sabrina. *You* called *me*."

"I called you, but there could be a dozen different ways to interpret your response when you show up like this. You could have just called me back."

"I thought this discussion deserved a face to face, don't you?"

His tone was controlled and even and a little bit threatening, and I wondered for a moment if I should be scared of him.

But I was always a little scared of him. Didn't I like that about him?

I crossed my legs, trying to ignore the pulse between my legs. "Face to face so you could seduce me into believing whatever you wanted me to believe?" If that was his plan, he needed to come up with a new one. I had my seatbelt on and everything.

"I thought it would be easier to talk honestly."

Something in my chest pushed out, like it was reaching. Like there was a part of me that was still holding out hope that we could put everything out on the table, and there'd be a way in there that we could be together.

But I knew better.

A of all, given the lengths he'd gone to, putting together my file over the years, I couldn't be entirely sure he wasn't a psychopath.

B of all, I'd already tried the honest approach and it had failed.

Besides, I knew the truth. I didn't need him to admit it, and I didn't believe for one minute that he would. But if he wanted to play the honesty game, then fuck it, I'd play his game.

I'd tell him his truth before he had a chance to tell me any other story.

I twisted in my seat so I could stare him dead in the face. "You want honesty? How about this for honesty—I know what it means. That you have all that stuff on me. I already know what it means, so don't bother trying to come up with some story to excuse it."

He tilted his head in my direction, humoring me. "Really. What does it mean?"

I stared him right in the eye. "You love me."

"I do."

He'd spoken them no louder than anything else he'd said, and yet those two words echoed through the car like he'd shouted them into a canyon.

"Oh," I said. My chest felt heavy. And hot. I was hot. "Oh," I said again.

I looked down, suddenly feeling dizzy and shaky and a little like I was going to throw up.

"Can you handle that?"

I looked back up at him, jolting when I met his eyes again. "I don't know." *Fuck.* I hated that he could see how vulnerable he made me. "I mean. You don't even know me."

He raised a brow. "Are you sure?"

"A file of papers about me isn't knowing me."

"I realize that." He leaned closer, close enough that I could smell the faint scent of his aftershave. "But I knew you then and I know you now. And I know."

My entire body vibrated in agreement, as though the cells within me were able to admit something that my brain refused to acknowledge.

Donovan Kincaid loved me.

I'd believed it, deep down, I'd thought it was the only thing that made sense. He'd loved Amanda and he'd done the same things with her. The pieces added up. It was a rational conclusion.

But emotionally I hadn't been so sure.

I dropped my gaze. My head was rushing back through everything, putting this new frame on every experience we'd shared together, seeing it through the lens of *he loves me*, trying to feel if it made sense.

Two weeks ago all I'd wanted was a chance that he might feel *more* one day.

He'd hurt me. Pushed me away. Pissed me off.

"If you're so in love with me, why did you insist that a relationship between us was impossible?"

He pressed his lips together. "You've discovered that I've been stalking you and meddling in your personal life for the last ten years, and you're concerned about why I didn't want to have a relationship?"

When he put it that way, it did sound kind of ridiculous.

I chuckled. I was losing it. *Yeah, he's a psychopath, but it's okay because he loves me.* I wanted him to tell me more about how he felt about me, but he was right. I needed to get my priorities straight.

I looked away for a moment to get my bearings. "I'm concerned about all that too." There'd been so many things I'd wanted to say about that when I'd called him. "I'm really bothered by it. I'm mad. I'm confused. I'm freaked out. I feel...violated."

"Of course you do. You should feel all those things." He wasn't patronizing, but not apologetic either.

"You're damn right I should feel those things." I was irked at his lack of remorse. "I think I hate you for it."

"Do you?" he challenged.

I opened my mouth to answer when he added, "Remember it's no fun if you're not honest."

"I hate you for it," I repeated, softer this time. I closed my eyes, scared of the next part, the words I hadn't said aloud to anyone, not even Audrey. "But I'm also fascinated. That you're fascinated with *me*. That does things to me. It makes me feel safe. And wanted. And looked after. It turns me on." I opened my eyes and looked at him. "I don't mean sexually." But I did mean sexually too. "Does that mean I'm crazy?"

He laughed softly. "Probably."

He stretched his legs out, more relaxed than he had been when we'd first gotten in the car. He scrubbed his hand over his face and let out a sigh. "I forget how much I can trust you. I should have done that."

There it was. Remorse. He felt remorse.

"Before running away to France?" I clarified.

"I didn't...run away. Exactly." He smiled ever so slightly, and my pulse beat double-time.

"You did run away. Because you didn't want me to find out about that file?" I was still putting pieces together, slipping them in where they seemed to fit best.

"When Amanda found out about *her* file, she was the one running away."

"So you thought you'd be the one to run away first this time?"

"I don't know, Sabrina," he said with a frustrated huff. "Yes." After he'd thought about it a second. "Okay, yes." He looked somewhere in the distance. "I don't trust how I would handle losing you. It's better if the ties are cut on my terms. It's safer for both of us. For you, especially."

"But you're here..."

His eyes returned to mine. "Because you called."

"Which means you're willing to consider the possibility of *not* losing me."

He searched my face. "Is that a possibility? *Not* losing you? Even knowing what you know now?"

Fuck, we weren't ever actually together and here we were talking in such enormity. Donovan had done that. Had put all this weight on our entire relationship by having been there for parts of my life I hadn't realized he'd ever been part of.

So even though I wanted to crawl into his lap or kneel at his feet, even though I ached to touch him, I couldn't. Not yet.

"I need to process this," I said, not allowing myself to sound regretful.

"Whatever you need. Just tell me." His eyes darted to my lips, and I wondered if he'd kiss me.

Or I wished he'd kiss me.

But kisses weren't what I needed. "I need answers. There's so much I still don't understand."

"I'll tell you anything you want to know."

I studied his eyes. "I think you actually mean that."

"If you're going to test me, Sabrina, just test me." He sounded almost annoyed, and I had to bite back a laugh. He'd tested me so many times, but turn the tables on him, and he couldn't take the heat.

"Not now. Now I need to go home." I glanced out the window. We'd been driving around Midtown aimlessly while we'd talked, but we were only a few blocks away from my apartment. "You should drop me off."

Donovan waited a beat as though he wished I'd asked for something else. But then he leaned forward. "Next time around, John."

"I won't be able to get out to open her door here with the snow piles," the driver warned.

"That's fine," I said, before Donovan could say otherwise.

We were quiet for the next few minutes, but both of us were right there, present, aware of each other's every move. Every breath. I wondered what he was thinking. But I couldn't ask because I didn't have room for anymore on top of all that I was thinking.

And then we were almost at my apartment, and I already missed him.

"We can talk after Audrey's gone," I told him, feeling terrible that I wished it wasn't a week away.

"When does she leave?" Was I imagining how eager he sounded?

"Sunday morning at ten-thirty."

"I'll be at your place at ten-thirty-one."

I chuckled. It felt good to laugh. No, it felt good to have a date planned, to have something to look forward to, to know that we weren't yet done.

I peeked over at him and found him staring at me. Really staring.

"What?" I asked suddenly self-conscious.

"I'm thinking about asking if I can kiss you."

My heart did the sort of acrobatic flip it hadn't done since I was a teenager.

God I wanted that kiss.

But I wasn't ready to admit that. "You say you know me, and all of a sudden you think I want to be asked?"

He smirked. With that devil's smirk that had taunted and teased me for so many weeks.

The car pulled over to the side of the road, angled next to a bank of snow.

I undid my seatbelt.

Then Donovan undid *his* seatbelt. And he leaned across me, caging me in without touching me. I was suddenly too hot again. My heart beat too loud. My breathing grew faster as I waited for him to bend down and press his lips to mine.

But all he did was pull the lever on the door and push it open.

My eyes pricked unexpectedly. I was going to blame it on the rush of cold air. It didn't matter. This was a start. We'd made a start.

I put one foot on the ground and bent forward to step out. Suddenly Donovan's hand was cupping my face, pulling me back, and when I turned, my mouth crashed into his.

I sighed into his kiss, letting his eager lips tell me all the things he hadn't had time to say. Letting his mouth remind me that he'd confessed feelings I had yet to absorb. Letting his tongue make dirty filthy promises of nights to come.

When he broke the kiss—much too soon—I stared at him with glossy eyes.

"You hold the cards right now, Sabrina," he said, his nose almost touching mine. "But don't begin to think I've forgotten who's in charge."

He brushed his lips across mine once more, then pulled away entirely. "You better go before your sister worries."

I was in the building and he'd driven away before I was sure I remembered how to breathe.

FIVE

"HE KISSED YOU?" I did not think that I'd be the one saying that tonight.

Turned out I wasn't the only Lind sister who'd gotten kissed on the way home by a Reach executive.

"More like *I* kissed *him*," Audrey said dreamily.

"You *kissed* my boss?" Jesus, I hadn't even gotten my coat hung up before she'd attacked me with this information, let alone gotten a chance to tell her anything about my car ride with Donovan.

She pulled her knees under her on the couch. "Dylan is not actually your boss. He's more like your boss's equal, if you want to be technical."

I threw my coat on the back of the sofa next to her along with my purse. Forget making it to a hanger; it wasn't happening. With my hands free, I put a fist on my hip. "If you want to be technical, he's old enough to be your father."

She rolled her eyes. "He is not. He's just experienced and wise."

"He's twenty years older than you."

"Maybe I have a thing for dads. Don't knock my kink. I don't knock yours."

That shut me up for a second. I hadn't actually ever told her my kink, but Audrey wasn't stupid. She could probably figure out enough to guess that I at least liked a good spanking.

"Fine." I dropped my hand. "I won't knock the age difference." I circled around to the front of the couch and plopped down next to her. "I don't actually care what you're into anyway, as long as it's consensual." It was the truth, too. I wasn't just blowing sunshine up her ass. "I just don't want you getting hurt. Dylan doesn't seem into relationships. You get that, right? Not to mention that you live on entirely different continents."

"It was just a kiss! God," she huffed, shifting so her legs were out in front of her. "I'm not planning to marry the guy."

"Just a kiss." I sounded skeptical only because, with Audrey, it was never *just a kiss*. The minute she decided she liked a guy, she *liked* a guy. She started doodling their initials on the back of napkins. She changed her Facebook status to *In a Relationship*. She gave her heart when she swapped saliva. She didn't do one-night stands. She didn't do casual hook-ups. She didn't do *just a kiss*.

Audrey sighed up at me with doe eyes. "I felt bad for the guy. All that doom and gloom. 'Love's dead. Grump, grump.' He needed something nice for a change."

Uh huh. "So you thought you'd kiss him and that would show him. Make him magically believe in hearts and romance again?"

"Shut up," she said with a pout.

That's what I was afraid of. Just a kiss and now she was head over heels for Dylan-love-is-a-myth-Locke. Thank God she was leaving in six days. And he was leaving. She might not even get a chance to see him again.

Audrey sank further into the couch beside me. "You think I'm naïve."

I looked over at my baby sister, ready to tell her all my worries, but stopped myself at the last second. I couldn't tell her to change how she felt any more than she could tell me to change how I feel about Donovan.

And she'd never try to tell me to change how I feel in the first place. She'd just encourage me to feel it.

So instead I kissed her hair. "I think you're amazing."

She peered up at me and grinned. It had been the right thing to say. Score a sister point for me.

She nudged me with her shoulder. "Hey. Tell me what happened with Donovan. He wasn't on a date with that woman, was he?" She said it with certainty, as if she had an inside scoop.

"He said he wasn't." I threw my feet up on the coffee table in front of us. "How did you know?"

She shrugged. "The way he looked at you." She followed me with her feet on the table too. "What else?"

"He said he came back to the States for me."

"To talk to you? To be with you?"

"That's what I don't know yet. We have more to talk about, obviously." I pulled a lock of hair down and twirled it between my fingers, replaying everything he'd said. There was so much I wanted to remember. So much I wanted to obsess over and hold too preciously.

"He said he loved me," I said softly. Well, he hadn't actually said it. I'd said it, and he'd confirmed. Was that the same thing? I was counting it as the same thing.

"Wow. That's big." Her excitement was hard to contain, but she was doing a pretty good job being cool about it. For me, I guessed. Probably trying to figure out how I felt about it before she let loose her own enthusiasm.

I nodded. It *was* big. But...

"But you already knew that he loved you," Audrey said, filling in the blank that I couldn't.

"Yeah. I did." That was the problem. Everything he'd said had only confirmed things I'd already suspected were true. I wasn't any closer to a solution where he was concerned. And it was going to be another several days before we got a chance to make any more progress.

"Still," Audrey said, "it had to be nice to hear."

I had a list of arguments why *nice* didn't matter. Then I remembered that I should just feel it.

"Yeah," I said, genuinely. "It's really nice."

———

I'D HEARD Donovan tell Dylan he'd be in the office the next day, I just hadn't really thought about it until it *was* the next day. Suddenly I was nervous and anxious and totally unprepared. All night I'd tossed and turned, and that was believing there were several more nights before I'd see him again. Now that there was a possibility I'd see him sooner, I was going out of my mind.

I settled on the simplest game plan—I'd hide.

My office was nowhere near Donovan's and since I was taking Wednesday off to spend with Audrey, I had a lot of work to keep me busy anyway. I just had to stay on task, holed up in my little corner, and everything would be good.

The plan worked well for the most part. By late afternoon, I'd gotten all my must-complete projects done and had gone the whole day without leaving my office.

All I had left to do was drop off some forms that needed to be signed off on. Forms that couldn't be emailed because they contained client payment information.

I walked down to the edge of the hall and glanced toward Donovan's office. It was dark, which should have made me feel relieved. And it did. Mostly. I didn't even know if he'd actually

made it in like he said he'd planned to. Now I wouldn't know at
all because I'd been too chicken to look for him.

I was seriously ridiculous.

I wanted to see him; I didn't want to see him. It was
confusing even to me.

Anyway, Weston's office was in the opposite direction and it
didn't matter if Donovan was in or not.

So I headed toward Weston's.

Halfway there, I passed the glass-walled conference room
and realized it wasn't empty. Weston, Nate, and Dylan were
sitting around the far end of the long table. And standing behind
them, as though he might have just walked in and hadn't sat yet,
was Donovan.

As soon as I saw them, I snapped my head away, back to the
hallway in front of me. They hadn't seen me. They were
wrapped up in their conversation. I didn't need to interrupt them.

God, my stomach was fluttering like a teenager's. Just
because Donovan was nearby. I didn't want to see him, but I
wanted him to see me. My face was flushed, and I couldn't
think and—

"Sabrina," Weston called through the open door, eyeing the
stack of files in my hands. "Are those for me?"

Adrenaline shot through me at the shock of being "caught." I
looked down at the pile, having almost forgotten what my original
agenda had been. "I was dropping them off at your office."

He used two fingers to gesture me toward him. "I'll
take them."

My heart was beating so loud I could hear it, and shit, I
suddenly couldn't remember how to walk in heels. Somehow I
made it to him without falling on my face, and without obviously
staring at Donovan the entire time.

"Executive meeting?" I asked as if speaking would make me
look somehow more collected than I was.

"Just shooting the shit, really," Weston said.

"Ah." Dumb, but fine. It was all fine. I'd gotten through it just fine.

But after I set the files next to Weston, I looked up, and Donovan was right across the table from me, staring at me in that way he always did. That way that saw into me and knew me.

It always rattled me when he looked at me like that. But today when he saw me, I remembered that he loved what he saw and the butterflies fluttered again inside me.

"Hi," I said quietly. Like a dork. Like a lovesick kid.

The corners of his lips pressed up just slightly, just for me. If we were alone I'd kiss him there. One kiss on each corner before—

"Donovan," Nate said, interrupting my daydream. "I meant to tell you—I saw the early footage from the France campaign. Sun Le Chen looks stunning."

And then it was all gone—the butterfly flutters, the racing heart, Donovan's smile. Left was stark, bleak reality.

"Sun was with you in France?" My voice was even because this wasn't shocking. This made much more sense than any of the amazing things he'd said last night.

He didn't answer. The silence in the room was answer enough.

"Excuse me, fellows." I turned and walked on steady feet out of the room, but not before hearing Donovan mumble "fuck" under his breath.

Unlike at the restaurant, he was right on my heels. "Sabrina, stop."

I didn't want to stop. But I could feel the eyes of the other men on me, and who knew who else was watching from their offices? So I stopped.

"What, Donovan?" I said through gritted teeth. "Go ahead

and tell me what you're going to say. You're going to make sure I hear it one way or another anyway."

"I explained last night that she is the spokeswoman—"

I interrupted him, my voice escalating. "You said you were negotiating terms. I didn't know she'd been with you all along."

"She wasn't *with me*." He was obviously frustrated. "She was—"

I glanced toward the conference room. Weston wasn't even pretending not to gawk. "People are watching us."

"I don't care who's watching us."

"*I* care."

Of course he didn't care. He owned the goddamn place. I was the one who'd be laughed at in this situation. Not him. Never him.

Half a beat passed. Then without any warning, he grabbed me by the elbow and roughly escorted me down the hall. At the first open room, he dragged me inside and shut the door behind him. After a second, he locked it.

I folded my arms across my chest and fumed, my eyes locked on his. At least now we were in the privacy of the copy room, and I could say what I really wanted to say. Ask what I really wanted to ask. "Did you fuck her?"

"I haven't fucked anyone since I last fucked you. And before that the only woman I'd been with was you since you showed up in town." He stood in front of the closed door and braced his hands in the frame, barricading me from trying to go past him.

"You were only in France two weeks. Seems her campaign got arranged awfully quickly to get her there that fast. And then she got back to the States when you did? That's awfully convenient." Models were scheduled months in advance. They didn't do shoots at the drop of a hat unless they were fucking someone.

But he had an answer for this too. "She'd been booked to do the campaign since Reach proposed to Elizabeth for Weston. You can look up the contract information yourself and check out the date. She was already in France when I got there. She left a week ago."

Okay. More plausible. "Still gave you lots of time together there."

"We weren't together at all." He took a step toward me. "What else? Ask me what you want to know."

I inhaled then exhaled, my cheek twitching. "Did you kiss her? Stick your face between her legs?"

He shook his head sharply. "I barely saw her off the set. And I never touched her."

God, it was maddening! There was no reason not to believe him. We weren't even technically together, and even without a commitment, all signs had pointed to him being faithful.

It was just that we were unbalanced in our relationship in general. We were on a teeter-totter with him solid on the ground, and me dangling in the air. He had so much more of the picture than I did, and it left me to grasp and reach at anything and everything.

"Too bad I didn't hire a PI to follow you around Europe," I said, acting petty and rash. "I have to ask you these questions instead of reading a report. How am I supposed to know you're not lying about all of this?"

"I guess you'll have to trust me."

I pouted. "Well that fucking sucks."

"That does suck. Having to trust me." He sounded a little annoyed and a whole lot dangerous.

He took another step toward me, and I started to step back, but there was a counter behind me, so I had to stay put. And maybe I wanted to stay put. He was only a foot and a half away from me now.

"But I haven't lied to you, Sabrina." His gaze never left mine.

"And I'm not lying when I say I don't give a fuck about anybody else's cunt but yours."

We stood there, not touching, not speaking, each of us standing our ground. But I had no basis to keep my position, and it felt like he'd won so much already.

I couldn't back down.

"Prove it," I said.

His expression flared, his eyes growing dark and mean, and I realized what I'd done. Donovan wasn't one to be provoked.

I'd just invited the devil out to play.

"Unzip your skirt and put your hands on the counter behind you."

My heart hammered and my belly twisted. My panties were embarrassingly drenched all of a sudden, and I *wanted* him. But I stood completely still. "I didn't—"

He cut me off. "No talking and unzip your skirt."

My mouth slammed shut, but I still didn't move. If I moved, I'd be asking for this. But if I talked, I'd be telling him to stop.

And I didn't want this to stop.

I just didn't want to ask for it because I was stubborn and stupid for wanting him in the first place.

But he would give it to me without the words, without my obedience. Because he knew me. He knew what I needed.

With his eyes never leaving mine, he found the zipper at the side of my waist and pulled it down. After that, the skirt was loose enough that all he had to do was tug it once and it fell easily to my feet. He nudged his knee against my inner leg, and automatically I stepped that foot out of the pool of material on the floor, widening my stance.

He gave a nod of praise, sending a jolt of warmth through my entire body.

Then he bent down in front of me.

Suddenly, breathing was harder than it should have been. My

chest moved up and down, air passed through my mouth, but I couldn't get enough of it to my lungs.

And he hadn't even touched me yet.

The sight of him alone—Donovan Kincaid, one of the most powerful men in the world, down on his knees in his black Ermenegildo Zegna suit—it was overwhelming and erotic, and by the time he put his hand at the back of my knee, I was already trembling.

He smiled up at me with his devil's smile, trailing his fingers up the back of my thigh, higher and higher still, to the round curve of my ass. His constant gaze kept my eyes pinned to his, and I knew he could read every thought, every emotion that ran through me. He knew exactly what he did to me with this caress of my skin, with that pinch of my flesh.

Finally breaking eye contact, Donovan brought his other hand around me and squeezed both of my ass cheeks as he buried his nose into the crotch of my white lace panties. My knees buckled when he inhaled audibly, and now I had to reach for the counter behind me. Just to keep myself from collapsing.

"I'm going to believe you wore these for me," he said before licking slowly up the center panel.

It wasn't a question so I didn't comment. Besides, I was too busy stifling a moan. If he'd made me answer—if I'd been able to speak—I'd have told him he was full of himself. It wouldn't have been a lie, but it wasn't all the truth. Of course I'd worn them for him. There was a chance I'd see him today, and I dressed thinking about that, thinking about all the dirty filthy things he might do to me if I let him.

I just hadn't actually planned to let him.

Keep telling yourself that, Sabrina.

"Fuck, you're already wet." He said this so quietly I was almost convinced it was for himself, but the gleam in his eyes told me differently. It told me I wasn't fooling anyone. I was as at least as turned on as he was whether I wanted to admit it out loud or not—and judging from the way he kept having to adjust himself, he was pretty goddamned turned on.

He sucked my clit into his mouth through my panties, and this time I couldn't keep my moan inside. There'd been too much want, too much need, and he sucked eagerly, driving me quickly to a frenzy.

But the material was an unwanted barricade. Like a condom, dulling the sensation, and I wasn't getting where I needed to be. Not all the way. I was still dangling. Always dangling.

Just when I thought I couldn't take it any longer, he dragged his mouth lower, and found my hole. With his thumb now on my clit, he used his tongue, to push the fabric of my panties inside me.

I jerked forward, caught off guard by how fucking good it felt, my hands landing on his shoulders.

Immediately, he sat back. "Hands behind you."

The rules, right.

Did he want my hands behind me because it was part of the game? Or because he didn't want me touching him? Or just because he said so?

It didn't matter. All that mattered was that he finished, that he made me come, and I was far enough along now that I didn't care about what I conceded in giving him my obedience.

I put my hands on the counter.

His mouth was back on me in an instant. This time he nudged my panties aside with his nose and resumed his attack on my bare cunt in earnest. With one hand wrapped around the back of my thigh, his other hand used the bunched material of my panties to cause extra friction on my clit.

He pinned my eyes once more, and maybe that was the most erotic part of the whole thing—the way he looked at me. The way he always looked at me.

I was whimpering now, bucking into his face, so close to coming.

Suddenly the door handle behind him jiggled as though someone was trying to get in.

I tensed in absolute panic, but Donovan didn't ease up at all.

A second later, the person knocked. "Anyone in there?"

I recognized the voice. It was Ted from creative. And Jesus, I was so close to coming.

"Melissa?" Ted called out to someone. "Do you have a key to the copy room? Does anyone know where a key is?"

I tried to push Donovan away, but his grip on me tightened. Without ceasing the massage of my clit, he took a break with his mouth long enough to say, "I'm not stopping until you come. So either relax and let it happen or be prepared to give them a show."

I knew enough about Donovan to not question his sincerity on this.

Giving my eyes back to him, I forced myself to ignore the commotion outside the door and focused only on the feeling of his mouth. Of his lips. Of his tongue. Of his fingers, and the expert way they played me—like he knew how to make me sing; like he had me memorized.

I didn't think I could relax enough, that I could come with Ted outside and the door locked and the lights off, but suddenly my orgasm shot through me like a freight train at a railroad crossing. Even though I knew it was coming, its speed still surprised me. I saw stars, my knees buckled, and a burst of pleasure ricocheted through my body. I didn't recognize the wail coming from me, low and unfurling like a ribbon of sound. Immediately, Donovan jumped to his feet to swallow my cry with a kiss, his hand still rubbing me through my climax below, and all I kept thinking was *yes, yes, yes, yes,* yes!

I was still shaking when he broke away a minute later.

Thankfully, I still had my hands on the counter behind me or I might have slumped to the floor. Donovan bent down and straightened my panties, then went to the floor, and picked up my skirt. I stepped into it, moving my hands to his shoulders for support while he pulled it up and fastened the zipper.

He didn't complain about the touch this time, and even gave me a half-smile as he wiped at the makeup under my eye. He leaned in and kissed me once more, hard, his tongue sweeping deep inside me. As deep as I wanted him to be. Even after he'd just made me come.

"I love the way your jealousy tastes," he said.

I frowned, remembering all of a sudden how this whole interaction started. "I'm not sure that—"

The doorknob twisted. Donovan dropped his hands and moved away from me just as the door opened and Ted walked in.

"You guys were in here the whole time?" he asked, confused. "The door was locked. I had to find a key."

"I didn't realize you were trying to get in," Donovan said without apology. "It's all yours."

He slipped out around Ted before he could say anything else. Before *I* could say anything else.

Maybe it was for the best. I didn't know that Donovan wanted to hear what I had to say anyway.

SIX

I SPENT the next day devoted to touring the town with my sister. I'd only lived in New York since September and hadn't made much effort to see any sights beyond those tied to spots used in the marketing campaigns I'd put together. Before that, the only other trip I'd taken to The Big Apple had been spent in Weston's bed. It was time that was remedied.

Together, we'd hit Macy's and much of the fashion district over the weekend. Today we hit One World Trade Center, The Met, and Rockefeller Center. It was warm enough that Audrey managed to convince me to get on the ice skating rink. I fell several times and didn't last long before calling it quits, but I laughed a lot more than I'd expected, despite the aches and bruises the adventure earned me.

Outside the office, it was easier to pretend that there weren't other things weighing on my mind. That Donovan didn't occupy my every waking thought. That every joke I made and every smile I gave wasn't laced with him, as though he had been grafted onto my DNA and every part of me contained a fragment of him.

I thought I did a pretty good job of hiding it, anyway. If I didn't, it wasn't until the intermission of the Rockettes' Christmas Spectacular that Audrey said anything about it.

"Is it a new thing? Or just all the old things?" she asked.

"Huh?" I'd been lost in my head, sure I must have missed the first part of what she'd said.

"You've been staring blankly at the stage for the past several minutes. And there's nothing happening up there at the moment. I'm guessing it's Donovan that's on your brain. Is it a new thing he did that's bothering you? Or all the old stuff?" Before I could answer, she clarified. "The old stuff is enough, by the way. I'm just curious."

I groaned and threw my head back on the seat. Which hurt more than I'd expected. So I groaned again. "Am I that obvious? Have I been a terrible drag all day?"

"No," she laughed. "You've been awesome. Now spill."

I grabbed a lock of hair and twisted it around my finger. "It's the old stuff. But there's new stuff too." I hadn't told her what had happened the day before, and I didn't plan on telling her. Not all of it, at least. "I found out that Sun—the woman from Gaston's—was in France with him."

"Not *with him,* with him, though. Right? Working together probably." She was so certain. It was enviable how certain she could be.

I studied her, wondering if she'd developed psychic powers while away at college that I was unaware of. "How do you know that?"

"I told you how. He came after you, Bri. He ran out of that restaurant for you. He looked at you like if you didn't hear him out he was going to be lost for a long time."

Oh, right. My sister wasn't a psychic. She was a *romantic.*

I closed my eyes so that I didn't roll them. It wasn't that I didn't believe what she said. I just couldn't base truths in our relationship on how he *looked* at me.

I couldn't base them on anything physical. Which was the current problem.

I opened my eyes. "Okay, yes. He said she was there for work," I admitted. "And then I..." I hesitated, looking for a way to convey the situation without telling her the actual situation. When he'd knelt in front of me and brought me to a mind-blowing orgasm with his tongue. "I let him...*kiss*...me." Yeah. That was a good way to frame it.

She tilted her head. "You let him kiss you? Why is that a problem?"

"It was a really serious kiss." I watched her to see if she understood. "Serious enough that he might think things are better with us then they are."

"Ah. I see." Her face got inexplicably red. "One of those kinds of kisses."

I didn't know exactly what kind of kiss she was thinking of, or what *kisses* she'd experienced herself to start her fidgeting the way she was, but I had a feeling she got what I was talking about.

"Well, you're just going to have to tell him the situation then," she said. "Set him straight." It was something she'd never do herself if she was in my shoes, but I would, and we both knew it.

"Set him straight," I echoed as the lights dimmed for the second act of the show. "Yep. That's what I have to do."

I might have already known that's what I needed to do. But doing so would require reaching out to Donovan.

Again.

LIKE LAST TIME, I waited until Audrey had gone off to the guestroom for the night. With a glass of scotch in hand and wearing nothing but a T-shirt and panties, I curled up under the covers with my phone.

After the show at Radio City Music Hall, Audrey and I had gone out for drinks at a piano bar. It was late now. Past two-thirty. Before when I'd called Donovan, it had been morning his local time. It was too late to call tonight.

But I could text.

Can you call me soon? We need to talk. It was embarrassing how long it took me to come up with those nine words. I pushed SEND, dropped my cell in my lap and sat back against the headboard to take a sip of my drink. Hopefully that would get him to call. If not tomorrow, which was Thanksgiving, then the next day. I didn't want to get my hopes up too high. The last time I'd texted him, he hadn't responded at all.

Thinking about the possibility of him not responding this time made me need to take another sip.

And then my phone started ringing in my lap.

I answered it quickly before it woke Audrey.

"You missed me," Donovan said, his voice as smooth as the Macallan 12 Year I was drinking.

My chest felt warm and fluttery. "What are you doing up?"

"What are *you* doing up?"

"Don't you already know?" I teased.

"Touché." There was a smile in his tone. "I'm nursing a scotch and talking to my girlfriend on the phone."

I suddenly felt dizzy, like I'd fall off the bed. I wrapped the fingers of my free hand tightly into the comforter. "You can't keep calling me your girlfriend."

"Because you're not? Or because you'd prefer a different term?"

"Because I—" I broke off. He always threw me like this. I didn't want to answer. I didn't *know* the answer. "Because I don't think we should be talking about that right now."

He let a full second go by. Then two.

"Fine," he conceded. "What *should* we be talking about?"

I said a silent prayer of gratitude, thankful to have been given the reins. "Yesterday." Then, because I did not want to start arguing about Sun Le Chen again, I clarified. "We need to talk about what happened in the copy room." I took another sip of my drink. I needed it.

"Ah. The copy room." His chair creaked like it was made of leather. A recliner? A desk chair? I didn't know. "I assure you, Ted doesn't know anything. He thinks he knows. He doesn't."

"That's not what I'm worried about." Though, now I kind of was.

"What *are* you worried about, Sabrina?" He didn't sound curious—he sounded annoyed. As though he already knew the answer to his question, but he had to go through the procedure of asking before he could challenge the response.

I didn't like that feeling. The feeling that he was two steps ahead of me.

But there was no turning back now.

I took a deep breath. "I'm worried that because I didn't stop you, I let you think that you can use sex to fix this. Fix us."

"I see." The reply was tight.

"And you can't. You can't use sex to fix this." There. I'd said it.

I swirled the liquid in my glass, waiting for him to say something. Anything.

But he sat silent, and I had to nudge him. "Are you going to say something?"

"Okay."

"Okay?" It hadn't sounded like he was challenging me, but it was so hard to figure out what a person truly meant from a two syllable word. "Can I have more than an okay?"

"I'm actually impressed you made it more than a day before you let this bother you."

And I was impressed that I thought for a minute he wouldn't be a dick about this.

"I am not predictable," I grumbled. Though admittedly, I might have given him grief about sex at times in the past.

But that wasn't this. This was different.

He chuckled. "I never implied that you were."

"You're implying that you knew I'd eventually complain about it," I huffed.

"*Are* you complaining?"

The low rumble of his question made me shiver. Add to that the memory of his hands on my thighs, his eyes pinned on mine, his mouth buried in my pussy...

"No." Except it never should have happened. "Yes. It won't fix things."

"But did you enjoy it?" Of course he wouldn't let me get away without the exact truth.

I closed my eyes as if that would make it easier to give this to him. "You know I did," I whispered.

"I just wasn't sure you remembered."

I bit back a groan of frustration. Donovan was not an easy person to interact with, but I wasn't a cakewalk either. I had my own issues. I was too proud. Too serious. And I had a borderline unhealthy comfort level with the kind of sex I liked.

We were both works in progress. I needed to be better about remembering that.

I set my drink down and pulled my knees to my chest. "I do remember," I said, softer now. "Which is why it took so long to make myself do the right thing and call. I want you, Donovan. I always want you. But we have to sort things out before anything like that can happen again. It can't be what we use to make this better."

"Okay." There was that damn two-syllable response again.

"I'm serious," I said, solemnly.

"All right. Got it." Without missing a beat he moved on to a new subject. "Where's your sister?"

"In bed. In the other room." I still wasn't sure if we were on the same page or not.

"Good. Now." There was a rustle like he was shifting the phone to his other ear. "What was your favorite part of riding my face?"

"Oh my God." Against my will, blood rushed to my lower regions. "Did you hear me, Donovan? We can't do this."

"I heard you." Unconcerned. As though he hadn't just been talking about eating me out.

The calmer he was, the more worked up I got. "You're not taking me seriously!"

"What did I do?" he asked innocently. "I just want to hear you tell me what you liked most about having your cunt pressed up against my face. Then I can tell you what I liked most. Would you rather I go first?"

"So basically you want to have phone sex." I pressed my thighs together, wishing I didn't want that as well.

I could hear the shrug in his voice. "I might pull out my cock later. Depends on how good you make the details."

"Donovan!" I rubbed my hand across my forehead, trying to convince myself I wasn't tempted. But I was tempted. And was it really that big of a deal? If we just talked about how good it felt to come with his fingers inside me pressing at just the right spot?

My resistance was waning.

But this relationship—whatever this relationship was turning out to be—was important to me. So I made another attempt at keeping my ground. "This can't be anything real if sex is the only thing you want from me," I told him pointedly.

"Think about it and tell me if I'm the only one who seems to want just sex from this relationship," he said just as pointedly.

I wrinkled my face, about to protest. Then I did think about it. Thought about the fact that I'd been involved with him in a pretty much sex-only relationship for less than two months. Even when I'd known him back in college, every thought I'd had about him, every instinct that had drawn me toward him had been sexual.

Donovan on the other hand, had noticed me before I'd ever really noticed him. He'd stayed involved with me for over ten years. He'd been there. Watching. Interfering. Manipulating. But he hadn't even tried to take advantage of me when I'd been most vulnerable—when he'd rescued me from being raped by Theo Sheridan.

Donovan was right. I was the one who appeared to be only interested in him physically. It was a blow to the gut to realize that so much I'd perceived about us was a misconception.

And it made me feel terrible.

It wasn't quite that simple, though. "To be fair," I said, trying to make myself feel better, "since I've been in New York, you haven't made anything else seem like an option."

"That is fair," he agreed. His breath came so clearly through the phone. I wished it were his thoughts, that I could hear what was in his head.

Then he told me. "I thought that somehow if I just fucked you it would be enough."

"Me too." That was exactly it. It wasn't that sex had been all I'd wanted from Donovan—it was that I'd thought that if I at least had that, I could live without the rest. "I thought that it would be enough if I, uh, did that too."

"Say it."

"Say what?" But I knew what he wanted to hear.

"No games, Sabrina," he said, impatiently.

"If I *fucked* you. Are you happy?"

"I'm hard." And so fucking smug.

"God, you're so..." I trailed off, too infuriated to find the words I wanted.

But as always, he wouldn't let that stand. "I'm so...what? You act like you're mad, but you also act like you like it, so tell me what it is that I am?"

"I don't know what you are!" That was the problem. I had no fucking idea.

I took a deep breath, and then more calmly repeated, "I don't know. Whatever it is, I can't stop coming back to look. I can't stop coming back, wanting you to tell me what it is that I am too."

I didn't know why I said it. Maybe because it was dark and we were on the phone, or because I was lonely, or because I really wanted him to know everything inside me.

Whatever the reason, I'd said it. It was out there. I couldn't take it back.

He was quiet a minute, and I imagined him stretched out in that leather armchair, I'd decided—his legs propped up on an ottoman in an office I'd never seen. He had to have a place like that in his apartment. A place where he was completely comfortable. Just one of many Donovan rooms I'd never seen.

He let a beat pass, and it didn't feel awkward because it was so full.

Then he asked, "Remember when you applied for that internship at BellCorp the final year of your graduate program?"

Of course I remembered, but how did he know about it?

Oh, yeah. He knew everything about me.

It was irksome, mostly because I didn't know what he knew and what he didn't, not because I minded that he knew things. I didn't really have anything to hide. It was also irritating because sometimes he'd made my only options seem silly and insignificant.

"You mean the graduate program at the *little school* that I attended after leaving Harvard? *That* internship?" I asked, bluntly.

"Yes, Sabrina, I've been a dick. Let's make sure we don't forget that."

"I won't." It was a small victory, but it was my turn to feel smug.

"Now can we talk about the internship?"

"I didn't get it." I'd been fairly disgruntled about it at the time. BellCorp was a financial industry giant and their internship always went to the top student in the master's program, which was me. Somehow, though, I'd been overlooked, and given a position at Citi Health while BellCorp's internship had gone to Abraham Decker, the cocky know-it-all who actually didn't know shit, but you definitely couldn't tell him that after he scored Bell-Corp. His ego had barely fit into a room before that.

The animosity hadn't lasted too long however, because two months into the year-long position, it came out that several Bell-Corp executives had been involved in insider trading. Abraham Decker spent the rest of his internship trying to help the marketing team put the best spin on the situation rather than learning how to run a successful firm.

My internship, on the other hand, had gone amazingly well. The company was in a growth phase and I'd been part of several campaigns. Citi Health had even earned a statewide community award that my boss had credited in major part to me.

"Actually, you did get it," Donovan said.

"Uh. What?" Because I heard him. Just...what?

"You did get it. But I called in a favor and asked them not to give it to you and they listened."

"Uh, what?" I asked again. And this was a favor to him?

"I know BellCorp's vice-president—they do a lot of business with King-Kincaid. I also knew they were about to go down for that insider trading scandal. When they did, I didn't think it would be good for your budding career to be caught up in it. Plus, Jeremy Shotts, the guy at the Colorado office, is a major blowhard who likes to fuck the pretty interns."

"I can take care of myself around execs with grabby hands," I snapped defensively, though I was pretty sure my track record didn't speak in my favor.

"Jeremy Shotts wasn't the reason I made the call, Sabrina," he said, annoyance underlining his tone. "Denying him was a bonus. Did you hear any of the rest of the story?"

"Yes. I heard you." I chewed the inside of my lip, trying to decide how I felt about this new information.

No, that was a lie. I knew how I felt. I felt good. I felt really good. Protected and looked out for and...loved. Things I hadn't felt in a long time. Sure, Audrey loved me, and she'd go to the ends of the earth for me. But not like that. Not fiercely. Not violently. Not to extremes. Not because she didn't care enough, but because that wasn't how she cared for people in general.

But Donovan did.

It was dazzling.

His love dazzled me.

It was rich and fierce and dazzling.

I could also name at least ten women right off the bat without thinking too hard who would tell me this was sick. That I was a victim of this or that misogynistic/patriarchal agenda. That I was weak. That I was malleable. Blah, blah, blah bad feminist.

"Stop thinking too hard, Sabrina," he said when a whole minute had gone by in silence.

I shook my head. "I'm sorry."

I didn't know what else to say. There was so much I wanted to say, but like the reasons he shouldn't call me 'girlfriend,' there were reasons I shouldn't talk about being dazzled. They weren't words for right now.

So I gave him what I could. "I guess I owe you a thank you."

He let out a frustrated sigh. "That's not why I told you about that."

"Then why did you?" I asked, just as frustrated.

"You wanted to know what you are."

"Okay."

"What you are is mine."

If there were such a thing as floating and sinking all at once, that was what I felt when I heard those words. Like I was one of the beloved giant cartoon characters that would be filled with helium and floated through the city in today's Macy's parade, and at the same time like someone who had just been thrown in a cold ocean with an anchor tied to her feet.

Mine.

His.

It was an answer to everything and nothing all at once. Something that seemed so unsure. Something that seemed so, so certain.

Could it be this easy?

I didn't know. I just didn't know.

"Finish your scotch and go to bed, Sabrina," he said breaking the silence. "You're not going to get any more of this figured out tonight. We'll talk more later."

"Okay," I said, still dazed. "Goodnight."

"Goodnight."

I put down my phone and picked up my tumbler, and wondered for a solid five minutes if I should text him back and ask him if he'd actually *known* I was drinking scotch too, or if he'd just guessed.

But I didn't because I wasn't sure yet if I cared what the answer was.

SEVEN

THE THINGS DONOVAN had said to me in the early hours of that morning stayed with me through the next day. So much of it was meaningless banter, but some of it was so poignant, so significant, that I played those words on repeat in my head.

What you are is mine.

I pulled that phrase out like a little pet. Stroked it and fed it. Listened to it purr. *Mine. Mine. Mine.*

I wondered how much he'd done behind my back. The story about BellCorp was a good one. It made me feel better about knowing him. But how many other stories like that were there? Would I feel the same about all of them?

I still didn't know if he was someone I could truly love.

But I was surer than ever that I wanted to find out.

We needed to talk. Really talk. And we would as soon as Audrey was gone. But a real relationship between the two of us wasn't just going to depend on what he had to say about the file he had on me. I couldn't pretend that was the only issue between us. I still didn't know him at all.

And then there was the idea that I only wanted him for sex. If

I wanted that to not be true, I needed to show it. To Donovan, but also to myself.

Friday morning, before leaving the apartment for another day in the city with my sister, I gathered the courage to call him once again.

"There's this thing we do every year," I said, pacing the living room with nervous energy. "This lasagna dinner tradition on the Saturday after Thanksgiving. Do you already know about this?"

"I can honestly tell you that I have no idea what you're talking about."

"Oh. Okay." It made me relax a little to realize there were still things about me that he had yet to learn. "Well, like I said, it's this Lind family tradition. I'm going to cook lasagna and there will be garlic bread and tiramisu—"

He interrupted me. "*You're* going to cook?"

This I expected him to know. Lind women were exceptional, bright, ambitious women. But neither of us could cook. We'd gone out for Thanksgiving because of our lack of skills in the kitchen. Also what was the point of making a big meal for two people?

But while our Thanksgiving was less conventional, we'd been sure to keep our lasagna dinner tradition intact. The custom had been passed down from our mother, always set for the Saturday of the last week of November. And while neither Audrey nor I were good behind a stove, this was the one dish we could both cook without burning the house down.

"It's not a big thing," I said defensively. "It's really just one main dish. Don't expect it to be amazing or anything. And we won't be alone. Audrey will be there, of course."

"Sabrina. Is this your version of introducing me to the parents?"

There he was again, one step ahead of me. I hadn't thought of it like that, but now that he'd put it in those terms, yes. That's exactly what this was.

I suddenly had to sit down.

"This is just something we do every year," I lied, unable to admit the truth out loud. "And since you're under the impression that I'm only interested in you for your—" I stopped.

He'd said something while I was talking, and I'd missed it.

"What was that?" I asked.

"I said I'll be there. Just tell me the time." He even sounded like he was looking forward to it.

"Awesome." My stomach had flutters and I couldn't stop grinning. Or shaking. "Seven o'clock."

"It's a date."

"HOW DID you spend your Thanksgiving, Donovan?" Audrey asked, as she filled the water goblets on the table.

I listened to the conversation from the kitchen as I pulled the food out of the oven. The evening had gone well so far, despite my anxiety about it. Donovan had shown up on time with an expensive bottle of red wine, looking more than amazing in his gray slacks and maroon sweater. I'd been an awkward hostess, too nervous to know how to handle small talk with a man who knew everything about me, who'd been inside me, who'd said I belonged to him.

So instead of trying to talk about the weather or rehash the Macy's Day Parade, I'd hidden in the kitchen, pretending that the salad needed more tossing and the vinaigrette needed whisking. I'd only come out once to grab a glass of wine after Donovan had popped the cork. He and Audrey had moved to sit around the dining room table, and from what I could see and what I'd overheard, my sister seemed to have the conversation more than handled.

But dinner was done now. I'd have to sit at the same table with him and hope I could contain the torrent of emotions that kept me flustered and prevented me from having coherent thoughts.

"I had dinner at my parents' apartment on the Upper East Side," Donovan answered casually.

"Is that a good time?" A question I probably wouldn't have been brave enough to ask.

"No. It's not. It's thirty or so of the richest, snobbiest, cattiest people that my mother feels socially obliged to impress, crowded into a Central Park mansion to celebrate what they own, who they own, and who they fucked over to own it. It was my first Thanksgiving in the U.S. in a long time. I'd forgotten how awful it was."

Steam rushed up to glisten my face as I opened the foil around the garlic bread. Despite it's delicious smell, it suddenly seemed like such a simple side. Embarrassingly simple.

How different this dinner must be to Donovan, who was used to servant-prepared meals and glamorous surroundings. And here we were in a two-bedroom in Hell's Kitchen that he owned and rented to people in much lower tax brackets, furnished almost exclusively from a Pottery Barn catalog, serving him a dinner that was heavy and rich with refined carbs.

I didn't even think I could pronounce the wine he'd brought.

This whole idea had been ridiculous. What had I been thinking?

If he hadn't realized by now how totally beneath him I was, he would after tonight. I might be making good money now with an executive job in his firm, but I was still the poor girl he'd met back at Harvard on scholarship.

Hell, I hadn't even managed to keep the scholarship in the end.

But I couldn't hide in the kitchen all night feeling sorry for myself. I quickly downed the rest of my wine then carried my empty glass and the garlic bread to the table.

"Can you grab the salad?" I asked Audrey. "We're ready to eat."

"Yep!"

She ran off to attend to her assigned task as I set my glass at my place and the bread in the center of the table. I avoided looking at Donovan, but when I turned to go back to the kitchen, he grabbed my wrist. Electricity shot up my arm. My skin burned under his fingers.

I looked back at him, my pulse speeding up when my eyes met his.

"Hey," he said.

"Yeah?" My voice cracked on the simple word.

He stroked his thumb along the inside of my wrist. "I want to be here. Okay?"

A storm of butterflies took off in my stomach. He never missed anything. Even behind a wall and a stove, he saw me.

"I mean it," he said when I didn't say anything. I couldn't say anything. "Okay?"

I took a deep breath in and let it out. It didn't completely relax me, but it helped. Expecting to be any more at ease was ridiculous with Donovan so close, touching me. Looking at me. Looking at me like he wished I were the main course instead of what I'd prepared.

"Okay," I said softly.

He didn't let go of me, though. He held on until my sister came bustling around the corner, her arms full with the salad bowl tucked precariously under one arm and the bowl with the vinaigrette I'd made in the other hand.

"Have you heard of making trips?" I hissed as I passed her on my way back to the kitchen.

"I think I'm doing just fine," she called back to me. "So if you weren't in the U.S. before, Donovan, where were you?"

"Tokyo," he answered. "Do you want to know the best thing about Japan?"

"Sure."

"No one gives you a hard time when you decide to work through the holiday."

Smiling, I shook my head and stuck a serving utensil on top of the lasagna dish.

Audrey giggled. "No wonder you and my sister get along. Workaholics."

"I heard that," I yelled, using hot pads to pick up the lasagna and carry it around the corner to the dining room. *He wants to be here,* I told myself. *He wants to be here.*

"Did she tell you that?" he asked, meeting my eyes when I returned to the room. "That we get along?"

Oh yeah, he wanted to be here. The way he looked at me sent sparks through my body. Every cell inside me was charged. Every molecule.

Jesus, how was I going to make it through this night?

Audrey pursed her lips. "Hmm. I don't remember."

"We don't," I said, teasing. "We bicker like crazy. He's a pompous asshole, and he never acknowledges that I'm right." Maybe it was only half teasing.

"That's not true. You're just so rarely right," he taunted right on back.

I set the dish down on the table and stared at Audrey. "See? Pompous. Asshole."

My sister thought it was funny. Donovan only shrugged as if to say, 'you get what you get.'

It made my chest pinch. I wanted to *get him*, pompous

asshole parts notwithstanding. For the first time, I started to believe it might actually be possible. That we might be able to work out everything between us, and we'd just get to *get* each other.

But that was for tomorrow.

Tonight I had to hope that my food didn't give anyone food poisoning.

After surveying the table for anything missing, I took my seat at the round table between Donovan and my sister. The next few minutes were spent refilling wine glasses. Audrey made a toast, and we all clinked. Then we began dishing up and digging in.

"How did the two of you spend the holiday?" Donovan asked Audrey as he passed her the salad bowl.

"Uh uh," I said before she could answer. "He doesn't get to know anything else about me."

Audrey looked from Donovan to me then back to Donovan. It wasn't that we'd done anything secretive. We'd gone to the parade and then the Holiday Shops at Bryant Park before having dinner at The Dutch. I'd tell him if he really wanted to know.

He just knew so much already. It was my turn to decide what he knew. My turn to hear about him.

So when she looked back at me, I narrowed my eyes into a warning stare.

"Sorry," she said to him. "Sabrina makes the rules around here."

He raised a brow. "Does she?"

"She does." Even as I said it I recalled the kiss he'd given me in his car almost a week before, and his parting words that made me shiver from head to toe. *Don't begin to think I've forgotten who's in charge.*

I hadn't forgotten where and how Donovan was in charge.

I hadn't forgotten the ways in which he took charge.

My inner thighs tingled, my belly tightened, my body

yearning for him like that now. For him to manage me. To control me. To dominate me.

"Hmm," Donovan said, the sound vibrating through me.

I crossed my legs, hoping to dull the steady ache. "Shut up and eat your dinner."

"Yes, boss." He was in on the joke, the fucker. It only made my want that much stronger.

I tried not to watch him as he brought his fork up to his mouth and took his first bite, but it was impossible not to. It was extremely intimate, watching him eat the food I'd made. Watching his lips. Remembering the last time they were on me.

"This is good," he said, and I blushed for so many of the wrong reasons. "Really good."

I kicked him lightly under the table. "Don't sound so surprised."

He only smirked and took another bite.

"It's our grandmother's recipe," I said, as if that explained why it was so delicious. It certainly wasn't due to anything I did.

"On your mother's side, I'm guessing." He took a swallow of his wine.

I tensed slightly. "You guess correctly." His guess was educated, probably based on the knowledge that our mother's mother was full Italian, the first generation born in the United States.

I exchanged a look with Audrey. I'd told her that Donovan had a file on me and that he'd obviously been watching me for years, but I hadn't given her many details about the contents. Had she realized there were places where her own life's information intersected with mine? Like our family tree? Had it occurred to her that my past was her past, that Donovan knew that too?

If it hadn't, she didn't seem too bothered by learning it now.

She had her own history on her mind, history that she also shared with me. "If it weren't for Nonna's lasagna, Thanksgiving would be a holiday that I'd be fine skipping all together," she said. "Our dad died over this week, so there are bad memories. But we had so many years of lasagna dinners with Mom that are tied into my memories of her—I can't get rid of this week and the bad memories of dad without losing the good memories of her too. It makes it a complicated time."

"I understand," Donovan said, piquing my full attention. "I lost someone over Thanksgiving too."

Amanda. I'd forgotten she'd been coming back to school from the Thanksgiving break when she'd died.

He looked only at Audrey as he went on. "But, a year later, I spent a really nice day in my office at Harvard with Sabrina. I can't wish one didn't happen without losing the other, too."

Audrey and I had talked repeatedly about this time being difficult before—losing Dad, remembering Mom.

And I often thought about leaving Harvard now too. About Donovan. About losing my virginity to him against a bookcase. About realizing I liked sex that was filthy and dubious and involved power plays.

I hadn't ever stopped to think about what this time might mean to him.

Yes. Complicated was right. For all of us. Then and now.

AFTER WE'D FINISHED DINNER, conversation was even easier. We didn't leave the table, choosing to stay there to pick at tiramisu and drink coffee and whiskey. Over a glass of scotch, I discovered that Donovan Kincaid was quite an expert in art history. He and Audrey debated long and hard the merits of modern art versus the classics—Donovan particularly liked the works of Jackson Pollock and Shiryu Morita while my sister preferred the romantics and gushed profusely about Carl Blechen.

I'd learned enough over the years from Audrey to add an opinion here and there, but I was happy to sip my drink and listen to these two very different, very important people in my life. It suited Donovan to favor the bold, abstract strokes of the modern expressionists, just as it suited Audrey to love the dreamy wistfulness of the romance period.

Did it suit me that I liked the pointillism of Seurat? Was I made up of small, distinct pieces that combined to form a bigger story? Was it easier to appreciate me from a distance? Was that what made a man like Donovan choose to love me so long from afar?

He was nearer now. In my life, in my home. Would he keep loving me when he saw me this close up?

Eventually, the discussion lulled and our glasses emptied. I got up to take our dessert plates to the kitchen. When I returned, I didn't sit, instead choosing to lean against the dining room wall.

The evening was ending, and I was unexpectedly nervous again.

Audrey stood and stretched. "It's almost midnight? I didn't realize it was so late. I need to get packed."

Donovan nodded toward her. "Thank you for letting me intrude on your last night in town. I hope I wasn't unwelcome."

She waved her hand, dismissing the idea. "Not at all unwelcome. We invite friends...and *boyfriends*...to this all the time." She glanced at me in time to see the death glare I gave her. "Besides, it gives me a chance to deliver the My-Sister-Is-My-Only-Family speech."

His brow rose. "I don't believe I know this speech."

"It's a good one," she promised.

"Audrey!" I hid my face with my hands. I was going to kill her later. I loved her, but I'd kill her.

She pivoted toward me. "This would have been a lot worse coming from Dad. Admit it. You can bear my version." She turned back to Donovan. "It's short. It's standard. But it's serious. Try not to hurt her. That's all."

Donovan focused on his finger as he ran it along the bottom of his empty tumbler. "Audrey, I'm going to be honest with you." He looked directly at my sister. "I've done and said a lot of the wrong things already in an attempt to not hurt her. But I came back from France to fix it."

"Okay then," Audrey declared. "Fix it."

Donovan nodded.

Satisfied, Audrey took his glass from him as well as her own and carried them to the sink.

I didn't move. Didn't breathe. Definitely didn't look at Donovan. I wasn't *in* this moment—I was outside it, looking on. If I let myself be in it, I'd feel it, and that would be too much. I'd hold it for later instead, bring it out when I was alone and try to feel it in pieces. Not all at once where it would too easily overwhelm me.

She came back quickly, announcing, "I'm going to my bedroom to pack now."

"I'll go," Donovan said with no motion to get up.

Audrey's expression grew panicked. "No! Don't! I'm going to my bedroom. I'll close the door. I'll turn on music. I'll pack. I'm not coming out. But I'm an adult. What that means is that you definitely don't need to go." She looked from me to Donovan and back to me, making sure that we both understood exactly what she was saying. That she was giving us permission to *be adults too.*

I wanted to crawl into the wall.

But God, I also wanted Donovan.

"Goodnight, Audrey," I said flatly.

"Goodnight." With a waggle of her brows she slipped away. A second later, music did indeed start playing from her room.

Now it was just us. Just Donovan and me. Alone.

I pulled a lock of hair over my shoulder and tugged at the end, trying to hide my flushed cheeks. "She's a meddler. I'm sorry. Protective but also overly sentimental. She believes that All You Need is Love and that kind of idealistic crap."

Donovan tilted his head, his gaze scorching every inch of me. "Whatever will you do with her?"

I shrugged. "Send her back to art school, I guess."

I dropped my hands and put them behind my back against the wall, hoping that might ground me. Because I needed to be grounded. I was floating right now, and I loved it and it scared me all at once.

Maybe I didn't need to be grounded. Maybe what I needed was to let go.

I forced myself to look directly at Donovan. "I'm really jealous of her right now, actually."

"How so?"

"Her head doesn't get in the way. Maybe if I were her, I wouldn't have all the noise in my brain that's preventing me from crossing the room and crawling into your lap."

I panicked the minute the words left my mouth. "I don't even know if you'd want me there." Then I panicked some more. "And that wasn't a desperate way of asking you to reassure me. Not at all."

Donovan's eyes darkened. "All I've thought about the last hour is bending you over the back of that couch, tying your hands with your apron strings, and fucking you raw."

I shivered. "Yes, please."

I became putty when he talked like that. In that gravelly tone that rumbled through my bones. In that way that made me feel his words as if he were already doing those things to me, already bending me and tying me. Already fucking me raw.

His gaze raked over me. "You're tempting. Very tempting."

"But...?"

"But a wise woman once told me that sex doesn't fix things."

Karma. I probably deserved this.

I scoffed nonetheless. "Wise? That doesn't sound wise. That sounds annoying."

"In my experience, wise is often annoying." He smiled, like that was a concession prize. His grin in place of his body. His admission that this was comically torturous for him too.

It was a terrible concession prize.

My skin was buzzing and alive. My pussy was aching and wet. But more urgent than my body's arousal was the itch inside me that couldn't be named or explained. The spot that burned when he talked about fixing things and wanting to be here and when he called me his.

"I don't want you to go." It came out almost as a whisper.

"We're going to talk tomorrow."

"That's so far away." *You're so far away.* Six feet too far. Might as well be miles.

"And after we talk," he said gently, "you might not want to fuck me anymore."

I nodded because he was right—he had to go. "But you should know I can't imagine that right now," I told him.

He nodded back.

A beat passed. Then, as if we both felt the energy shift together, he stood up at the same time as I moved to the closet to get his coat.

"You still want me to come over tomorrow?" he asked as we walked to the front door.

"About that," I'd been meaning to bring this up. "As you've mentioned already, the apartment is awfully...distracting. I thought we could meet instead at the office?"

He looked at me carefully for several long seconds. "You really think it matters where we are?"

No, it didn't matter where we were. If he wanted to fuck me, he'd fuck me, and having him remind me like that made my pussy throb with need.

But I had my reasons. I needed to be at the office.

I shrugged. "Humor me."

"The office it is."

I opened the door and he walked past me out to the hall. When he turned back toward me, I wanted him to kiss me, but I knew he couldn't, that if he started, neither of us would be able to stop. Instead, he reached his hand out and traced his thumb along my jaw.

"Goodnight," he said.

"Goodnight."

I was glad he made me shut the door and lock it before he left so I couldn't watch him walk away. It already felt too much like when we'd said goodnight, we'd really meant goodbye.

EIGHT

WITH AUDREY LEAVING and the talk with Donovan loom-
ing, I didn't sleep well. It was still dark outside when I finally
gave up on sleep. I took a long shower. I shaved—everywhere. I
plucked my brows. I gave myself a pedicure. I put on sexy lacy
panties and a matching bra and stood in front of my bedroom
mirror. If no one saw it but me, at least I knew I looked good.

I finished dressing, pulling on black leggings and boots and a
cream sweater that fell to my thighs, and when Audrey woke up,
we walked down the street for a last breakfast together.

Afterward, I'd planned to accompany her to Grand Central
to see her off, but she vetoed that plan.

"That's stupid and out of your way," she said. "We can say
goodbye here just as easily, and then you can get to Donovan
sooner."

I wasn't usually the affectionate one of the two of us, but I
pulled her into a tight hug. "I love you," I told her, worrying
suddenly that I didn't say it enough, that she didn't know how
deeply I felt it, that she would walk away now without understanding.

"I love you, too." When she pulled away her eyes were wet. I had a feeling she got what I'd meant. I had a feeling her words meant more than they said too.

Thirty minutes later I was at the office.

It was too early for Donovan to be there, which was a good thing. It gave me time to sit down at my desk and get my head straight. I needed to go into this with the right mindset. Like it was an interview. A trial, even, and I was the prosecutor.

Because as much as I didn't want to be cold or harsh, Donovan was on trial. He'd done things to me—he'd violated me in very real ways—and he was going to have to answer to that.

I just had to make sure I didn't let him in my pants before then.

But that wasn't the reason I'd chosen to meet at Reach.

Another half hour later, I heard the elevator open. My light was the only one on. I knew he'd find me, and I waited for him to do so. A minute more and there he was, standing in my doorframe dressed in another pair of dark gray pants, this time with a crisp white dress shirt and a black pullover. The scruff on his jaw was more rugged than usual, his eyes a little less green, and I wondered if he'd had a hard time sleeping too.

I wouldn't blame him. This was going to be hard for me. But I had a feeling this was going to be even harder for him.

"You want to do this in here," he asked without preamble.

My heart thudded against my ribcage, but I managed to keep my voice steady. "I was thinking the conference room."

He nodded, and I stood up, but before I'd moved out from my desk he asked, "Do I need to go get it or are you already prepared?"

Now it felt like my heart was in my throat. He knew. He already knew what I had planned.

I blinked, unable to speak.

"Because you and I both know that I'd just as easily fuck you on the conference table as anywhere, so that can't be the real reason you wanted to meet here."

I nodded, acknowledging he was correct in his assumption. Acknowledging that we were here because I didn't just want him to tell me about it, I wanted him to go through everything *with* me. I wanted all the details explained.

I wanted him to get the file.

"I didn't want to go through your office," I told him earnestly, sounding timid.

He cocked his head. "I think there's some irony there, don't you?"

"I'm well aware." I swallowed. The air between us stretched taut and thick.

And his eyes, where they'd been so warm last night, seemed cold and shielded today. As though he didn't want me to see anything inside of him.

I might not have walked in prepared, but he did.

"I'll meet you in the conference room," he said. Then he turned to walk to his office, and I turned and walked the other way.

Five minutes later he joined me, the overflowing manila file tucked under his arm. He studied me for a second. I'd chosen to sit at the middle of the table, unwilling to choose the head for myself, not wanting him to choose it either. In his eyes I could see him deliberate—should he sit next to me?

He chose to sit across from me. It was the right choice. We weren't here together today. At least, we hadn't come together. We might *leave* together—that remained to be seen—but for now, we were on opposite sides.

Donovan slid the folder across the table in my direction. I reached out to take it from him, my fingers on the edge closest to me, so far from where his hand still gripped the side, and pulled. He didn't let go, and I looked up to meet his eyes. They were empty, and I realized that might be the closest to afraid that I'd ever seen him.

It almost made me feel sorry for him.

Then I glanced back at the thick folder, its contents practically spilling out from its seams. This would be hard for us. But if we had any chance together, we had to get through it all.

My eyes still locked on his, I tugged on the folder again. This time he let go, and the whole thing slid easily to my side.

With a shaky hand, I opened up the front cover and smoothed it down onto the table.

"So," he said. "Where do you want to start?"

God, there was so much in there. So many papers and photos I had questions about. So much I needed to know. "How about the beginning?"

"A very good place to start." He leaned back in his chair, but he was by no means relaxed. His shoulders remained tense, his jaw tight.

That wasn't my problem.

I took the first paper out of the folder and scanned it. It appeared to be a receipt for a wire transfer from Donovan's bank to the mortgage account in my father's name dated shortly after his death.

I turned the paper around and scooted it toward him. "What's this?"

Donovan glanced quickly at it. "It seems to be proof of payment of some kind."

I drew my eyes into narrow slits. "Is this really how you want to play this?" I asked. Admittedly, it was almost easier if he did want to be an asshole. Then I could be an asshole right back.

He cocked his head this way and that ever so slightly, and I understood it wasn't me he was wrestling with—it was his own need for control. His own drive to hold the reins. To deal the cards. To run the show.

Eventually he let out a short audible breath. "It's the payoff for your father's mortgage. I paid the balance after his death."

"Why?"

"For you." For him, the answer was plain as day.

When my father died, everything had been left in my name. I'd been as surprised then to find out my childhood home had no mortgage outstanding as I was now to hear Donovan proclaim his reason for paying it off. I'd expected to be paying that loan for ten more years. When I didn't receive a statement for several months after the funeral, I'd even gone to the bank and questioned it.

"The loan officer told me that my father had made extra payments over the years," I told Donovan. It seemed impossible at the time. My father had saved every extra penny to send me to Harvard. Where had he gotten the money to pay off his mortgage? But I hadn't been about to argue with the bank.

His mouth twisted. His jaw ticked. "I have friends," he admitted. "A friend. He made the register appear the way I wanted it to appear." He was about to leave it at that, but then, as if realizing I'd demand more, he added, "I knew if there'd been a lump sum, you would've gotten suspicious."

"You didn't want me to find out it was you." I couldn't decide if I was mad or grateful. Having the mortgage paid off had been a real blessing. It would have been really hard for me to go back to college and pay for my sister's expenses with house payments on top of it.

But he'd done it behind my back! He'd done it in secret!

"Are you wanting me to thank you?" My words were sour, poisoning whatever gratitude I meant to show.

"No," he scoffed. "That's not why I did it."

"Then why did you do it? Why did you care about me enough to do that? Because of what happened in your office? Because we had sex?"

He frowned as though offended. "Do you really think that was when this began for me?"

No. I thought it began that night at The Keep.

But I wasn't giving him that. I wasn't giving him anything.

"How can I have any idea when you haven't told me shit?" My voice was already raised. I was already swearing, and we were only on the first item.

Good thing I had nowhere else to be, because I was going to stay until this was done. Until I knew everything I wanted to know. I hoped he was prepared for it to be a long day.

"I noticed you the first day you walked into that classroom, Sabrina," Donovan said. "*That's* when it began for me. And it never stopped."

Goose bumps scattered down my arms despite the sudden warmth that filled me inside.

We'd barely known each other, and yet he'd noticed me. Out of everyone. Out of an ocean of people, he'd found me.

But I had to ignore that—had to ignore the way it made me feel. It didn't benefit me at the moment.

What I needed were facts. Details. Confessions. The more, the better. "So you anonymously paid for my house? So that I would...?"

"So that you would be taken care of," he said with pronounced candor.

I closed my eyes for a beat.

Then I opened them again. I couldn't spend too much time on this one thing, large as it was. There was simply too much to go through. I took the receipt back and put it face-down on the inside cover of the folder and moved on to the next item.

The next several papers in the file were related to school. Recommendations he'd sent that I hadn't known about, items related to the internship from my master's program. We went through every single document, Donovan explaining each connection and his reasoning for interfering. Every time, it had been for my own good. As though he'd been my secret fairy godfather, showering me with the best opportunities at every turn.

"If you were this determined to butt in," I said after learning that the article I'd been asked to write for University Today had been suggested to the editor by him, "why didn't you just bring me back to Harvard? I was certainly trying hard enough to get there. Couldn't you have pulled strings there?"

He stared at me with a dull expression. "I'm flattered that you think so highly of my influence. It was *Harvard*, Sabrina. I can pull strings, but I'm not a miracle worker."

On and on it went through piles of invoices, receipts, copies of contracts, and school papers and essays I'd written. The head-hunter I used to find a job in California had worked for Donovan. The management company that had overseen my first apartment was owned by Donovan. The new security system that had been installed in my second apartment hadn't been paid for by the landlord as I'd believed. It was all Donovan.

Memories reshaped and took on new form. It was like when I learned that Santa Claus wasn't real; that all those gifts I'd been given had really been from my parents instead of some magical being. Now I was learning that situations I had always attributed to good luck or good fortune, other situations that I hadn't even thought more than two seconds about, all had been gifted to me by Donovan.

I couldn't help but ask over and over, "Why? Why? Why?"

And always, always it was the same answer. "For you."

We'd been at it for a couple of hours when I came across a paper that didn't make any sense. "Why is there an employment contract for Brady Murphy in here?" I hadn't noticed it the first time I'd been through the file.

Brady Murphy had been someone I'd dated for a short time

while working in California. The relationship had never been very serious, but I'd been more serious about him than most of the guys I dated. He was too nice maybe. Too soft in bed. But a good guy. We might've stayed together longer than the four months that we had if he hadn't gotten a job offer from an up-and-coming tech firm in Japan.

...and suddenly I had a feeling I knew the answer.

"Brady Murphy was never right for you and you know it," Donovan said in answer to my question.

"So you got him a job that took him out of the country?" I didn't bother keeping the incredulity out of my voice.

Donovan shrugged. "If I'd found him a job in the states, there was too great a chance that you would have moved with him. And you needed to break up."

Indignation fumed inside me. "You sent my boyfriend away so that we would break up? Oh my God. I can't fucking believe you!"

"It would have been too easy for you to settle down with him. And that's exactly what you would have been doing—settling. It was for your own good."

I spoke over him, my words landing in unison with his. "Don't tell me it was for my own good. You didn't do that for me. That was for you. You were jealous."

Donovan gave me his version of an eye roll, a slight shift of his gaze. "Oh please. There is nothing to be jealous of about Brady Murphy. He's a weak, whiny sap. I was looking out for you."

I didn't believe him. "You didn't want me with another man." I was almost more flattered than I was mad. Or something deeper than flattered. Just like his jealousy was primitive—because he *was* jealous no matter how much he denied it—the emotion it ignited in me was equally primal. Equally base. It turned me on. It aroused me.

"How many other relationships did you meddle with?" My

mind started to race through all the other boyfriends I'd had, the other men I'd casually dated. Donovan had messed with Weston and I by arranging for him to be part of this fake marriage with Elizabeth Dyer. I knew that. It only made sense that he would've interfered with others.

"Roger Griffin?" I asked. "His grandmother wasn't really sick, was she?"

"Are you accusing me of luring a man away from you with a fake sick *grandmother*?" Donovan stared at me unblinking.

"Okay. I didn't really think that one through."

"But if his grandmother *hadn't* gotten sick, I did have an arrangement in the works," he admitted.

My interest was piqued. "What kind of arrangement?"

"Turns out Roger had a weakness for high-priced call girls."

I scowled. "I don't even want to know how you knew that." I chewed on my lip, taking in this new information. It wasn't as if any of my previous relationships had really been ones that I'd wanted to continue. Every man I'd been with before Donovan had just been a placeholder, someone to fill my time while I waited and wondered if anyone could ever truly know and love me.

And all along there had been someone.

He just never bothered to tell me, instead choosing to watch quietly from the wings.

It took another hour to finish going through the rest of the folder. Close to the end, there were papers that showed he'd paid to move me to New York, that he'd negotiated the extra benefits in my employee contract. I was becoming numb to it by this point. I wasn't shocked anymore by new discoveries. I was overwhelmed, but no longer surprised.

Then I reached the final slim stack of papers that addressed Theodore Sheridan. I'd saved them for last on purpose. There was a narrative I had created about these documents, and I wasn't sure that I wanted to find out my story wasn't true.

I slid the pile across the table to Donovan. "Tell me about these."

"Those are the court papers for the trial against Theo Sheridan," Donovan said, gliding the pages right back to me. "He's currently serving time in a prison in upstate New York. He was sentenced to seven years. He's got four left."

A mystery that had been unsolved since college found its answer.

"You framed him at Harvard." It was an accusation, but it didn't carry judgment.

After Theo had assaulted me, he'd been arrested for possession of drugs with intent to sell. He'd had to drop out that semester. I'd never found out what had happened after that, though I'd searched online from Denver. I'd always had a feeling that Theo's arrest seemed too convenient. Too easy. But I hadn't ever really thought Donovan was involved.

"Those charges didn't stick," Donovan said dismissively, confirming my suspicion by not denying it.

"And so you set him up for a sexual assault charge seven years later instead?" I couldn't hide the hostility in my voice. I appreciated the intent. It was a sweet gesture, noble even. Of course he'd done it as revenge for me. But I had serious problems with sending a man to jail on trumped-up charges. I told him so.

Donovan tilted his head and stared at me with a strange expression on his face. "Those weren't trumped-up charges," he said slowly. "Theodore Sheridan *raped* Liz Stein."

And that was *exactly* what I didn't want to know.

"No," I said, shaking my head back and forth vehemently. I didn't want to believe it. I grasped for other possibilities. "You found someone, paid someone to say these things. For me. To get him back for what he did to me."

"Are you looking for honesty? Or do you want me to tell you what you want hear?" It was remarkable how Donovan could be so obviously irritated and incredulous, and still retain a note of compassion in his subtext.

I didn't want compassion. I wanted the truth.

"I want you to be fucking honest. For fucking once. I want you to fucking tell me that you made this fucking happen."

His jaw worked. But he stayed silent, and the silence told me everything. That he'd already been honest. That he'd been honest all day. That the truth hurt.

I shot up from my chair and crossed to the window. I bit my lip and folded my arms across my chest, hugging myself. It looked cold outside, like the temperature had dropped. The snow banks at the side of the road lit up as cars passed them, the exhaust slowly discoloring their purity.

I didn't hear him, but I felt Donovan move up beside me. His hands were tucked safely in the pockets of his pants. He wouldn't dare touch me. Not after everything we'd gone through today. All the disclosures and revelations had been laid out, but had yet to be weighed. Who knew which way the scale would tip—in his favor or not?

Still, I could sense his desire to connect to me physically.

Or maybe that was me.

"I've only ever thought about myself," I said, my eyes never leaving the road below. "I thought about what people would say about me if I called the cops that night. What it would do to my life. I didn't once, for a single moment, consider what he might do to someone else." My voice was steady, but inside I was cracked. Theo hadn't even had his dick inside me, and he'd wrecked my life. What had he done to this woman? What had I done to this woman by letting him go free?

"You couldn't have changed anything. The only reason he's behind bars is because Liz Stein had a good case and a good lawyer. And she only got the good lawyer because I had people monitoring Theo so I could be there in case he ever got into trouble like this." He wasn't just being kind. It was rational. Somehow, I understood that.

It didn't relieve my guilt.

"I could have at least tried."

"I tried *for* you," he insisted, turning to face me. "I couldn't get the drugs to stick, even when he'd been caught with them. I had a better chance at that than you did with your assault case, and you know that. I'm sorry if it's hard to hear."

It *did* hurt to hear, even though I already knew. I'd always known. It was why I hadn't pressed charges in the first place. Because I'd always known that a girl crying assault at a college party—a scholarship girl no less, accusing a rich, white prep boy— never went anywhere.

Knowing didn't make it any less painful. Not then, not now.

I turned toward Donovan. "Tell me what happened to her. Tell me what he did to her. I need to know."

"If I tell you, are you going to hate yourself if you're turned on?"

Fuck you.

But I didn't say it. Because I couldn't promise either.

"Tell me how he did it."

Donovan regarded me briefly. "He worked on Wall Street. He met her in a bar that he frequented after work. Her friends abandoned her, so he volunteered to walk her home. He took the subway with her, walked her to her door, then asked to use her restroom before going home. Inside her bathroom, he saw her robe hanging on the back of the door. He pocketed the belt of the garment before joining her again. She offered him a drink.

"While she was making it, he came up behind her, secured her wrists with the belt, shoved her up against the counter, pushed down her pants and penetrated her. He held his hand over her mouth so she couldn't scream. And when she fought too hard, he covered her nose with his palm as well so she couldn't breathe, until she settled down. He untied her before he left and threatened to ruin her and her family if she told anyone. She immediately went to a neighbor and they called the cops. He didn't use a condom. He came inside her which made it easy to collect his semen in the rape kit."

I wasn't turned on. I was sick.

I moved to lean on the conference table. It was horrible, and horribly true. Hearing her story brought back all the things that I remembered from my own night with Theodore. How he'd pushed down *my* pants. How he'd covered *my* mouth and *my* nose with his hand. How I'd fought. How it had been hopeless.

Until Donovan had shown up.

"He took her robe belt. She might've even just offered if he'd waited." And she might not have ever been there with him if I'd done something first.

"He's a predator, Sabrina. He's not interested in an offer."

Right. He was a predator.

But what about Donovan? Was *he* a predator? Was he interested in *my* offers? Or was he only interested in what he could take from my life without my permission?

I stared at my hands, angry with him, with Theo, with myself.

I walked back to where I'd sat, closed the file and slid the file across the table. I didn't want it anywhere near me anymore. I didn't deserve the good deeds inside it, and I didn't want to think about the mess that Donovan had cleaned up on my behalf.

"That wasn't so bad," he said, crossing back to where he'd sat, and I wasn't sure if he was saying that to me or to himself, but he did look a lot more relaxed than he had when we started.

Too bad I didn't feel the same.

"I'm not done yet," I said. I had more one more question to

ask, the question I'd been wondering for weeks. It felt even more relevant now that I'd wondered about the exact definition of a predator. "Are there cameras in my apartment?"

Donovan's skin seemed to sallow before my eyes. He paused. Then swallowed. "They're rarely ever on."

My stomach dropped like a boulder into the ocean. "But sometimes they're on."

"Sometimes they're on," he confirmed, heavily.

I knew this. In my heart of hearts, I knew this. Too many times, he'd known things. Things he shouldn't have known. About how little I slept. About the details of what I was doing.

"What do you watch?" I asked, my voice surprisingly steady, even though my heart felt like it was beating in erratic waves.

"I'm sure you don't need to ask that." His voice was low and warning.

"I'm asking because I'm imagining what you *could* watch. You might as well just tell me so I'm not imagining something worse." And I was very definitely imagining the worst, me at my most intimate. All the nights I'd used fantasies of him to lull myself back to sleep after being woken by nightmares from the past...

"You're not imagining something worse."

My skin prickled. My stomach twisted into knots. My skin got hot, and my blood felt like it was boiling. A low level of rage had simmered beneath the surface of my emotions all afternoon. Now it bubbled to the top. It had been one thing when his violations were in the past. It was quite another to find out he was still invading my privacy, even now, even when we lived in the same city, even when all he had to do to be with me was *choose* to be with me.

I pushed my chair into the table so hard the other chairs rattled.

"Sabrina," Donovan implored. "Don't make this more than it is."

"Don't make this more than it is?" I echoed. "Which part? The part where you butt your way into every relationship I've had? Every job? Every situation I've been in—none of which you were ever invited to be a part of. That part? Or the part where you spy on me, like a common peeping Tom? Or did you mean the relationship that we have right now, the relationship where I actually wanted something with you, wanted something real with you? Where I asked you for it and I begged you for it, and you pushed me away? Is that what I'm not supposed to make too much of?"

I was trembling with anger and hurt.

Donovan rounded the table to approach me, reaching his arms out toward me in the way I'd wondered if he wanted to earlier. "Sabrina," he said again, softer.

"Don't!" I said, backing away. "I don't want this."

He lowered his arms, but he didn't move away from me. "You don't want what? You don't want *this*?" He pointed to the file. "Or you don't want *me*?"

I shook my head, unable to answer.

"Because they're one and the same, Sabrina. This file is who I am. You don't get one without the other." His tone was sharp.

It cut at me where I was already bruised.

"You never gave me a choice." The sum of everything I'd learned. My eyes were wet. I blinked to keep tears from falling.

"I'm giving you a choice now." He took another step toward me. "I fucked up when I pushed you away. But I'm here now. And you have to decide."

I shook my head again. He was so close I could reach out and touch him if I wanted to. And I had wanted to touch him for so long. The yearning and desire from the night before were still inside me, still layered just underneath my skin. Pressing at my edges, begging for his skin on mine.

But the wall that I had hoped would be gone after today was still there too, perhaps less thick than before, but a barrier just the same.

"I think this is enough for one day," I said, wrapping my arms around myself. "I'm ready to go home."

Whatever decision was going to be made, it was going to have to wait for another day.

NINE

I LET Donovan give me a ride home. His driver was already at the curb when we got outside the building, and it seemed petty to refuse and wait for a cab. Especially considering how cold it was outside.

We were quiet as we drove through town. I couldn't even look at him. Instead, I stared out the window, my thoughts lost in the overwhelming scraps of discovery from the day. There were too many new pieces of information; too many things that startled me in beautiful and amazing ways. Pieces of my past I now had to look at through an entirely different lens, stories that took on entirely different meanings. Some of them moved me in ways I never thought I could be moved. As if I'd been a boulder stuck in mud that finally had enough rain washed upon it to sweep it down the mountain.

But some of it was too raw, or I was too raw. Donovan's symbols of affection felt like lemon juice against paper cuts. He'd been well-meaning, maybe. But I never asked for that. I'd never asked for him. I'd never asked for his *invasion*.

The worst part was knowing how many times I would have

wanted that invasion. How much of my life had been lonely? How many years had I longed for anyone, any *man* to love me? No, to *get* me. To understand. It wasn't fucking fair of him to love me in secret.

Dylan's description of the way Donovan had loved Amanda echoed in my mind. *Too much. Loved her too much.*

And now when we were finally together, Donovan pushed me away over and over in every way he knew how, all the while watching me, invading my most sacred moments...

Could I forgive him for that?

I didn't know if I felt betrayed or hurt or violated or desired, or all of those things combined. But I was wound up; my insides a whirlwind, a tornado.

Too much.

And next to me, Donovan sat still and quiet like he was in the eye of the storm. Like it didn't matter that I wasn't talking to him. Like it didn't matter that I had just put him on trial for the last several hours. Like it didn't matter that the jury was now out deliberating, and that the verdict didn't look good.

I was jealous of his ability to remain stoic. Of his ability to have no emotion.

Except it was a lie, and I knew it now. I had seen a whole file that proved how much emotion he had where I was concerned.

And yet sitting together in the backseat of his car, I felt further from him than I had in days.

I didn't know how to fix it.

I didn't know if I should even try.

When his driver pulled over to the curb in front of my building, I didn't wait for him to get out and open my door for me. I bolted. As if I could run from these volatile emotions within me. If I could just get far enough away from him, from Donovan, from the way he invaded and possessed and obsessed and cared...

Halfway to the front door of the building I came to a halt.

What was I doing? I was mostly angry because Donovan had kept himself away from me for so long, and now I was pushing him away further? How did that help things?

I didn't care anymore about what he'd done. As long as he didn't drive away. As long as he kept loving me *too much*. Maybe *too much* was *just enough* for me.

"Sabrina?" Donovan called from behind me.

I spun around and found his car still at the curb. He had slid across the seat. The back door was open; he was half out of the vehicle. "What's wrong?" he asked, his expression etched with concern.

"I don't care," I said testing the words out. Finding them true.

"What?" The note of hopefulness was unmistakable even in that one word.

"I don't care," I repeated, stronger.

He shut the door the car, and in two strides he was at my side.

"Sabrina?" He said only my name, but I heard what he was really asking. I heard how eager he was for me to give him the words that I was feeding him.

"I don't care. I really don't. About any of it. I know I should. I should be mad. And I *am*, though not for the right reasons. I'm only mad because it took you so long to invite me in."

I had more to say, more to explain. But he cut me off, pulling me into him, his mouth crashing against mine. His lips were hot, his kiss desperate. Or maybe it was *my* kiss that was desperate. My hands were already all over him, wandering up inside his coat, stroking along planes of his chest, my hips grinding against his.

Too soon he pulled away. "I'm coming inside with you." Confident. Sure. As if it was his decision.

"I know."

There wasn't anywhere else I wanted him to be.

Donovan nodded to his driver, then laced his hand in mine

and tugged me toward the building. We breezed past the doorman and caught an elevator that we shared with a father and his teenage daughter, the latter as distracted with her phone as I was with the heavy curtain of sexual tension between Donovan and me. I couldn't even look at him. I was certain that if I did, I would end up ripping off all my clothes despite the other people in there with us. Even the slight touch of his thumb rubbing up and down the length of my finger was almost too much, enough to make me wet and fully aroused. Ready to explode.

When we arrived at my floor, I stepped out, appearing calm and collected, despite the torrent of urgency inside me, with Donovan right behind me. But as soon as the elevator doors shut, I was rushing down the hall, swollen with need, my hand still laced in his.

At my apartment, he dropped my hand so he could move my hair from my neck. With his body pressed up behind me, his erection pushing into my ass, he kissed along my skin, nipping at the spot where my shoulder curved upward while I dug in my purse for my key. A door opened down the hall, and he stepped slightly away from me. He grinned politely at the elderly lady as she passed by us in the hallway, but under his breath he whispered to me in a low rumbling voice, "If you don't stop fumbling with that lock and get the door open, I'm going to fuck you in this hallway, and I don't give two shits about who watches."

I almost melted into the floor right there.

And hallelujah, the door finally opened.

I burst through the entry, not bothering to turn on the lights, dropping my keys and my purse and my coat as quickly as I got into the room. Stripped of my accessories, I spun around into Donovan who shut the door behind him with his foot. He tossed his coat on the floor.

And then we were there, in each other's arms, ravishing each other.

I moaned against his lips. His tongue was driven and aggressive, plunging inside my mouth, scraping against my teeth. I grabbed the edges of my sweater and pulled up, breaking from him only long enough to pull it over my head and toss it aside.

He took the moment our mouths were apart to push his hand under the waistband of my leggings, inside my panties to stroke along the length of my slit. When I met his eyes again, they gleamed with satisfaction, and I knew it was because of how wet I was. How drenched.

"Please," I begged, pushing into him. I got my hands under his pullover, plucking his shirt from his pants, desperate to feel his skin. "Please."

I was too frantic.

Donovan liked control.

With his free hand, he grabbed my wrists, and in one quick motion whirled me around so that I was pressed against the wall. He held my arms stretched above my head, and I let out a groan of frustration. I needed to touch him. I needed to feel him.

"Donovan, I need—"

"I *know* what you need." Proving his words were true, his hand, which was still inside my pants, rubbed ruthlessly against my clit. My knees buckled at the intensity.

Jesus, I was going to come quickly at this rate.

"I've thought of so many ways I want to fuck you." He whispered in my ear. "So many ways I want to make you come. Every way I can imagine. That's how many ways I'm going to make you come. Every way I can imagine."

He maneuvered his hands so that his thumb was still pressing against my nub and his fingers could reach down lower, inside my hole. Two long fingers stroked inside me, massaging exactly the right spot. He didn't warm me up. He didn't need to. He didn't take his time. He went right for the kill, intent on making me come hard and fast.

And I did. Fast and hard, so hard I couldn't stand.

He let go of my hands so he could anchor his arm around my waist to hold me up while sonic waves of pleasure rippled through my body.

I hadn't even recovered when he turned me around again, turned us both around, so that he could walk me backward, his arm still around my waist, the other now snug in my hair. His mouth again claimed mine. Devoured mine.

And I was dizzy, dizzy, dizzy, and wanting more.

When I hit the back of the couch, Donovan lifted me up and set me on top. He broke away from me and pulled off my boots. Then I lifted my hips so he could pull off my leggings and panties. As soon as I was bare, I reached for the fly of his slacks, assuming the command before he gave it.

"Take out my cock," he demanded, his voice warm like scotch.

I was already halfway there, tugging first his pants down, then his boxer briefs, just far enough to get to the prize. Out he fell, heavy and thick, his angry pink tip dripping with pre-cum.

I threw my arms around his neck and wrapped my legs around his hips, pulling him toward me, pulling his cock toward the ache between my thighs.

He took his dick in his hand and dragged it down the length of my pussy, and for one terrible torturous second I feared he was going to torment me, tease me, make me beg before he filled me. But then his crown was notched at my hole, and, with his hands gripping my hips, he rammed inside me. Then again. And again. Over and over, pounding into me with a frenzy that matched the agitation within me.

"Fuck. There. Right there. Oh, shit."

I was an unneeded director. Even if he didn't know how to touch me, how to make me feel good, he wouldn't listen to me telling him what to do if he didn't want to. My commentary might even have provoked him to change tactics, because a moment later he was pushing my knees back so that my feet rested on the back of the couch. And now when he drove into me it was so far, so deep, it was as though he reached the very center of me.

He *did* reach the very center of me, I realized. Not just with sex, not just with his cock, but with everything he did. He was the only man I knew, the only man I'd ever met who could reach so far into me that he could see my darkest secrets and understand my most intimate self. Even before he'd manipulated my life and put cameras on me, even before he stalked me, even before he violated every bit of my privacy, he'd known me. He'd seen me. He'd noticed me.

Now he noticed me with his fingers tangled in my hair. He pulled my head back, exposing my throat, then with his free hand, he plucked down the cup of my bra and twisted my erect nipple between his thumb and finger until I squealed at the pain. Immediately he brought his mouth down to suck on it and soothe it, alternating licking with biting, sending jolts of shock and pleasure straight into my pussy, which throbbed and screamed, at the brink of coming again.

"No, I can't," I said, when he moved his hand down to brush against my clit. It wouldn't take much before I was erupting.

"You can," he insisted.

"No. No. I can't. It's too much." *Too much.*

"Keep saying no. That only makes me more determined." I could feel him grinning, even as he went back to nursing on my tit.

I clamped my jaw shut, intent on keeping silent, but my protests seeped out in high-pitched one syllable *no-no-no's.*

Donovan angled his hips and rubbed his thumb and pulled at my nipple with his teeth in just the right, right way—that right way that only he knew. And then I was coming again, exploding. Trembling. Convulsing.

"Fuck, baby, that's it," Donovan urged. "Come all over my

cock. Just like that." He shoved against me as I tried to push him out, his pace slowing as my pussy vice-gripped around him. He rode out my climax, a satisfied smile on his lips.

When he pulled out, his eyes moved down to stare at his cock, dripping with my cum.

"You look so pretty on my dick," he said. He stroked his finger along the length of himself and rubbed my wetness along my lips. Hovering just above my mouth he whispered, "I bet you taste so pretty, too."

He kissed me, licking my cum into my mouth. I could taste myself. Sabrina-flavored lip gloss.

"Don't you think you taste pretty?" But he didn't let me answer, instead kissing the breath right out of me.

He didn't let it go on long, though. Soon he cut off sharply and pulled me down to the ground. When I was steady on my own, he let go of me and wrapped his fingers in the hem of his pullover. "Go to your bedroom. Take off your bra and your socks. Bend over the bed, your ass up, and wait for me." He didn't wait for me to leave before pulling both layers of shirts over his head.

I stalled, my eyes drinking in the sight of his naked chest. It had been so long since I'd seen it. So long since I'd touched it freely. I felt like an inmate who'd been newly paroled, drunk on the absence of bars between me and my man.

But that man didn't appreciate my delay.

"Go." He smacked my ass, and I dashed toward my bedroom.

Once there, I stripped the rest of my clothes off and situated myself on the bed like he'd asked—ordered, more like—tilting my head so I could peer in the direction of my door under my arm. I wanted to watch him walk in. Wanted to watch him see me. Wanted to watch as much as he'd let me see.

Was this how he'd felt all these years?

Maybe I understood that feeling more than I thought I did.

But even more than liking to watch Donovan—I liked it when he watched me.

He made me wait, arriving a long five minutes later, naked now himself. He leisurely stroked his cock as he walked in, and I felt my jaw drop. He was magnificent. So magnificent to look at. Even in the dark, with only the light of the city streaming through the window. I'd already had two massive orgasms, and at the sight of him, all power and man, I was aching for him to be inside me again.

This time, he did taunt me. Instead of plunging inside me, he stared at me, his eyes glazed and filled with lust.

"Sabrina, you can't imagine the things I think about, seeing you like this." He came up behind me, and swiped his free hand across my wet pussy, dragging my cum up higher, to the rim of my asshole. "So, so pretty." He pressed his thumb just inside.

I bucked forward, surprised by the invasion.

But he persisted. "You'll let me in here, if that's where I want to be."

And I would. After every other invasion, it seemed almost inevitable. I did trust him. I had a safe word.

Still, I wasn't sure I was ready for that now. Not when what we had was still so fragile and, not *new*, exactly, but raw.

My heart sped up as he pushed in even farther. "Don't worry, Sabrina. Not tonight. But when I say."

Then his cock was at my entrance, sinking into me, slow this time, so I could feel the length of him as he fell in. His thumb remained where he'd put it inside my other hole, and with both parts of him filling me, I felt so full and tight, like I was inflating, like everywhere was being pressed against at once.

I let out a moan, long and low as he rode in and out, massaging all my nerve endings.

I couldn't think in words anymore. Couldn't think in details. All I was aware of was this feeling of abundance, a feeling that existed not just in my lower regions, but everywhere inside me. As though the tiny speck of contentment that existed in me at all times had suddenly ballooned, reaching out along every vein, along every bone to the ends of my appendages, from the top of my head to the ends of my toes. Tears gathered at the corners of my eyes, and the final orgasm that Donovan teased from me stretched and lingered like a new morning on a spring day, tightening and pulling, screaming from my being.

When everything was drained from me, I collapsed, listless, on the bed. Donovan secured his grip on my hips and pummeled into me, racing toward his own climax, eager to join me. Soon, his pace lagged and his thrusts deepened until finally he stalled. With a ragged grunt, he spilled his release inside me and fell on the bed at my side.

I opened my eyes, barely conscious, fighting against exhaustion. We had needed each other like this. Needed to let our bodies speak to each other in the dirty, filthy ways we knew best.

Now there were other things to be said. We had no course set for where to go from here. I needed a road map. I needed to know we were in this together. I needed to know exactly what *this* was. And I was afraid that if I let sleep take me, I'd be alone when I woke up later.

But when I met his gaze, steady and piercing, I realized the fear was unwarranted. Whether or not he was in my bed in the morning, I knew the truth now—Donovan was always with me. He never really left me alone.

TEN

"HAVE LUNCH WITH ME," Donovan said, interrupting my daydreams.

I looked up to see him standing in the doorway of my office. I'd just been thinking about him, remembering the night before. When I'd stared into his eyes, dark and vague in color in the lightless room. *"What are you thinking?"* I'd asked.

"I'm thinking you probably want to be fed before I fuck you again. But I don't know if I care."

He'd left my house late in the night, but I'd seen him around the office already this morning. We'd brushed past each other at the Monday morning executive meeting, my body immediately going on high alert, and though our conversation had been benign, the tone and subtext of our meaning was heavy. *I belong to you. You belong to me.*

Even though we never actually said those words. We had barely said *any* words the night before, spending most of our time preoccupied with reacquainting ourselves with each other's physical landscape.

Which meant there was still part of our relationship in limbo.

But wasn't every relationship in some form of limbo, until someone put a ring on it?

Shaking off the dizziness that the sight of him brought on, I rushed to see if anyone noticed him sneak into my office. Thankfully I saw no one but Ellen, my secretary.

"I can't go to lunch with you," I said, pulling him in and shutting the door behind him. God, just the touch of his hand on mine made my entire body spark.

"You can. Your schedule is free. I already checked with your secretary." His fingers were playing with mine, but my eyes were on his smirk.

"That isn't why I can't have lunch with you," I whispered, as if I'd be heard even behind the closed door. "People will talk."

He dropped my hand and crossed the room, turning to lean on my desk. "You have lunch with Weston, don't you?" He didn't look at me, instead poking nosily at the papers I had laid out on the workspace behind him.

"That's different. He's my boss." I walked over to my desk and straightened my papers as I spoke.

"*I'm* your boss." This time he gave me the full piercing weight of his hazel eyes, and I hated that I was going to have to defend Weston, but I was.

"You're not the boss I report to."

He let that sit for several seconds. It was impossible to refute. Weston was in charge of marketing. Donovan was in charge of operations. There wasn't a reason for me to have lunch with the chief of operations.

Unless I was banging him.

"So people will talk," he said, deciding where he stood on the matter.

I was flabbergasted. This was not the man I'd been with the last few months. That man had winced at the slightest hint of scandal between us. Yeah, things were different now, and he wasn't worried I'd find out his deep dark secret—that he'd been secretly in love with me for years. But just because things *were* different, I wasn't sure I wanted people thinking I was slutting it up with one of the presidents of the company.

"I—"

Donovan cut me off, apparently bored with the conversation. "Sabrina," he said, standing. "I don't give a fuck about other people. Come to lunch with me."

Twenty minutes later we were seated downstairs in the New York Minute Grill with our meals on the table in front of us. The restaurant had been Donovan's choice, proving how much he really didn't give a fuck about other people, seeing as how the New York Minute Grill was located in the very same building as Reach.

Quietly, I'd been on the lookout for anyone from the office for the first quarter of an hour, but despite the location of the restaurant, I hadn't seen anyone I knew and was forced to relax and admit it hadn't been a bad decision after all.

So a few bites into my pear pecan salad, I set down my fork, took a swallow of my ice water, and smiled at the man across from me. "Thank you for dragging me out of my cave."

It was actually really nice to be out in the open with Donovan. It was like a real date, and we hadn't really had one of those. Sure, we'd gone to the Japanese restaurant and Gaston's, but one had been a weird feeling-each-other-out scenario and the other had just been a precursor to sex. Today's meal was something else entirely. It was two people wanting to spend time together because they liked to spend time together.

"I had ulterior motives," Donovan said over his steak salad.

So much for two people wanting to spend time with each other.

"Of course you did." Why did I ever think anything different? "And they are?"

"Primarily, spending time with you."

Well, then. I felt my cheeks pink, delighted my initial feeling about our date was the correct one. Except, he did say *motives* in the plural.

"And?"

His grin made me feel he was impressed with my intuition. "And we left things unfinished last night."

I could feel the flush in my face deepen. I'd been thinking about last night all morning, but his mention of our carnal interlude made me as hot and weak as if he were undressing me.

"It sure didn't feel like we left anything unfinished." I shoveled a forkful of salad into my mouth, hiding my brazenness behind the act of chewing.

My body felt the aftermath of him. My thighs were sore; my stomach ached. The flesh between my legs was tender and raw from how he'd used me. How I'd let him use me.

"Oh, Sabrina." The rumble in his voice made my belly do back flips. "There are still a thousand ways I intend to make you come, and another hundred thousand I haven't thought of yet."

"Ah," I shivered, "I, uh, well. Sure." I drank half my glass of water just to cool down.

He laughed low in his throat. "That's not what I'm talking about, though. I think you know that."

"Actually, there *is* more to say." I'd meant to say more on the sidewalk before he'd come running after me and cut me off with that incredible kiss. "I said I didn't care. And I don't. But you should also know I felt a lot of other things too. Hearing about those things you did for me—for my family—it really stirred things inside me. Part of me is still pissed—"

"Understandably," he interrupted.

I ignored him, raising my voice ever so slightly. "I never asked you to do those things. I never expected it. You didn't have the right, but then, *didn't* you? Doesn't...*caring* about somebody give you a right?" He'd yet to say *"love"* himself since I'd brought it up that night in the back of his car, so I steered clear of that word in particular. "I don't know. I spent so many years as a girl with nothing in my pocket, daydreaming about a knight in shining armor. As so many young girls do. And don't we all wish the rich would give more to the poor?"

I laughed at myself then shook my head. "But this isn't about the money. Or this isn't *just* about the money. The time you invested... It means a lot. I know you're not looking for a thank you. I'm not going to give you one. I don't know if I'm exactly grateful. But I'm not exactly mad. And I am...moved. And turned on. In some way that I think is probably sick and unhealthy."

Donovan tsked. "You worry too much about what arouses you. If you're turned on, just go with it." His gaze drifted briefly down to the neckline of my blouse before returning to my eyes. "And I am not a knight in shining armor."

"No," I laughed. "You're not." I sobered. "And yet you are."

We held each other's gaze for several seconds. Something deep inside me tugged. Or tore. Or tightened. I dropped my eyes.

But I couldn't let him be a hero in this. That wasn't right either. "You're also the villain, don't forget that."

"Lucky for me you're the kind of girl who likes to fuck the villain."

I pressed my lips together hard, unwilling to acknowledge how true the statement was, even though we both knew it.

My stubbornness seemed to amuse him.

Then he grew serious.

"Fucking around is usually all the villain ever gets," he said, studying me to see if I understood what he meant.

I didn't. "I'm not sure what you're getting at."

"I'm asking what you see as happening next."

I sat up straighter in my chair, tension rolling down my spine.

I'd been in this position before with Donovan. I'd laid it all out on the line, told him what I wanted. I'd gotten hurt.

"I don't know what to say," I said slowly, cautiously. "I don't know where to go next. What to—"

He helped me out. "Maybe start with telling me what you want."

I was silent. It wasn't—of course it wasn't—but it felt like a trap.

He shifted in his seat. "How about I start by telling you what I want?"

This. This sounded interesting. "Okay."

He wiped his mouth with his napkin then returned it to his lap before drilling his eyes into me. "I want more. I want a relationship. I want to be open about it. I want people to know we are together. No hiding or worrying about having lunch together. I want to be able to assume a blowjob comes with the meal." I bit back a giggle at that, which he noticed and acknowledged with a grin. Then, quickly, he was somber again. "What are the terms in order to get that?"

I blinked.

Just three weeks before, I'd proposed almost the same scenario, minus being open about our relationship and I'd said nothing about blowjobs—though I wasn't against them.

The whole idea made me giddy and lightheaded.

Terms, though. "What, we negotiate like a business deal?" I hoped he wouldn't notice how bothered I was by his choice of words.

Or maybe I hoped he did notice. I couldn't decide how passive-aggressive I wanted to be.

"If that's how you want to look at it."

Okay. Aggressive-aggressive then. Because that was not how I wanted to look at it at all.

"I don't. I mean, where's the romance?" I could hear myself, and it annoyed me. "God, I sound like my sister."

But annoyed as I was that I sounded like Audrey, I still wanted that. Still expected that. Still expected some sort of hearts and flowers from a man who supposedly loved me.

"Where's the *romance?*" His face wrinkled with disbelief. "I'm not asking you to prom, Sabrina."

I dropped my fork and threw my napkin on the table, no longer interested in my meal. The warm fuzzy feeling I'd had a few minutes ago had disappeared, leaving irritability in its wake. I was seconds away from going off, but before I said anything I would regret, I wanted to get full clarification. "What exactly *are* you asking?"

He pushed his dish aside and leaned over the table. "I'm asking who you need me to be in order to get you."

He was asking about the files. And the surveillance. And the ways he manipulated.

He was asking who he had to be to be with me.

My insides felt gooey like liquid chocolate. Goosebumps rose up my arms. I ran my teeth along my bottom lip, afraid I might get teary if I didn't keep myself together. After I'd caught my breath, I said, "I told you. I don't care."

I fiddled with the hem of the napkin and Donovan reached out to put his hand over mine. "You told me you didn't care about what happened in the past. You seem to care a lot about what's happening right now."

My brows pinched together. "I don't understand. If we are together, why would you need to do any of—"

My gaze landed on a Christmas tree in the lobby, the blue and gold ornaments as obvious as the realization that entered my mind. Even if we were together, even if we were a couple, Donovan had no intention of giving up his stalking, his interfering, his private viewing from the cameras in my apartment. He'd done all those things while he'd been with Amanda. It was how she'd ended up dead.

I moved my gaze back to his. "It's because that's who you are." He'd said it himself. Said it as plainly as he could.

He nodded, but doubled down by answering as well. "Yes, Sabrina."

"But you're asking who I need you to be..." I let out the air in my lungs, slowly. "So am I to assume that you're willing to give up some of who you are in order to be with me?"

He nodded again. "Or all of who I am. It's up to you to decide how much."

My stomach twisted and braided with both the intoxication of such crazy power and a little bit of disgust. Or a lot of disgust. And also something else—something sentimental and tender, some sort of emotion that would probably fit a lot better inside Audrey than in me.

But here it was inside of me all the same, and I had to figure out what to do with it and how to make decisions with it. I had to figure out how to answer the question that Donovan was waiting for me to answer now:

"So, tell me, Sabrina—who do you want me to be?"

ELEVEN

I NEEDED A MOMENT TO PROCESS.

It had been less than twenty-four hours since I'd learned the extent to which Donovan had infiltrated my life in the last ten years. I still hadn't worked through all of the emotions I had about that. I hadn't been away from him long enough, hadn't had enough time to truly think and let it all sink in.

And here he was asking me to make major decisions based on those emotions?

It felt impossible.

Fortunately the waiter came then and left the tab at our table. Donovan swiped it before I had a chance to even offer.

"I don't expect you to pay for my every meal," I said. A prickly subject perhaps, but much safer than the one we were on before.

"I do." He pulled his gold card from his wallet. "I just told you I wanted a relationship. This is part of a relationship."

"Maybe in the 1950s. I'm a modern woman. You should let me take a turn now and then."

"Is that part of your terms, then?" He had me there. This subject was more related to the one before than I'd realized. He'd been my benefactor for years, hadn't he? Was that Donovan's idea of a relationship? Taking care of someone? Paying the bills? Coming to the rescue? Had he been taking care of me for too long? *Was* the ability to pay my own way part of my terms?

This was even more complicated to answer than it sounded. And it had already sounded complicated.

"You can pay for my lunch." I was chickenshit. It was easier than continuing the debate when I wasn't prepared to argue.

Donovan nodded with a knowing smile and caught the eye of the waiter as he passed by again. He handed him his card and I watched as the server disappeared, wishing I could look at the man across from me instead. Wishing I knew what to say.

"I can ask for his number when he comes back if you want me to," Donovan teased.

I glared in his direction. "I'm not interested in our waiter."

"He sure seems to have your attention."

I sighed. "It's not him who has my attention. It's you. Always you. I don't know how to answer you. I'm bit overwhelmed here."

His forehead wrinkled as he considered. "Tell me what you need."

He sounded so sincere, and why shouldn't he? He was good at that. Good at giving me what I needed. I just never realized how good he was at it. I wondered if it was as hard for him to share it with me now as it was for me to understand the fullness of it.

"I need some time to think." I needed time to put things into boxes, sort out the good from the bad. Divide the right from the wrong.

Or maybe it was all wrong.

He paused, and in that pause I could see his doubt. I could feel his concern. I wanted to reassure him, but before I could, he gave me my release. "Take all the time you need."

AN HOUR LATER, I sat at my desk in front of ad sketches for a new electronics line, barely seeing them. I was supposed to be creating a timeline for product release, but instead I was reviewing my mental notebook of all the instances Donovan had interfered in my life. I was still collecting inventory and hadn't gotten to the point of breaking down which were good and bad when I realized my stupid mistake—I'd given him the wrong answer.

I didn't need time to think. I should have been able to answer instantly. I could kick myself over it. Immediately, I called down to his office but was told he was in meetings all afternoon. My revelation would have to wait.

So as soon as Ellen was gone for the day and the halls began to darken, when all but the most committed employees made their way home for the evening, I locked up my office and headed down to his.

His secretary Simone was at her desk, her purse on her shoulder, obviously about to leave.

"He's on the phone," she said, a fact that was evident since the walls to his office were currently clear and there he was behind his desk, the receiver cradled under his neck. "But you can go right in."

Uh...odd.

First, it was unusual for him to keep his glass clear. Was that because, as I'd always suspected, he'd kept them opaque to hide from me? Did his transparent walls now suggest a greater transparency than just the literal one in front of me?

Also strange was the permission to walk right in. The last time I'd tried to see Donovan in the office, Simone had, at Donovan's behest, requested I make an appointment.

Things really were changing between us.

Emotion lifted in my chest, a contradiction to the grimace on Simone's face. Apparently she wasn't as happy with the change in events as I was.

Yeah, I got it, sister. If I were his secretary, I'd have a crush on him too.

Ignoring her pout, I thanked her and moseyed over to the doorway as the click-clack of her heels sounded her exit down the hall behind me. I leaned against the frame, much the way he'd leaned against my doorframe earlier in the day. Simone may have instructed me to go on in, but I preferred to have an invitation from the man himself.

He looked up at me immediately, a sly smile forming on his lips as he continued his phone conversation.

Warmth spread within me. It was a nice thing to feel wanted.

"I'm glad I could help you out," he said into the phone. "Or *not* help you out, as the case may be. I'll pull my man off the case immediately."

He was quiet for a moment, obviously listening, but all the while he ate me up with his gaze. Slowly, he traced up my Dolce & Gabbana knee-high boots, higher along my tight-fitting pencil skirt. Then he scaled the curve of my abdomen and the swell of my breasts to follow the arch of my neck, the line of my lips.

By the time he reached my eyes, my skin was hot and my panties were slick. He shifted in his seat and I wondered if he was turned on.

"I hate to interrupt you Cade, but an urgent matter has just made itself known." He paused, and I bit back a giggle. "No, no. Nothing to worry about. I can handle her. Er, it. I'll see you later this week."

I crossed my arms casually across my chest. "Cade *Warren?*" It wasn't my fault that I'd been eavesdropping. He'd been the one to leave the door open. "Was that the Cade you were talking to?"

Cade was the fifth founder of Reach. He ran the Tokyo office and rarely made it to the United States. As such, I hadn't met him yet.

"Yes, as a matter of fact. He was having a little trouble finding someone he used to know. I was helping him out with some of my resources." Donovan leaned back in his chair and crossed one leg over the other at the knee.

"You are good with those resources, aren't you?" Everything he'd done for me without me knowing? That took a man who knew people.

"That I am. But he's found who he's looking for now. So he doesn't need me anymore." With barely even a breath to note the change in subject, he said, "I'm hard."

"Because of Cade?" I teased. "Apparently he'll be here later this week for Weston's wedding. We'll have to make sure you two schedule some alone time."

Weston's *fake* wedding. It seemed silly that Cade was traveling halfway across the world for that. But I was looking forward to meeting him.

"Not because of Cade." With a nod of his head he gestured for me to come farther into the room.

I waited a fraction of a beat then pulled the door closed behind me. Anyone lingering around the office might be able to see us through the glass, but they didn't need to hear this conversation. It was private.

"Something on your mind?" he asked as I walked toward his desk. "Because if you just stopped by to visit, I am more than willing to occupy your time."

I had to clench my thighs together to distract myself from the buzz between them. There'd be time for that later. There'd be time for everything later.

First...this.

"I wondered if your offer was still on the table." My voice

sounded breathier, more seductive than I meant it to. Or maybe it was exactly as seductive as I meant it to sound.

"Why yes, Ms. Lind." Even with his devilish grin, his statement managed to sound sweet. "Are you ready to get down on your knees?"

I rolled my eyes. "We're still negotiating."

He raised a brow. "Then you're ready to negotiate?"

"I'm ready, yes. I'm ready to tell you what I want." I felt shaky all of a sudden, excited. I was eager to say what I had to say.

If he was nervous, he didn't show it. "Sit," he said, and pointed at the chair across from him.

"Like a real business meeting." I slunk down in the chair. I crossed my legs, letting my skirt ride up my thigh. "Nice." I was being sassier than I needed to be simply because the business terms still prickled at me.

"Keep provoking me, Sabrina, and we'll both have a good evening."

A delicious shiver ran down my spine. I had to keep focused. Because the sooner I got through this, the sooner I'd have his mouth on me.

And I really needed his mouth on me.

"I hope that's a promise," I pushed one more time.

It was perhaps pushing a little too far because his response was serious. "What do you want, Sabrina?"

I swallowed, letting my tone match the somberness of his. "You. I want you."

My words hung in the air like the tinsel and the mistletoe of the season. Donovan heard them, absorbed them. I saw them sinking into his skin, saw the flicker of his eyes as they started to form meaning inside him.

I went on.

"I wanted you at Harvard. I couldn't admit it to myself back then, but I wanted you. I wanted you all the years we were apart.

Every night in the dark, it was you I thought about. I wanted you when I got here, from the moment I saw you. I wanted you even when I was with Weston. I wanted you when you flew across the ocean to get away from me. And when I found the file showing me all the ways I had you? I wanted you all the more."

He tilted his head just a bit to the right, not enough to disturb my train of thought. Just enough to show he was listening.

"And if that file represents who you really are—which isn't all of you, trust me, but let's say it's a significant part of you—then I don't want to change any of that."

Not any of it.

Okay, maybe some of it. Small modifications. But we'd get there momentarily.

Donovan's eyes narrowed. "I don't think you know what you're saying, Sabrina."

"Don't do that. Don't patronize me like that. I know what I'm saying. I'm saying go ahead and butt in. Interfere. Take care of me." Wasn't that what even Cinderella wanted?

He started to say something else, but I jumped in. "With some understandings in place."

"Right. Terms." He didn't sound angry about the idea. In fact, he seemed quite comfortable with this direction. "Name them."

I glared at his word choice but decided not to argue about semantics. "Mainly, transparency. I want to know what you're up to. If you're maneuvering things behind the scenes, I want to be behind the scenes with you." I winked, just because it sounded dirty.

"The benefit of maneuvering behind your back," he said purposely changing my choice of words, "is that I don't have to justify myself to you." Apparently he *did* want to argue over semantics.

"Oh, like you mean if I might not agree with your choices for *my life*?" I over-enunciated the words '*my life*'.

"Something like that." His lips were tight, his jaw tighter.

"Then I guess we'll argue about it until one of us wins, like all couples do. I think that's the very definition of a relationship."

I stared hard at him.

His shoulders loosened as he chuckled. "How very quaint."

My mouth gaped and I fluttered my eyelashes in bewilderment. "Were you not serious about negotiating terms? Was that just a thing to say to sound noble?"

"Were you not serious when you said you took me how I am?"

I scowled. He smirked.

I must've won because then he said, "Yes, I was serious. Very serious. If you need transparency, I'm happy to give it to you." His teeth were clenched as he said it, but his expression seemed sincere.

I believed him anyway.

"Thank you. I appreciate that." *Point for me.*

Scratch that. *Point for us.*

"Is there anything else you desire, Ms. Lind?"

There was so much I desired. And all that was wrapped up in on Armani suit and sitting two and a half feet away from me.

"Along with transparency, I think honesty is a given. But I'll mention it anyway because it's important." This was mandatory. I would not tolerate lying. "I need to know that everything is out in the open. That there are no more secrets. I don't care if you have someone tailing me and I'm unaware. I'm pretty much going to assume that for the rest of my life now, you know. But decisions that affect my life? Those things can't be kept from me. You have to tell me, or it's a deal breaker."

He nodded before I'd finished my monologue. "Of course."

"I mean it, Donovan. I know you're a secretive person. Things affecting me though, you have to keep completely out in the open." I sounded redundant. But it was well worth repeating.

"I get it. Complete honesty."

He was already looking me straight in the eye, and I didn't want to beat a dead horse, but I had to be sure. "And there's nothing from the past? Nothing left that I don't know? Now would be the time to tell me if there is."

He paused as if mentally going through a tally of the years, making sure that everything was checked off. It was a little unsettling that he couldn't answer right away. I would've been even more unsettled if he had.

"Everything was in that file," he said after a few seconds. "You know everything."

"Okay." I let out a slow breath of air that I didn't know I'd been holding. "Okay," I said again. We were really doing this.

"Then we've come to an agreement?" Donovan asked with a tone that hinted of hopefulness.

I considered but was already nodding.

"And exclusive commitment," I added, as he got up from his chair and walked around to lean on the other side of the desk just in front of me.

"We already have an exclusive commitment. So that goes without saying." He was semi-aroused. Hard to miss when his crotch was now at eye level, but let's face it, I probably would have looked anyway.

"Except we've never said it. I had no idea you weren't sleeping with anyone else." I pressed my hand along the inside of his knee. It was right there. It was impossible to resist.

"If you had any idea what goes on inside of me, Sabrina, you would know—I'm not sleeping with anyone else. There's not going to be anyone else."

I pushed my hand flat, on his inner thigh and stood so we were face to face. "You know that's what all cheaters say."

"I guess you'll just have to trust me." His thigh muscle flexed under my palm.

"And I guess you'll just have to... Well. You have private eyes on me." My hand drew closer to the bulge in his pants. He was now fully erect.

Before I could reach the prize, however, he grabbed my hand and brought it to his lips. He sucked one long finger into his mouth. "And are those private eyes going to bother you?"

"The private eyes won't." I shivered as he drew my next finger into his mouth along with the first. "I'd like the cameras off, though."

"We'll only use them to make dirty movies." Three fingers in his mouth now, and I wondered if I'd be able to come just from this. "And you agree we can be public?"

This one I'd been iffy about. On the one hand, we couldn't really have a grown-up relationship if we were sneaking around everywhere. On the other hand, his reputation was secure. Mine, not so much. I was still really new to the company. I didn't need my whole team thinking their leader was only here because she was fucking the boss.

Though it was kind of true. Just wrong boss.

"How about we don't announce anything?" I offered as a concession. "We can be private without being secretive. We don't need to be obvious."

He rocked his head back and forth, considering, then drew all four of my fingers into his mouth, sucking on them hard before answering. "I suppose I can agree to that."

Next, he licked his tongue along the surface of my palm. I shifted my weight from one hip to the other, entranced by the erotic tingles that traveled down my spine.

I had no idea how I had the sense to remember the last thing I had on my agenda. But somehow I did. "Oh, and I'd appreciate a little more romance."

His eyes burned into me. "And I'd appreciate a few more hand jobs."

I nodded as his mouth closed down over mine. His kiss was

teasing, nipping at my lips. He pulled my hand down to his pants, a silent command, and I began unbuckling him eagerly.

"Darken the glass," I whispered against his lips.

"I'll worry about the glass. You worry about my cock." He didn't darken it.

So much for not being obvious.

We'd played this scenario out before, touching each other when others were nearby. The risk of being seen thrilled me to no end. My heart was pounding. I was breathy, as though it were his hands on my sex organ rather than my hands on his. Some responsible area of my brain shouted a warning to me, begging me to ignore the high I was riding and demand some privacy.

But another part of me reasoned: it was late. Most everyone was gone. And hadn't I just agreed to let him take care of me?

So he'd take care of me. He'd watch out to make sure we weren't caught. And in return, I'd take care of *him*.

His cock was thick like steel in my hand, still wet from his attention. It was slick enough to run down the length of him, up and down. A burst of pre-cum formed at his tip and I drew it down his shaft, pumping him the way I knew he liked. Soon he wrapped his hand in my hair and pulled my face up so he could kiss me as I stroked him. Deep, lush, possessive kisses. Kisses that told me exactly the way he imagined fucking my cunt.

It was so fucking hot. His mouth. The low groans in the back of his throat. Knowing there could be anybody walking by behind us made me moan along with him.

When he was close, he broke his kiss so he could ask, "Where do you want it?"

I was prepared to swallow, but I'd let him choose. "Wherever you want to put it."

"I want to put it on your tits."

My knees buckled. Thank God he was holding onto me or I might've lost my balance. The image sounded so sexy.

But the windows...

"Trust me, Sabrina." He could read my hesitation every fucking time. "Or don't. But you have to hurry." The strain of his voice told me, even if his words hadn't, how near he was to climax.

"Unbutton my shirt," I told him without another minute's pause.

He was fast, and my shirt was undone and my bra cups tugged down before I could second-guess myself. Then he put his hand over mine, taking over the action of the hand job. I knelt down as he stood, just in time. With a guttural moan, he shot his load over my bare breasts. Cum dripped along my décolletage, down over my nipples. I was covered with him.

I peered up and grinned, feeling as satisfied as if I'd been the one to orgasm.

He matched my grin with one of his own. After tucking himself away, he helped me to my feet. "If I offered to go get something to clean you up, would that count as romantic?"

Considering how sex had ended often for us in the past... "I'd say that's a good start."

THE NEXT AFTERNOON, I received flowers by delivery. A large beautiful mixed bouquet that was impossible to miss as the deliveryman walked in through the office. Everyone was talking about them, about who sent them. At least that's what Ellen said when she brought them in to me.

"Some are saying you have an admirer," she said. "But most are sure you must be seeing someone."

Yeah, the secret wasn't going to last. Particularly since it seemed like Donovan didn't care if it didn't.

Well, people could talk. It didn't mean they *knew*.

"Are they from Kincaid?" she asked.

Okay, she knew. And if *she* knew, it wouldn't be long before *everyone* did.

"I guess I should open the card." I found the envelope buried in the stems and tore it open. Inside was a simple note in Donovan's handwriting. He must have gone into the shop and ordered them in person. *Would you be my date for prom (a.k.a. Weston's wedding)? –D.*

He definitely had no intention of keeping our relationship low key. If I showed up as his date to Weston's wedding, everyone in the office would know we were together.

But, wow.

What a way to ask. Here was the romance I'd requested. My heart was racing and I could feel the flush on my cheeks.

Suddenly, I didn't really give a fuck who knew about us either. I would go to his prom with him. I would be his date.

In fact, I couldn't think of anything better.

TWELVE

"HOLY SHIT," I exclaimed as we walked past the divider in the middle of the ballroom, leaving the ceremony portion of Elizabeth and Weston's wedding to go to the reception. Everything about the event was incredible, from the décor to the uniforms of the wait staff. The location itself was very highbrow—the Park Hyatt's Onyx Ballroom, a luxurious venue, steeped in glamor with floor-to-ceiling watercolor panels.

"That's what I said when I saw you walk out to the car this morning," Donovan said, squeezing my hand.

I heard him, and my chest did a silly little flutter, but I was too wrapped up in the scene in front of me. Though it had been an early evening wedding, hors d'oeuvres were the only food being served. There were probably too many guests to accommodate a full-service dinner logistically. But it was an open bar, and the food on the trays that the waiters passed seemed substantial. A live band played jazz music, and there was a table with a nice sized-gift bag for every guest to take upon their departure.

"All this for a fake wedding?" I wouldn't even do this much for a *real* wedding. Of course I'd always planned on eloping somewhere, so maybe I wasn't the best judge.

"Hush." Donovan scanned the nearby vicinity to make sure nobody had heard me. "You want to be careful what you say. Elizabeth apparently has a few family members suggesting this marriage is a sham. There's nothing like a fifty-thousand dollar wedding to say true love."

My jaw might have dropped.

Well, if that's what it took to access her trust fund... I assumed her inheritance was exponentially more.

"I guess I'm amazed she could pull it off so quickly." They'd only had a handful of months to plan the whole shebang. If I ever *did* get married, I was definitely hiring her wedding planner to handle everything.

And why was I thinking so much about my own possible wedding? Spending so many nights with Donovan the past week, maybe. Funny how having a relationship got me thinking long term, even when it was such a newly formed relationship.

"It helps to have friends." He pulled two glasses of champagne off a tray as a waiter passed and handed one to me. "The hotel belongs to the father of a friend of mine. Elizabeth knew the woman who brought in the flowers. Her wedding dress came from Mirabelle's. Mira is Hudson Pierce's sister. Hudson has done some business with Reach recently, as you know. They agreed to only one attendant each, which made the rehearsal quick and simple for everyone, especially when Weston realized Brett would be a more enthusiastic best man than I would. It all came together."

"You mean, *you* made it come together." If there was one thing I was learning about Donovan, it was that he knew how to maneuver. Knew how to pull strings. No wonder he'd once had the nickname The Puppet Master.

"I know what's important. And this is important." He took a

swallow of the champagne then so I couldn't read his expression. Couldn't tell if the importance was because of the business merger this union created, because he believed in their marriage, or because it had made Weston unavailable to me.

Perhaps it was a little bit of all three.

"For what it's worth, I don't think you have anything to worry about on the believability front." I raised my voice just slightly in case anyone nearby was listening in. "It's obvious how much love they have for each other. They gazed at each other during the ceremony like no one else existed in the universe." I lowered my voice. "I actually mean that."

He frowned skeptically. "We'll see. There's already a pool going around with the guys on how long before they file for annulment."

"Isn't filing for annulment part of the plan?" I whispered.

He smiled and nodded at someone across the room. "It is," he said through his grin, "but a date hasn't been set for it yet. It was left to be determined. The guess is how long they'll last. Do you want in?"

It was my turn to frown. "No, I do not." I didn't know what bothered me so much about it. We'd made bets on Weston regarding Elizabeth before. But that was when I truly believed that they were just pretending their way through this whole thing.

Now I wasn't so sure that they were. "It doesn't seem right to bet against somebody's happiness."

My date swung his attention back in my direction. "Jesus. You really believe this could work out, don't you? That's cute."

"Thank you for being so patronizing. I truly appreciate it," I said sarcastically, folding one arm over my breasts so I could sip my drink with a scowl. So apparently he didn't believe in their relationship. It stung for some reason, as though he'd said he didn't believe anyone should get married, and as though I cared what he thought on the matter.

And maybe he didn't. He'd once been engaged, but he might have changed his perception of the ritual, but why I cared about his opinion was unbeknownst to me. It wasn't like we were getting married.

"No, I really mean that. You're adorable." He tugged my hand away from my chest and pulled me toward him. "I'm not saying I don't believe in marriage," he said, as though he knew exactly what I was thinking. "I'm saying that this marriage has obstacles. Weston is a playboy. He hasn't stayed with one woman for longer than two weeks in his life, and here you are with faith in him. I think that's cute."

His mouth was near mine but before he could kiss me, I said, "That's not true. He's been faithful for months to Elizabeth." I tipped my chin up, cueing him to press his lips to mine.

"Then the rumors are true," an unfamiliar voice exclaimed beside us. "Donovan Kincaid has found himself a girlfriend."

Instinctively, I backed away from the man I'd been about to kiss. I'd accepted that people were going to talk about us—I really had—but it was one thing to say I was cool with it and quite another to actually *be* cool.

"I'm the one who told you that rumor, you asshole," Donovan said clapping the back of the stranger in front of us. He was of average height; his hair cut short, almost military style. He appeared to be in his mid-thirties, bulky where Donovan was lean. Hard where Donovan was chiseled. Mean where Donovan was mischievous. "Sabrina, this is Cade Warren. Cade, I told you about Sabrina."

"No. You told me about our new Director of Marketing Strategy. *Weston* told me about Sabrina." He shook my hand in greeting—a firm shake, just gentle enough to prove he remembered he was shaking the hand of a woman. "Pleasure to meet you. Everything I've heard has been quite... complimentary."

I bit down the anxiety threatening inside. I hated not knowing what he had learned from Weston versus what he had learned from Donovan, but at least it had been Donovan who had told him we were together.

I also hated that I knew almost nothing about Cade except that he worked in the Tokyo office. It made it hard to make small talk.

Fortunately, Donovan knew things about him, and he came to my rescue.

"Cade's story that he's here for the wedding is only a cover," he said—a pointed jab at his partner. "He's really in the States to meet up with a woman from the past."

Cade's eyes narrowed. "Hey—"

"Payback's a bitch." Donovan wrapped his hand around my waist and pulled me in to his side, possessively.

I liked it. A lot.

"But that was supposed to be a secret," Cade said with a note of menace.

I knew good and well that Donovan wasn't afraid of Cade. But maybe he should have been. Cade seemed tough. The kind of tough that covered up that he had once been broken. Broken badly.

I knew that kind of broken.

But I'd never seen this kind of tough. It was a myth, as far as I'd been concerned. I'd never believed people could build walls that strong.

Apparently I was wrong.

People with walls that strong were to be feared. They didn't have anything to lose.

"Sabrina and I have no secrets," Donovan said, his thumb drawing circles on my hip.

Goosebumps shot down my skin from his touch and from the words he said. It felt good to hear them. To know that they were true.

"Well, isn't that precious?" Cade rolled his eyes. He seemed like the kind of guy who didn't believe in relationships that required no secrets. He probably didn't believe in weddings either. A hundred bucks said he'd made the first bet in the 'Weston and Elizabeth get an annulment' pool.

"Don't worry," I assured Cade, because I was more than a little afraid of the man, even if Donovan wasn't. "Your secret is safe with me."

He grinned. "It's a good thing too. With you dating this guy, you're gonna need all the friends you can get." He turned his focus to my date. "How long do we have to stay at this thing anyway?"

But I wanted to address what he'd just said about me.

I put my hand on his bicep, which was larger than it had first seemed under his tuxedo. "Oh." *Shockingly* larger.

Anyway. "Wait a minute—what do you mean 'I need friends'? Are people talking? People are upset that I'm dating him, aren't they?"

He took a swig of the beer he'd been holding and shrugged. "You're dating one of the bosses. And you're fuckhot. And from what I hear, smart as shit. Of course people are talking. Have I heard anything? No. But look at them." He gestured at the crowd around us. "There's sure a lot of whispering and glances."

"It's because it's our coming-out party," Donovan said. "They're surprised. That's all. Ignore them, Sabrina. Ignore him." To Cade he said, "And you need to stay until the bride and groom arrive. They're getting their photos taken and then they'll be in."

"Fine." Cade took another swallow from his bottle, and when he did, I noticed the edge of a tattoo as his sleeve pushed up on his arm. "I'll stay until then. But then I'm out of here."

Yeah, this guy did not do weddings.

This guy did not do romance.

I made a mental note to ask Donovan where he found him later on. He seemed more like ex-military then a guy who ran an international advertising firm in Japan.

But I knew better than to judge by appearances. And I knew better than anyone that smart, creative people came from all walks of life.

"Maybe we should mingle while we're waiting," I suggested. I, at least, needed to say hello to the people from our office. I didn't want to appear stuck-up on top of everything else.

Cade let out a hearty laugh. "You're still trying to win their hearts aren't you? She's cute, Donovan."

I pressed my lips together tightly so they didn't say anything that I'd regret to the man that I just met, who was technically one of my bosses.

Donovan surveyed me, likely noting the glare I was holding back, and let out a laugh of his own. "I was just saying that." He moved his hand to my neck, just below where my hair sat tightly in a knot. His fingers on my sensitive nape sent shooting stars of want down my spine. "It looks like a bunch of the staff is gathered by the bar. We can go say 'hello.'" Then he bent in so that Cade couldn't hear him. "He's a dick, but he's a good guy. I'll make it up to you later."

I didn't know what exactly he was making up to me, or why he considered any of it his fault except that he'd been the one who'd wanted me to come with him to this thing. But the feel of his breath on the shell of my ear and the promise of something good to come was enough to make me relax. A bit.

"I'm holding you to that."

We'd just made it over to the bar when a buzz spread through the crowd, not just directly around us, but throughout the ballroom.

"Ladies and gentlemen," I recognized the voice that came across the speaker system as Brett Larrabee, Weston's best man and a fellow student from Harvard. "It's time to welcome, for the first time, Mr. and Mrs. Weston and Elizabeth King."

Applause erupted as the couple entered the room holding hands. Both were smiling, but neither looked at the other, each directing their attention at their guests.

Was it all an act? Were the glances passed between them just for show?

It was one thing to be sleeping together. It was quite another to be married and be serious about it.

Maybe Donovan was right. I'd likely spent too much time recently with my sister. Just because Weston was having a good time with his business arrangement didn't mean he'd found a happily ever after.

"They do a lineup or something, don't they?" Cade asked, finishing his beer with one long swallow.

"I think they plan to mingle," Roxie said, as our group joined hers.

"Fuck this. It will take forever for them to get through all these people. I'm taking off." Cade tossed his bottle into a nearby trashcan. "Can I borrow you for a moment, Donovan? It was nice meeting you, Sabrina. I'll probably see you around the office before I head back to Tokyo."

"Ditto." It seemed safe enough. Polite but noncommittal.

Donovan looked to me as if asking my permission. I scanned the faces of those gathered, noting who I'd be left with if he abandoned me. There weren't many staff members. Not many had been invited, mainly just the top employees who worked under Weston. My team members, Roxie, and a few other key staff members. Basically all the people who'd be the most pissed at the advantages I'd gain at dating the boss. In other words, I'd be alone with the wolves.

No. Not the wolves. My staff. My people.

"Go ahead. I'll be fine." I didn't know if it made things better or worse that he kissed me on the cheek before walking out to the lobby with his partner.

"You came with Donovan?" Roxie didn't even wait until he was out of earshot. He glanced back at me at the sound of his name, and I tipped my head up in reassurance. I had this.

I didn't have this.

"Uh, yeah. I did. He's my date. He's my..." *Say it. Just say it, Sabrina,* I willed myself. "I guess we're seeing each other." *Chicken.* "No guessing. We *are* seeing each other."

"Ah," Roxie said, a whole ton of subtext in the single syllable, and hell if I knew what any of it was.

Tom Burns, my lead team member, on the other hand, was pleasantly surprised. "Good for you." I hadn't really talked to him about me and Donovan, but he had walked in on an intimate moment and had a pretty good idea there was something going on between us besides a working relationship. He'd encouraged me to pursue it. "Glad to see you two together."

"Yeah. Me too." I didn't mean to sound so sketchy about it. I really was glad. Just nervous, too.

"Speaking of dates, this is my wife Daisy," he said, gesturing to a petite blonde with bobbed hair. "She just talked me and Frank into going off in search of more cream puffs."

"And more of those grilled shrimp kebabs," she added, eagerly.

"And shrimp kebabs. Got it. Would you like to add anything to the order, Sabrina?"

"No, thank you. You can take my empty, though, if you like." I handed him my champagne glass, which I'd been carrying around for the last several minutes even though it had nothing in it.

"Sure thing. We'll be back." He took off with Frank, Roxie's husband, in tow.

As soon as they were gone, Daisy's infectious smile disappeared. "So. Sabrina. Tom's been with Reach since it opened. Worked his way up from the bottom. Then you came in and stole that top position right from under his nose. By all rights, that promotion should have been his. And now we find out you're sleeping with one of the main men? That's not fishy at all."

Every muscle in my body tensed. My throat felt like I'd swallowed a desert instead of Moscato.

"Not just *one* of the main men," Roxie added. "I still say she and Weston were together to begin with."

I gaped, unsure what to say. I wanted to defend myself, defend my talent and resume, but nothing they said was untrue.

And I'd expected this might be a problem, but not from Tom Burns. Not from his wife. Not from Roxie. She was supposed to be my friend!

"I'm so sorry, Ms. Burns," I stammered. "I didn't—"

Daisy suddenly burst into laughter. "I'm just fucking with you. You should've seen your face." Roxie joined in the hysterics.

"Then ... you're *not* mad at me?" I was confused. Relieved, but confused.

"Mad?" She shook her head, her hair bouncing as she did. "I'm grateful. Tom wanted that promotion, but we have three kids. I would never have seen him, and I didn't want to be a single parent. I'm grateful they found someone competent instead of persuading him to make the jump. And Tom says you're good! Glad to see more women in those exec positions. Congratulations!"

Roxy was still laughing. "Her face. Her face!"

And now I was laughing a bit too. "Thank you. I think."

"I bet you get those kinds of comments all the time," Daisy said. "I should know. I work in an office with all men myself. Real estate. Men don't think we know how to sell anything except our bodies, am I right? But I have the second-highest sales in my team this year. Look at us go!" She patted me on the arm, as though we were old chums now.

"Go us!" I said awkwardly. I liked her. Despite her strange teasing and the fact that it was hard to get a word in edgewise, she was spunky and fun. I was neither. It was always nice to find common ground with someone different.

"If anyone gives you a hard time about dating that fine piece of Kincaid—which all the ladies are jealous about, by the way—don't you even listen to them. You do you, girl. Stand up proud knowing that you deserve to be where you are." Her eyes scanned the crowd as she talked. "Roxie, Frank got distracted by the fondue again. If we want our food, we're going to have to go get it ourselves."

With Roxie and Daisy gone, I looked around and realized the rest of the staff had dispersed too. I wasn't so sure that they were as unbothered by my relationship with Donovan as Tom and Daisy—I'd seen the uncomfortable exchange of looks as we approached—but Daisy was right. I needed to do me. And I did deserve to be there. Even though I *had* fucked not one, but two, men to get there.

Turning, I casually looked for someone to engage with. I spotted a client across the room, but I didn't want to end up talking shop, so I waved instead. Nate Sinclair was nearby, a woman I didn't recognize on his arm. He seemed engrossed in conversation with the couple standing next to him, and I didn't want to interrupt. Elizabeth was taking selfies with the trio of older ladies—aunts, if I remembered correctly from her engagement party. Weston was no longer with her. They must've separated from each other in their mingling.

I searched for him, looked for his face amongst the sea of tuxedos and suits, and then stopped suddenly, my heart racing faster, when it landed on a familiar profile. One I hadn't seen in ten long years. His face was fuller than I remembered, his hair shorter, his neck longer.

But I'd never forget that jawline. Never forget those eyes that invoked pure terror in me.

No way in hell would I ever forget Theodore Sheridan.

THIRTEEN

I WAS FROZEN. Torn between moving closer to be sure it was him and running far, far away. The oxygen in the room felt thinner. My lungs felt weaker. My legs were pipes of lead.

Before I could do anything at all, the man in question—Theodore—turned fully in my direction, and I could see for sure that it was him. The man who had held me down, who had covered my mouth and had stuck his hand down my panties, who had very nearly taken my virginity without my permission, was in the same ballroom with me, not twenty feet away.

Emotion bubbled up through me like vomit. My mouth dropped open in a soundless scream that heaved through me, causing sweat to bead at my brow. What was he doing here? He was supposed to be far away. He was supposed to be behind bars. He was not supposed to be drinking champagne and laughing with Elizabeth's maid of honor.

He was not supposed to be here.

I was struck with a sense of duty to go and warn her, the woman I didn't even know. Melinda, I believed was her name. I'd never been good with names.

But even after what I'd learned about Liz Stein, I couldn't bring myself to do it. I couldn't bring myself to go anywhere near the fucker. I had to be away. Far, far away.

I needed Donovan.

I whirled toward the door he'd exited through half an hour ago, determined to go after him. At the very least, I intended to get as far away from Theo as possible. But when I turned, I smacked into a hard, warm, familiar body.

"Hey, hey, what's wrong?" Weston asked with all the concern and compassion of someone who cared about me.

"Theodore Sheridan." I was practically hyperventilating. "He's here. I have to leave." I tried to move but Weston had his arm on mine, securing me in place.

"He is? Are you sure?" His eyes swept the room behind me, his brows tightly knit. "With Melissa?"

Melissa, that was the maid of honor's name. I nodded, unable to speak.

"That's Theo's little brother Clarence. They sure look a lot alike, don't they?"

"What?" I still couldn't get a breath. I braved a pivot to look where I'd last seen Theo/Clarence and squinted at the man's face. There *were* differences from my memories of him, but it had also been ten years. "You're positive?"

"Yeah. I'm sure. There's no reason for Theo to be here. He's ... Well. He's not here. That's the polite way to say it. Clarence went to school with Elizabeth, though. Small world, isn't it?"

"That's not Theo," I said again. Weston probably thought I was crazy. I'd never told him about the assault, and I doubted it was something Donovan had ever brought up.

He looked me in the eyes. "That's not Theo. Swear on a bible."

"Oh." I believed him, I really did.

And I was relieved.

But the weight of my panic had been extraordinary, and now that I'd been reassured that fight or flight was unnecessary, I had to deal with all those extra endorphins the panic had produced inside me.

I started to cry.

Not a full-out sobbing, tears-rolling-down-my-cheeks kind of cry. But my eyes leaked and my lips trembled and my shoulders shook.

"No. Oh, no. This is..." Weston patted my arm where he held me, looking around, perhaps for someone to help him. Maybe he gave up, or realized he could handle me on his own, because a second later he pulled me into his embrace. "Don't do that. I mean, weddings are for crying, but not this one. Well, maybe this one. But not for the usual reasons, and that's not really a comforting topic right now. What I mean to say is, what can I do? I'm not really sure why you're upset. I am terrible with women crying. Are you okay?"

With my face buried in his lapel, I worked on pulling myself together. This wasn't the place to cry everything out of my system. I needed to just get the valve under control, put on a happy face, and get back to the event.

Weston was helpful thankfully, rubbing my back as he rambled. Both were soothing. Both distracting.

When I could finally swallow past the lump in my throat and get out a coherent sentence, I broke away from his chest.

"I'm sorry," I said, accepting the handkerchief he offered. "This is really embarrassing. I just really thought it was Theo. Which I'm sure doesn't explain anything and you just think I must be truly bananas."

Weston continued to rub my arm. "I can actually fill in the blanks, I think. Elizabeth told me Theo is currently serving time for rape. Am I making unreasonable connections?"

"Um. No. Not unreasonable." I turned my face away, feeling another wave of tears threaten.

"Hey, that's not what I wanted." He swiveled on his shiny black shoes, trying to decide what to do with me. We were off to the side and out of the way of most of the crowd, but my display of emotion was definitely not well suited for Weston's wedding.

I was about to apologize again, tell him I wasn't his problem, when he said, "Oh, let's do this. Come join me on the dance floor. They just started a slow song. We can talk—or not—and sway, and no one will be the wiser."

As much as I didn't want to be his burden, I was still shaken up. "Okay."

I let him take my hand in his to lead me to the center of the dance space. It was warm, but nothing magical happened at his touch. It was funny that I once thought I might have a future with him. I'd always belonged to someone else.

And, maybe, so did he. "Aren't you supposed to have the first dance with Elizabeth or something?"

He shook his head. "We aren't doing any of the traditional things like first dance or cutting of the cake. It seemed strange under the circumstances."

Was I wrong or did it seem like there was a note of disappointment in his tone?

"Makes sense." I pressed easily against him, grateful for both the familiarity and the friendship. "While I'm disappointed to not see the two of you have a first dance, I appreciate this."

"That's what friends are for, right? Want to talk about it?"

"I prefer not to, if that's okay." The tears had stopped, but there was a layer of pure terror just under the surface, like heavy clouds after a rainstorm. There was more inside me waiting to get out. I was barely holding myself up, and it was with Weston doing most of the holding.

"Completely fine. I just have to say, I'm here for you. You have to know that. Things might not have gone the way," he lowered his eyes from mine and cleared his throat, "I once intended for us, but maybe this is better. Whatever *this* is, I have a feeling it lasts longer."

He sounded forlorn. More so than I expected a man on his wedding day might, even a fake wedding day.

"Uh oh. That sounds like there's trouble in paradise already. Things not going so well between you and the Mrs.?" It was nice to be able to have something to joke about. Not that I wanted Weston to be miserable. I just didn't want to focus on the reasons *I* felt miserable.

But Weston apparently wanted to play the same avoidance game. He shrugged. "It's a strange situation. I guess, all in all, things are going exactly as they should, and I'll leave it at that."

We shuffled together in silence for a little while, both of us lost deep in our complicated psyches. Then all of a sudden, Weston exclaimed, "Hey! You came to this with Donovan?"

I leaned back to look at him, smiling. "Oh, yeah. You've been preoccupied. I didn't know if you knew."

"Word gets around. Especially when it's juicy."

"I suppose it is pretty juicy," I said, not even caring anymore that I was the center of gossip.

"But is it good? Is he treating you right? Donovan's my guy, but if he doesn't take care of you I won't hesitate to kick his ass." He'd said words like this before, and while I didn't really believe Weston would ever take Donovan down, his intentions were sweet.

"Yes, Weston. He's taking care of me." Donovan Kincaid redefined what it meant to take care of someone.

"Good. You deserve it."

I wasn't sure I deserved it, but I wanted it. I wanted all that Donovan gave me and every way he gave it.

I also wanted the best for Weston. "You deserve it, too. To be loved. To be taken care of. To take care of someone."

He looked away as though he wanted to reject what I was saying, but I put my hand on his cheek and pulled his face back front and center. "I'm serious, Weston King. If that means growing up, do it. We aren't kids anymore. I know Donovan would want you to know the same."

He rolled his eyes. "I'm sure he would."

The song ended, and we parted.

"Speak of the devil..." He nodded toward sidelines where Donovan was standing watching us.

I headed toward him immediately, still worked up and eager to have his arms around me. Weston followed.

"You're here," I said, pressing into my date.

He paused a second, maybe surprised about my show of affection. Then he wrapped his arms around me. "I was only in the lobby with Cade. I've been here the whole time."

There was a slight hint of tension in his voice that I felt mirrored in his body, and I wondered what had happened between him and Cade to put him in this mood, but my curiosity wasn't strong enough to make that question a priority.

"I thought I saw Theo," I told him, desperate to share what had happened—even though it had turned out to be nothing. "I thought he was here, Donovan. I freaked out."

Immediately, his mood shifted. He was on high alert, my protector. "You saw Theo?" He scanned my face, urgently.

"I thought I did. But I was wrong."

"Clarence Sheridan," Weston explained. "He's friends with Melissa."

Donovan nodded, understanding.

"They look so much alike." My throat tightened again. "I thought it was him, and you weren't here..."

"I'm here now." Donovan drew me in tighter, wrapping an

arm around my waist and placing a hand at the base of my neck. He kissed the tip of my head. "Are you okay?"

I nodded against him. "Weston helped calm me down."

"Thanks, King. Much appreciated." He didn't let me go as he extended his gratitude to his friend.

"It was no trouble, really," Weston said behind me.

I felt something transfer between them. Something that maybe only men understood—only men who were good friends. But because I couldn't see either of their faces from my position, I couldn't even see what it was to know.

I pulled out of Donovan's arms, uncomfortable with the feeling that I was being left out of the conversation. My eyes darted from one man to the other, but I was unable to read either of them.

"Congratulations are in order, I suppose," Donovan said, changing the subject. He took my hand in his.

Weston nodded his chin at me. "I hear the same should be given to you."

Donovan didn't say thank you, but for that matter neither had Weston.

They held each other's gaze for several seconds that might've been tense or might have just been seconds passing. I didn't really read men very well. I'd never been good at it, and I wasn't suddenly good at it now simply because I was dating Donovan.

Finally, Weston said, "So Cade already left? That motherfucker didn't even wait to see me."

And the mood shifted.

Donovan shrugged with one shoulder as if to say *you know him*. "He's staying in the States a while. He might still be here when you get back from your honeymoon. I still can't believe you're actually going on one of those."

"Gotta make it look real." Weston waggled his brows, indicating the real reason he was looking forward to a honeymoon, despite the sham marriage between him and his bride. "Do me a favor and keep him out of my office. Last time he was here my signed copy of *Sandman* went missing."

I wasn't sure if that was directed to Donovan, or to me since I was the one covering Weston's job for the most part while he was out of the office.

Before either of us could respond, others were gathering around us to wish the newlyweds congratulations. Frank and Roxie, Tom and Daisy. Some of the guys from the marketing team. Soon there was joking and laughter and small talk that didn't require my full attention.

I was glad to let others handle the conversation. It hadn't been Theodore, and I should have recovered by now, but I still felt topsy-turvy. My stomach was still in knots. It was ridiculous.

Even though it wasn't Theodore, it wasn't just that I'd seen a man who looked like him that had been the reason for my turmoil. I hadn't been thrown into such fright simply because my memory had been jogged. I lived with those memories all the time. They were always in the corners of my mind. They haunted my dreams on a regular basis. It was almost a comfortable companion—the dreadful horror of those memories.

What threw me today—what had me still so worked up—was knowing how few degrees of separation there were between me and Theodore right now. If he were released from jail—*when* he was released from jail—his little brother would still be friends with a woman who was currently married to one of my bosses. To a man I was close to.

The chances were good that Weston and Elizabeth would be over in a matter of weeks; and that there would never be an occasion when I would even be in a room with Clarence again.

But what if I was? What if Weston and Elizabeth stayed together by some miracle, and a few years down the line, at a holiday party or a charity event or the launch of a new business venture, I turned unexpectedly and that time it *wasn't* Clarence?

It was a lot of what-if's, and I'd learned not to live on what-if's. But tonight the what-ifs were an infestation taking over the most vulnerable parts of me, wearing me down to just smiles and nods.

I lost track of how long I'd been disengaged from my companions when I felt Donovan's hand settle heavy on my hip.

"Come with me," he said with no further explanation.

Without giving excuses to the others, we slipped away through the open doors of the ballroom, out toward the restrooms in the lounge. I wondered for a moment, if we were leaving altogether, but he passed the coatroom and the stairs, and led me to a room across the lobby.

The door was slightly ajar, and after looking around to make sure no one was watching, he pushed it open and pulled me inside. He shut the door behind us and when he turned on the light I saw we were in what looked like an apartment of some sort, a series of rooms with a kitchen and dining room and living area.

"What is this place?" I asked, pretty sure we weren't supposed to be here, whatever it was.

Donovan unbuttoned the jacket of his tuxedo. "It's another event space, this one designed to look like a residence. The wedding party rented it as well. They used it earlier for the family breakfast and then later for last-minute prenuptial paperwork and photographs. No one is using it now though, and I for one, could use a break from all that chatter."

In my distress I'd forgotten that he'd been tense since returning from his chat with Cade. I wasn't going to pry. He would tell me if and when he was ready, and hopefully I would have my own shit together by then so I could be there for him when he did.

Meanwhile, a break from the chatter sounded like exactly what I needed.

I made my way to the closest couch and slumped down in the center seat. Donovan wandered around the room, checking out the décor. I watched as he fingered the heavy curtain sash, then as he crossed to the Christmas tree, decorated with large red and gold bows.

I closed my eyes and leaned back, opening them only when I felt the sofa cushion depress next to me a few minutes later.

"Give me your foot," he said, loosening his bowtie.

Without question I put one strappy heel in his lap. He unbuckled the sandal and removed it, then motioned for me to give him the other so he could repeat the gesture with my other foot.

"Do you need anything? A drink? Some water? Something to eat? Need to use the restroom?"

I rubbed at the inside corners of my eyes, thinking I could probably use a mirror but not having the energy to go look. "I'm good. You're being very hospitable." Maybe that hospitality would extend to a foot rub if I played my cards right.

"I am. Because if you don't need anything else, I'm going to make sure you remember your safe word. And then you're going to make me believe you don't want me to touch you when I do."

For the second time that night, I had a rush of endorphins. My heart sped up double time. My hands began to sweat. This time though, my blood was hot and the catch in my breath was excitement.

We'd played this game before. I liked this game. I was good at this game.

I bolted up to my feet, but Donovan was fast and he pulled me straight back down, hard, drawing me closer to him than I had been. I tensed my shoulders and slammed my thighs together tight. It wasn't hard to pretend I didn't want him. Not only did I have real experience with sexual assault, but I also practiced on a regular basis turning my fears of men into fantasies. How many times had I turned nightmares of Theodore into erotic indulgences, my head filled with thoughts of Donovan as I rubbed myself to climax?

As I said, I was good at this game.

Donovan moved his mouth to my face and licked along my cheek, which was somehow the perfect blend of smarmy and hot. It sent shivers down my back. With one arm keeping me tight against him, he pushed his other hand up the skirt of my dress, demanding access. I clamped my legs even tighter.

"Now don't be like that, pretty girl. You want me to keep things nice. Don't you?"

I turned my head away. He knew the perfect words to use. Substituting my name with misogynistic terms for women. Reducing me to nothing but my looks and my purpose, to nothing but what I did to him, what I did *for* him.

It made my pussy pulse with desire.

I fought not to moan.

Not earning entry between my legs, he found another way to violate me. My dress was mostly backless and had prevented the wearing of a bra. Now, the hand that gripped me at my waist took advantage of this, reaching under the material at my ribs to palm my breast.

His hold was tight, and it hurt, his trimmed nails digging into my skin. I would have bruises from this.

It was perfect. Such a perfect scenario. I could imagine it. I was a smart young woman trying to get a leg up, working extra hours with her seemingly detached boss, not realizing that his devilish grin was really dangerous. Not realizing that once he was alone with me, he'd want more from me than my reports on supply and demand.

God, I was dizzy, it was so hot.

Except, no.

Liz Stein hadn't had it this easy. Rape was rape—I wasn't saying that one rape was easier than another—but I needed this rougher.

And I was positive that was why Donovan was doing this—for me. Because he knew this was exactly what I needed.

So as he kissed my neck and continued to fondle my breast, I bent down and bit his arm, sinking my teeth through the layer of his white tuxedo shirt until I hit skin, until I hit blood.

He jerked away, shaking his hand. "Fucking bitch."

But in that brief moment that he was distracted, I escaped, crawling across the coffee table to get to the hallway that connected the residence rooms. There wasn't anywhere to run, really. The next room had more seating in a different arrangement but nothing else. Nowhere to hide. I breezed past it to the dining area, where a long banquet table ran the length of the room.

Donovan was right behind me.

I knocked over a chair behind me, stalling him, and running along beside the table. I would have to double back along the other side, I realized quickly, since this room ended in a wall.

The chair was barely an obstacle. I looked over my shoulder in time to see him jump it. Which was terribly sexy and wild. Then, as I rounded the table, he climbed up and across it, getting off on the other side. Before I could switch gears and go back the other way, he'd caught me.

"And now we're going to have to do it the hard way." Something told me he wasn't too disappointed.

I was panting like a dog, my panties so wet they were slippery as he pushed me toward the banquet table. But I struggled, kicking him high in the thigh with the back of my foot when he tried to bend me over, barely missing his crotch.

For a second he lost his grip again, but when he regained it, he was pissed. I could feel it in the way he clutched me, the way he slammed me against the wall. I'd have bruises from this too.

"You hurt me and you're going to hurt more." With that venom in his voice, I almost believed him. Or maybe I *did* believe him, that it came from somewhere so deep inside him that it was absolute honesty. That if I *did* hurt him, if I broke his heart, then he would, whether purposefully or unintentionally, hurt me more.

Or maybe I just wanted to believe that, that that's how much he loved me, because it turned me on to believe that.

He was actually hurting me now. My shoulder ached from how he wrenched it behind my back to tether my wrists. I could feel him fastening them together with a rope of some kind. His bowtie maybe, but he'd left that on the couch.

I glanced behind me and saw a flash of gold at my skin. *One of the ribbons from the Christmas tree.* When he was walking around the room he'd been preparing. Just like Theodore had done with Liz.

Perfect. Donovan was so perfect.

He knew that one day, inevitably, I would have nightmares about what Theodore did to Liz. I would create images where, instead of Liz, it was me that Theo wrapped up with the belt of a robe and raped. Especially after tonight, after seeing Clarence and believing he was the man who'd wanted to hurt me long ago.

Donovan was giving me images to replace those before I'd even created them.

I'd been hesitant to say I was in love. I'd been falling for so long, but I wanted to be sure before I told him. After all the years and energy he'd invested in loving me, I had to make sure my emotions were significant enough to match his. And I had to really understand what he felt before I could even make a comparison.

Right then, right there, with my hands tied behind my back,

my cheek pressed against the wall, and his hand clasped at my throat, I finally understood the depth of what he felt for me.

And so I surrendered.

Even as I jabbed him in the ribs with my elbow. Even as he tore my thong and I wiggled and writhed. Even as he used his knee to separate my legs, and I flailed against him, I surrendered.

Surrendered everything.

And when he shoved inside me with his hot angry cock, he pounded all the tension and torment of the evening from my body, leaving me limp and weary and *his*.

We came together, both of us grunting out our releases like they'd been days coming. Like we'd been just practicing before, and this was the performance. A performance meant only for two.

Donovan let go of me, leaning back against the table to catch his breath. Meanwhile, I sunk to the ground, my hands still tied behind my back. I kept my eyes closed, my cheek pressed against the cool wall and allowed myself to revel in the blissful feel of nothing.

Suddenly, Donovan was kneeling in front of me, turning me to face him. He reached behind me to untie my wrists and then ran his palm down my cheek. "Talk to me."

He was checking in. Good man. Last time we'd played this I'd ended up sobbing in his arms.

"This was definitely a whole lot better than chatter. Just what I needed." It was a lot more complicated than that, but the point was, I was good. "How about you?"

His shoulders eased, his face relaxed, and words rushed out of his mouth like air out of a balloon that had just been untied. "I love you. I want to be the one to take care of you. I'm not going to share you anymore. Not even with Weston."

God, I was such a dummy.

He hadn't been tense because of Cade. He'd been tense

because of *me*. Because he'd walked in and seen me in the arms of a man who'd once been a potential threat.

And all I'd wanted was Donovan. Wanted Donovan to comfort me, wanted him to say he loved me. How could he not understand that? Hearing it now for the first time for real shook me to the core. It was the balm I'd sought all night. He was the refuge I'd sought all my life.

I flung my hands around his neck and tipped my chin up to kiss him. Then I pressed my forehead against his.

"Okay," I said because there were no words for this, for all the words inside me. Just... "Okay."

FOURTEEN

THE NEXT MORNING, I studied Donovan across the kitchen bar as I licked yogurt off my spoon.

"Is it weird to have me here?" It was the first night I'd spent at his house since we'd been officially together, and what *I* was finding weird was how weird it *wasn't*.

Donovan looked up from his tablet, where he was reading the Sunday morning paper. "It's *nice* to have you here."

"But does it interfere with your routine? Am I in the way? Am I distracting?" I wondered what he had done with his days off in the past. Besides sit around and check up on me all the time.

His attention returned to his iPad. "I've thought about it enough for it not to seem too jarring," he said dismissively.

I set my spoon on the counter in front of me and leaned forward. "You've thought about it?"

He put his iPad down. "Yes, Sabrina. You aren't the only one who's had fantasies."

I bit my lip as I grinned. He really did have the romance thing down.

"Granted," he swept his eyes over my body, currently clothed in his tuxedo shirt from the night before, "in my fantasies, you were usually naked."

I shrugged with one shoulder. "Real life, man."

He was already coming around the bar for me. I shrieked with my hands held out to stop him from whatever wicked torments I was sure that he meant to implement.

"You've already attacked me once this morning."

"I've heard no mention of your safe word." He rested his hands on the arms of the kitchen barstool, caging me in, and bent down to kiss my neck. He normally had a bit of scruff on his face, but he hadn't yet shaved so his jaw was extra bristly, tickling my sensitive skin.

"No, no," I howled, laughing. "You can't! I promised to call Audrey. You have to stop!"

He lifted his head. "Okay." He kissed me, long enough and deep enough to get my lower belly fluttering, then he pulled away. "I need to work out anyway. Want to join me?"

I pretended to think about it for all of three seconds. "No thanks. I have that phone call to make and everything." Besides, hadn't we gotten enough of a workout last night?

A thought occurred to me. "You haven't bugged my phone, have you?"

"I have not bugged your phone. I told you, you know everything." He swatted the side of my bare thigh.

"Just checking," I teased. "But to be sure—there aren't cameras in *your* house are there?"

His expression, annoyed as it was, was also hot and searing.

"Make yourself at home, Sabrina," he said, refusing to address my last comment. "Join me in the shower later."

"I'll see if I can fit you into my schedule."

He threw me a warning glare over his shoulder. That, and the magnificent view of his backside—his torso naked, his ass covered with sweats hanging low on his hips—sent delicious tingles down my body.

I sighed, my gaze still fixed on the kitchen doorway long after he'd left. I was sore and exhausted, and I couldn't remember the last time I'd been this happy.

I waited until I heard the treadmill start in the other room before going upstairs to get my cell phone. I'd brought a small overnight bag with me and had included my charger so my battery was full. Lazily, I stretched out on Donovan's bed and perused social media, something I rarely indulged in. Elizabeth had posted a few candid pictures from the wedding and I wondered if they were more crumbs for doubting family members or if they'd been real moments she'd wanted to capture.

Maybe Weston would never change. Maybe he was a wild playboy who could never settle in one bed. But seeing him with Elizabeth made me want to believe it was possible.

Or maybe it was being with Donovan that made me want to believe that love was possible for Weston. Because I wanted it to be possible for *me*.

Did I love Donovan?

That was a question better left for the experts.

I closed out of the social apps on my phone, found Audrey's name in the favorites list, and clicked to call.

"Tell me everything," she answered.

I laughed. "Hello to you too." To be fair, I hadn't talked to her since I'd parted with her the week before, and a lot had happened in the last seven days. Not that I was going to tell her every detail. But I planned to tell her the major points.

"I wouldn't have to rush to the meat of the subject if you maybe called me a little more often," she berated.

"I know," I admitted guiltily. "It's been a busy week. But I do owe you a rundown." I stood up. This was going to require pacing.

I roamed the top floor of Donovan's apartment, giving Audrey the highlights of the last week. I didn't tell her that I had put him on trial, but I did tell her that we had gone through everything from the past, and that he had explained himself satisfactorily. That may have been somewhat simplifying the situation, but it was *our* relationship. Our business. Not anyone else's.

Then I told her we were making a go of it; that we were trying out something real.

"Has he said it yet? Has he told you he loves you?" Audrey's tone was as bright and eager as when she'd been ten years old asking me about Santa Claus.

"He has." I sounded especially young, too. Who was I? I wandered into the study. "Yesterday, he did. I didn't say it back. Maybe I should've said it back. Should I have said it back?"

"Did you *want* to say it back?"

"I wanted to say it back. I just wanted to make sure I meant it first."

"And you're not sure?"

I pressed my cheek against the cool window frame and switched the phone to my other ear. "I'm afraid that what I feel isn't worthy of what he feels for me."

It was the first time I'd said it out loud, the first time I'd formed it into words and I had to pause for a second to make sure it was what I meant.

It was.

"What have I done for him? Spread my legs? Sucked him off? Let him get a little rough? I can't be the only woman willing..." I trailed off, not wanting to make the conversation uncomfortable for my sister by discussing specifics of the kink I liked.

"He's not in love with you because you're a slut."

"I'm not a slut!"

I could practically hear her roll her eyes. "That's what I'm saying. You're *not* a slut, so that's not why he loves you. And people don't love other people because of what they do for them, anyway. If they say they do, they're wrong. That's not real love."

"Then why is he in love with me?"

"Oh, sister dear. You are wise and smart beyond your years, and yet you are such a fool."

It was my turn to roll my eyes. My sister's fountain of drama floweth over.

"The heart wants what the heart wants," she went on. "It is not ours to ask why. As for you and how you feel—there is no point in comparing your emotions with his actions. He did what he did because he wanted to do it, not just because he loved you. He didn't do anything that he wasn't completely comfortable doing whether you knew he loved you or not. He certainly wasn't waiting for you to give him something in return or he would've told you about his secret actions long ago. My guess is that he's out of his mind happy just having you wake up in his arms right now."

"Did you come up with that on your own or did you steal it from Hallmark?" If I didn't mock her, there was a chance I'd tear up.

Besides, mocking her was my job as her sister.

But maybe she had a point. Donovan's comments from earlier replayed in my mind. He had fantasies about me being in his life. He'd said so himself. Maybe he really was just happy to have me here.

"I'm just giving you a hard time," I said now. "I appreciate what you're saying. I will keep that in mind as I go forth with my declarations of affection."

I walked over to the large wooden desk and plopped down in the brown leather chair in front of it. I meant to be present in the conversation with my sister, but at the same time I was thinking, *This is Donovan's desk. This is Donovan's chair.* Was this where he sat when he thought about me? When he watched me? When he called me and I imagined him nursing his drink?

Is this where I'd be sitting when I figured out my own feelings about him?

"It's complicated," Audrey said, as if reading my mind. "I get it. But I have every faith that you'll figure it out, and when the time is right, you'll say the right words."

I wasn't quite so confident, but there was a power in sitting amongst Donovan's things. It made me more wistful, and my hope less tentative. "I'm sure you're right."

We talked for a few more minutes about school and plans for Christmas and then we hung up with the usual *I-love-you*s and *keep-out-of-trouble*s. And when her voice was gone, for a few minutes I missed her more than I had before I'd called.

I sat in Donovan's chair and swiveled back and forth, flipping my phone absentmindedly against the desk while I thought about what Audrey had said, and about Donovan, about where I wanted our relationship to go. After the phone slipped through my hands one too many times, I got bored of the activity and let it lie. My eyes caught on the manila folder sitting on the desk in front of me, not unlike the folder that had contained all of Donovan's connections to my past. This one was thin, and I turned it to read the label that had been printed on the notch. *Sun Le Chen*.

I sat forward, my heart hammering against my ribcage. Why did Donovan have a file with Sun's name on it?

I opened it up.

There was very little inside, just a stack of black-and-white photographs. All were candid shots of the gorgeous model, seemingly taken without her knowledge as she shopped in a street market. I couldn't say for sure if they'd been taken recently, but they didn't seem to be in the United States. The style of the streets and the architecture appeared to be European, French maybe. And if it was France, it could have been recent. It had snowed here the last month but not there.

So Donovan had photos taken of Sun while she'd been in France?

"I'm sweaty," he said, suddenly standing in the doorway. "And I'm ready to make you sweaty."

I twisted my chin in his direction. "Why are there pictures of Sun here?"

He folded his arms across his chest and leaned one muscular shoulder against the frame of the door. "Have you been going through my things?"

"Is that a problem?" There was a hint of laughter in my agony.

He worked his jaw, not giving an answer. "They're part of the France campaign," he said finally, thankfully choosing not to debate my snooping further. "They were delivered the day I got back. I've barely looked at them."

"They're candid." I flipped through them again. "She's unaware of the camera." I looked up at him, pleading for a more satisfactory answer.

He cocked his head with incredulity. "Sabrina, you can't be suggesting..."

"Can't I? Secret photos taken of a woman—"

He cut me off. "She knew about the camera. It's called acting. The whole shoot was taken in that style. It doesn't mean—"

"How am I supposed to know that?" I let that hang, our gazes locked. To his credit, his eyes were stormy and tormented. "Do you have feelings for her, Donovan? Is this folder like mine?" I couldn't help the tremble in my voice or the heat of the tears in my eyes.

He rushed to me, coming around the desk and turning the chair to face him. "No. No, Sabrina. You are the only one. You are the only woman alive that I have spent any time... The only one I've wanted to... watch and *know*. Everything has been you."

I'd never seen him struggle so much to get a thought across, and it made me want to climb into his arms and believe everything he told me.

But...

"You've slept with her." He'd told me that he had. He'd had his mouth on her pussy. He'd even described how he'd gone down on her.

And if he'd slept with her—like he'd slept with me—then couldn't he *feel* things for her too?

He didn't move, didn't lean forward or draw away, just stood there holding his ground with his hands planted on the armrests of the leather chair. "And you slept with Weston."

Ouch.

It felt like a punch.

I slumped back into the chair, absorbing the shock of his words. I knew what he was getting at—that I should understand that sleeping with someone did not equate to feelings. But what I heard was: *you hurt me, I hurt you.*

And he still had the upper hand.

"The thing is," I said, "you can just ask your private detective whether or not I'm sneaking off to see Weston behind your back."

Now he straightened. He considered for a moment, circling around the front of the desk. He was caught. If he asked me just to trust him, he would be a hypocrite.

When he was at the center of the desk, he turned to face me, placing both palms on the flat surface. "Is that what it would take to fix this? If you had someone watching me the way I have someone watching you?"

I turned the chair so it was pointed at him, and wrinkled my nose. "I can't really afford to hire a detective to follow you around everywhere, Donovan, if that's what you're getting at."

It was also dumb. If I wanted to know something about him, I'd just ask him.

Of course, he could always just ask me as well and that didn't seem to be good enough for him.

"No, it's not what I'm getting at. I take care of you, remember?" He reached over and grabbed the phone that was secured to the landline and dragged it over to him. Before I could ask what he was doing, he picked up the receiver and dialed a number he knew by heart.

As it rang, he said to me, "You're in luck. The guy I had working for Cade is free now, but he's still on retainer, which means he's—" He moved the mouthpiece to his lips. "Ferris. It's me. I have a new job for you."

I was beginning to understand where he was going with this. "This isn't necessary. Really."

He ignored me. "It's going to sound odd, but here's the details: your contact is Sabrina Lind. Yes, the same Sabrina Lind."

So, I'd been Ferris's subject before. Great.

"You're going to send the bill to me," he continued. "Anything she asks you to look into, you do it, no questions asked, even if the subject is me."

"*No,*" I mouthed. "Hang up."

But he didn't hang up.

He moved his eyes so he wasn't reading my lips. "I don't want any copies of the reports. They all go straight to her. You got it?"

"Donovan..." I warned.

Stubborn and alpha-minded, the man disregarded everything I'd said so far and held the phone out to me.

"No!" I couldn't even entertain the idea. I wouldn't.

"It's already done. Just take the call and give him your information." He pressed the receiver toward my hand.

"I said no!" I jumped up from his chair, away from him and his stupid phone call. "I'm not doing it, Donovan," I hissed with finality.

It might be tempting to go along with the investigation—for

somebody else. There was so much I didn't know about him, but I didn't want to learn about him from a report. I wanted him to show me who he was in person. I wanted to uncover him, layer by layer, the way that people do when they meet someone that fascinates them so entirely that they can't get enough until they hear everything from his own lips.

Donovan's jaw set, his mouth pressed together in a tight line as he held me in a hard unmoving stare. Several heavy beats passed.

Finally, he brought the receiver back to his own ear, and I let out the breath I'd been holding.

Until he started talking. "Ferris, the order is for a complete background report on me with surveillance. Solo surveillance only. No need for a tail if Sabrina is in my company. Photos. No videos. Send to the email that you have on file for her but send the invoice to me."

I crossed my arms under my breasts and tried to decide if I was angry or disappointed.

Donovan finished the call and hung up the phone with a sharp clack that suggested he was as frustrated as I was, and for some reason that lessened my irritation a degree or two.

"You don't have to look so wounded," he said, coolly. "You said I didn't have to give this up."

"That didn't mean that you should try and force me into the same behavior." How could he not understand?

"This is what I know, Sabrina. You wanted answers; this is how I know how to give them."

There was a sincerity in his tone that awoke something in me, made *me* the one to understand—he wasn't trying to make me mad. He wasn't trying to hurt me. He wasn't trying to overrule my wishes. He was doing the best he could with what he knew, and *this* was what he knew. Surveillance. Stalking. Sneaking around.

It was up to me to teach him differently. I'd have to teach him trust.

And to teach him trust, I'd first have to show him trust.

"I don't need that report." When it came to my email, I'd just delete it, I'd decided. "But if that's what you need to do, I understand. Right now, what I need is for you to tell me once again that you don't have feelings for Sun." I took a deep breath—this was going to be hard. "And I'll believe you."

He came to me in three easy steps. Putting his hand on my chin, he tilted it up to meet his eyes. "I don't feel anything for Sun. I've never felt anything for her. She was always just a distraction so that I wouldn't go crazy from how much I loved you."

My chest tightened and a knot formed in the back of my throat. I pushed up to the balls of my feet and pressed my forehead to his. "Thank you. I believe you."

FIFTEEN

MONDAY CAME FASTER than it seemed possible, as it often did. With Weston gone, my workload had doubled. On top of his absence, the end of the year always brought new campaigns. Existing clients wanted to get a head start on the new year; new clients were knocking on the door with resolutions for a better business going forward.

Fortunately, I had little time for worrying about office gossip or private investigators. I didn't even have time to eat lunch. By afternoon, I realized how easily I could be buried under the demands. I canceled everything unnecessary and came to terms with the fact that I would be running back and forth between my office and Weston's all week.

Wednesday morning I gave up, gathered what was important from my space, and moved into his.

"You look good in a room this size," Donovan said when he came in to check on me that evening.

I looked up from the stacks of strategy reports in front of me and blinked several times. I'd darkened the glass walls of the office so that the other staff members wouldn't distract me, but it had the downside of closing me off to the world. My phone had died hours ago. I glanced at the window behind me and realized for the first time that it was dark. Nighttime dark.

"I guess I lost track of time." I stretched my legs out in front of me and flexed a foot. I'd long ago slipped off my shoes.

Donovan sat in the chair across from me and rested his ankle on the opposite knee. "You've been doing that a lot this week."

It wasn't exactly accusatory, but I had the sense that he was trying to tell me something.

"I'm sorry I haven't had any time for you. I had no idea this would be so hard. I didn't think Weston did anything."

"Weston *doesn't* do anything. This is the best his job has ever been done. The rest of us are never going to let you leave." He smiled, and I knew he wasn't saying it just to be kind. "And don't worry about me. I'm taking you away this weekend."

I cocked my head, intrigued with this new information. "Oh really?" I had planned on working all weekend. There was no other way to get through everything I needed to without doing so, even though I'd worked until almost ten every night so far this week.

"You can't work every second of your life and still expect to do a good job, Sabrina. Trust me, I know. You have to have a little downtime."

I folded my arms under my breasts. "And you have so much downtime. Tell me Mr. Kincaid, what hobbies do you have? What occupies your weekends besides work?"

"You."

Okay. He won.

"And I will allow you to have time to work this weekend as well, as long as you occupy part of your weekend with me."

The only reason I didn't say anything right away was because I was too busy melting inside. "You make it really hard for a girl to argue."

"That's the whole point." His brow wrinkled as if he were thinking. "I have to admit, it's a whole lot easier just telling you to go places. Though it was more fun devising ways to get you where I wanted you to be."

"Asking me. You *ask* me to go places. You don't tell me."

"Yeah. That's what I do." He smirked, and I couldn't decide if he was indulging me or if I was indulging him, but when I thought about it, I didn't really want to find out.

"So where is it that you want me to be this weekend?" I asked, gathering the papers in front of me into organized piles for the morning. I'd worked long enough today. My brain was mush at this point. "Do I get to know? Or is it a surprise?"

He considered before answering. "My parents' country house in Washington, Connecticut. They will be there as well. I apologize for that. My mother hates the city in the winter, and she pretty much stays in Washington from the weekend after Thanksgiving until New Year's. But it's a big house, and my father is just as much of a workaholic as we are, so we won't have to spend very much time with them."

I couldn't stop smiling. "You're taking me to meet your parents?"

He raised a brow. "Did you hear anything else I said?"

"Not really." I was practically giddy. Schoolgirl giddy. "Meeting the guy's parents, Donovan... That's a big deal. I'm really kind of flustered right now."

His eyes grew warm and soft like melted cookies. "You're a big deal to me," he said quietly, and the air left my lungs. With more energy, he went on. "I'm serious, though. My parents are cold and formal. Don't expect much from them. They will engage with you transactionally."

I thought it wasn't a good idea quite yet to remind him that *he'd* engaged with me transactionally as well. "Then why their country house? We could go someplace else."

"Because it's beautiful, even in the winter. *Especially* in the winter. I want to share it with you."

Almost as an afterthought, he said, "And I want them to meet you. Even though they don't deserve to know you."

Silently, I ran my hand flat along the surface I had just cleared on the desk, overwhelmed by the things he'd just said. When I found my voice again, I agreed. "I'd like to go there. Please. I'd like to meet them."

"We're driving out at four sharp on Friday. Have everything you need here and ready by then. We'll take a driver so we can even work on the ride up. I can help you with anything you're behind on. I should have all my operations projections in place before we leave."

"All that sounds really fucking fantastic."

He was staring at me, hard and deep, the way he did when he was unearthing me, bringing what was buried inside me to the surface.

Also the way he looked at me when he was scheming. When he wanted to test my boundaries. When he wanted to play.

I was afraid to ask. "What?"

"Take off your panties."

"What?" I'd heard him, I just didn't know if he was teasing or not.

"It's after nine. You and I are the last people here. Take off your panties."

What was I thinking? He was never just teasing.

"Why?" I wasn't disagreeing. But I wanted to know.

"I'm going to fuck you on Weston's desk."

Oh God.

Now I *needed* to take off my panties because they were drenched. Why did that turn me on so fucking much? Because it was someone else's property? Because it was my boss's desk?

Because I could sense the primitive alpha reasoning behind Donovan's desire to do it?

"There are probably cameras," I said, scanning the most likely spots for their location.

"I *know* there are cameras. They are visual only. Weston will be able to see everything we do if he decides to look through the security footage. Don't tell me that doesn't turn you on, because we both know it does."

Yep. That sure did.

My breath shuddered as I drew it in. The reality was Weston would have no reason to look at the footage. I'd been there for three months and we'd never looked at security footage. In all my years at Now, Inc. we'd never once looked at the cameras. They were always there, "just in case." "Just in case" never happened.

But. There was always the possibility that Weston *could*.

I was already going to do it. I was already slipping on my shoes, standing up, coming around the desk to Donovan.

"What about you? Are you into this because the voyeurism turns you on as well, or because you want to show Weston I'm yours?" I pulled the skirt of my dress up so that my panties were visible and turned, as if making a show of it for the cameras. Then I tugged them down my legs seductively, maneuvered them over my heels and handed them to Donovan.

His expression said he was pleased with my performance, if not also a bit surprised. He took the panties I offered him, sniffed them, and tucked them in his front suit pocket. "Both," he answered. "Definitely both."

He pulled me to him and kissed me, sucking on my tongue, before swiftly turning me around and bending me over the desk. The skirt I was wearing was full and easy to gather. Donovan pulled it up around my waist so that my pussy and backside were on display.

I felt vulnerable and exposed—so very exposed—knowing

that there were cameras in the room. Knowing that Weston could see any of this one day. Even certain that he would never watch, I wasn't sure I would do this if it was anybody *but* Weston. He had seen me naked before. He wasn't seeing anything new.

But what about Donovan? How did he feel about exposing me to another man? Was he not bothered by the idea that Weston, specifically, might see me?

I was both tormented and turned on by that strange juxtaposition of ideas—Donovan wanting to keep me to himself and also owning me so completely that it was his prerogative if he wanted to show me off.

It turned out he had his own conflicting desires.

He removed his jacket, undid the cufflinks at his wrists, and put them in his pocket. After he pushed up the sleeves of his shirt, he glided his palm along my ass. "All of this, Sabrina, belongs to me," he said, definitively. "No one gets to touch your ass but me." He moved his fingers to my pussy and dipped inside. "No one gets to touch your pussy but me. No one gets to see any of this but me."

I moaned as he stroked in and out of my hole. He hadn't even touched my clit, but I was so aroused, I didn't need it.

"Do you understand? This, right now, in front of these cameras, is on my terms. And it's the last time Weston has a chance of ever seeing you like this. Tell me you understand, Sabrina."

"I understand." Two words and they were so hard to get out while he was massaging that spot inside me.

But I understood. I got it. Donovan was claiming me, and I had absolutely zero problem with it.

Suddenly, his hand was gone. Then it was back, landing on my behind with a crisp smack.

I jumped with a yelp but Donovan was already smoothing away the ache.

"That was for teasing me, Sabrina. For flirting with Weston in front of me that night at the restaurant."

Uh, what?

He spanked me again, this time on my other cheek, harder. I whimpered as he chased the pain with a circular massage of his palm. "This is for dancing with him at his wedding when you should've been in my arms."

He was punishing me. Punishing me for being with Weston.

Fuck. That was hot.

I pressed my thighs together as though that could ease the buzz between them, as though it could stop the liquid dripping from my cunt.

Another smack and my orgasm was already building. "That was for accepting the job when he offered it to you, when I worked so hard to provide you with a nice career in Los Angeles." His tone was more strained, more ragged with each new strike.

The next hit came closer in spacing, with barely enough time to achieve relief from the last. "This is for the doe eyes you gave him every day for half a semester at Harvard. And this one is for thinking even for one minute that he could ever give you anything you needed."

That blow was the worst, the pain bringing tears to my eyes, but it wasn't any worse than hearing the pain in Donovan's voice, pain he'd carried for years. Pain I'd never known about, that he'd never truly blamed me for, and if I could in this small way feel it for him, then I would take a hundred more blows.

But that wasn't what he had in mind for me.

"And this," he said as I heard his belt being worked open, his zipper being drawn down. "This is for spending a weekend in his bed. You were never his to give him what you let him take."

I reached across the desk and held onto the opposite edge, attempting to prepare for Donovan's thrust.

Still, he caught me off guard, slamming into me with such

force that it felt like he was hitting the very end of me, like he'd found every single part of me there was to know, every last secret, every last hidden sin, and had driven it out of me with his entry.

He didn't let up, pounding into me with quick, frenzied, punishing strokes, and I knew he was chasing his own demons, and that this fuck was maybe more for him than any other time I'd spread my legs.

But this was for me too, as everything he did was for me. And any last worry I had about Sun Le Chen was fucked into a bad memory. There was no way that he could need me this much, be this hurt by my relationship with Weston, and be carrying a torch for someone else. It just wasn't possible. He'd said to me once that if I could see inside him that I would know that there was no one else.

Well, I couldn't see inside him, but I could *feel*. He was making me feel everything he felt, and it was raw and jagged and dirty and hard.

But it was love, and it was rich, and he lavished me with it.

His speed and tempo were erratic. His balls slapped against my clit. That, plus the erotic scenario sent me toward climax, despite the lack of manual stimulation. Donovan still came before I did, rutting into me as he released, even after he was completely empty, as if he needed to be sure that every drop had been spilled inside me. And when it was, he lifted me so that my back was against his chest, then reached around and massaged my clit. Just a little nudge was all it took before I was spiraling into a sea of bright lights and warmth and pleasure.

I was still spinning when Donovan turned me around to face him and kissed me sweetly, luxuriously, for much longer than I would have expected considering that we weren't in our own space. It were as though I were his oxygen, and he'd been flying a bit too high, or diving much too deep, and he needed me to catch his breath, to fill his lungs, to make him right again.

Finally he broke away. "I don't want to stop touching you," he said, straightening my clothing.

I kissed him again. And again, because I didn't want to stop touching him either. But I hadn't brought any clothes with me to stay the night at his house, and I had to be to work too early in the morning with too much to do the next day to risk not getting a good night's sleep.

But it didn't mean he couldn't come to my place.

"You could—" I started to say.

"I'm coming to your place," he said at the same time.

"Good." I had a feeling it was the only way we were getting out of here tonight. I pulled myself away and went to the closet to get my coat and purse while he straightened out his sleeves and put on his jacket.

"Ready?" I asked, standing at the doorway.

"Just one thing first." He went to one of the shelves where Weston kept his comic books displayed, and picked one up. "I wanted to borrow his first edition of The Walking Dead," he explained on the way out.

I was too tired to make anything of it at the time, even though it was immediately strange—Donovan reading comic books? But it wasn't until I was drifting off to sleep in his arms much later that night that I realized:

When Weston found his possession missing, he was going to watch the security tapes.

SIXTEEN

WASHINGTON, Connecticut was two hours outside the city. We left on Friday afternoon shortly before four o'clock so that I could stop by my house and pick up my weekend bag before hitting the road. I hadn't wanted to take it to the office with me. Even if most of the staff knew that I was dating Donovan, they didn't need to know what we were doing with our free time. I certainly didn't want to feed their imagination.

We took the Tesla, which was equipped with an all-wheel drive system that made the car exceptional in all weather, according to Donovan. Apparently he was quite proud of his cars and extremely willing to boast about them when prodded, a rather fascinating fact to learn about him. Since he'd brought his driver along, we were both passengers, and the two of us knocked out a bunch of the work that had lingered from the week on the ride up, so by the time we turned down the tree-lined lane, white from snow, I felt relaxed and ready for some social engagement.

The car came to a stop at the end of the long driveway in front of a sprawling two-level mansion. It was gorgeous from the outside, a well-kept home with sweeping vistas over hundreds of acres of preserved land. It was private and hard to get to, a real getaway location, and much too big for a family of three—two, now that Donovan was grown.

"Only your parents live here?" I asked, stepping out of the car.

He nodded with an embarrassed sigh. "And only part-time, at that."

"Wow. There's certainly a lot of room." We hadn't made it inside yet, but I was guessing it was probably ten thousand square feet. I'd grown up in a house that was barely twelve hundred square feet.

"My parents like to have the option to keep as much distance between themselves as possible. You'll see. Let's get out of the cold."

He led me to the door, which opened before we had the chance to knock, and there stood a tall, middle-aged gentleman dressed in slacks and a sweater, too young to be Donovan's father.

"Mr. Kincaid," he said in greeting, eyes cast down. "Welcome back to the Pinnacle House. And welcome to your guest."

"This is Sabrina Lind," Donovan said in introduction as he helped me remove my coat. "I apologize; I don't remember your name."

"No apologies, sir. It's Edward. I can take that for you." He took my coat and hung it in a nearby closet, then returned to take Donovan's.

The driver entered behind us to drop off our luggage. "Where shall I park the car?"

"The third garage is empty," Edward said. "I'll meet you there in a moment to open it for you. Your mother suggested I put you in the upstairs master, Mr. Kincaid, is that still fine with you?"

"That will be perfect."

"I'll bring your things directly if you'd like to go up and wash for dinner. Your mother wishes I remind you it will be served at six thirty precisely."

I watched the exchange between the two men. Donovan was always guarded and stoic, but I found it interesting how reserved the butler—or whatever his title might be—was. He was the person designated to greet us. He'd been hospitable, technically, but nothing about his words or actions had felt warm or welcoming.

Maybe that's how servants were supposed to act; what did I know? I'd never been around any before.

"Yes, dinner at six thirty precisely," Donovan said with a bit of annoyance. "Heaven forbid my mother's schedule vary even a minute from her routine."

"Is that a message you'd like me to give her, sir?" There was a bit of a challenge in those words from Edward, despite his formality, as though he were loyal to his employer, which I suppose he should be.

"No," Donovan laughed gruffly. "No message. We'll be there." He shifted his attention to me. "Sabrina, I'd love to give you a tour but we can't right now. We have just enough time to change if you'd like. Shall we?"

He offered his hand, and I took it. The entryway opened into a large free space with plush rugs covering the wooden floor and fancy brocade couches in front of the fireplace. The far wall showcased a giant window that overlooked the land below. It was too dark outside and there were too many lights inside to fully capture the view, but I had a feeling it was going to be breathtaking.

To our left, a grand staircase wound upward. Donovan led me to this, and once we'd reached the top, he steered me down the hallway to a room at the end of the house with double doors. These opened into a grand master suite with a large four- poster bed, a fireplace with a fire already burning in it, a sitting area with a desk, and an en suite. A set of glass doors opened up to a private balcony. I peeked outside. The snow had started falling softly though, and I couldn't see very far in the dark.

Donovan came up behind me and put his arms around my waist. "It will be beautiful in the morning, especially as the sun comes up. Trust me. But right now we have fifteen minutes before dinner. Will you be ready?"

I turned to make a comment about not having my bag yet, but a knock on the door said that Edward was just outside. He came in and placed my luggage on a bench at the foot of the bed, and set Donovan's bag on the floor next to it.

Immediately, I opened up my suitcase and started digging inside for something to wear. I hadn't actually planned on changing for dinner, but now I felt obligated. Thank goodness I'd thrown in an extra couple of outfits so I would be prepared for any spontaneous occasion.

Except even with all the choices, I had no idea what to choose. I was already in an A-line business skirt and jacket. Was I supposed to dress up or down?

"I don't know what to wear," I said, frantically throwing a couple of items over the bottom of the bed to better view my options.

Donovan came back from the closet where he'd hung up his suit jacket. "The Ann Taylor," he said, "with the black. I'm going to wear slacks."

I grabbed the skirt—a feminine floral pattern—my makeup bag, and the sweater in question, turned to him and gave him a quick peck on the lips. "Thank you."

Then I ran to the bathroom to change.

I came out ten minutes later wearing the new outfit, my mascara and lip gloss freshened.

Donovan was waiting at the door, as though he had just been about to knock. He had changed too, and was now wearing slacks and a burnt red pullover that brought out the green in his eyes.

"You're beautiful." His gaze said he maybe didn't want to go downstairs as much as he had just a minute ago.

"But am I *appropriate?*" I was suddenly nervous, I realized. My throat was dry and my palms were sweaty.

He looked as though he were debating the answer, or at least as if he had something that he wanted to say but wasn't sure if he *should* say it or not.

But before I could get too worked up about it, he said, "You're perfect." He glanced at his watch. "And we've got to go."

I slipped on my pumps and followed him out the door, ignoring the gnawing feeling that he wasn't telling me something, an emotion that was hard to distinguish beneath the fear that I was woefully unprepared.

Downstairs, we crossed through the free area we passed when we walked in, then another living area, into a formal dining room with a beautiful cherry wood dining set and an ornate crystal chandelier above it. French doors led out to a patio, and I could imagine that in summer the room could be opened up that way to hold generous banquets.

But it was still winter. It was dark outside, and the table, which had seats for twelve, was set for four. An attractive gentleman with silver hair and a beard sat at the head. Next to him was a stunning redhead with a long neck and green eyes.

The man stood when we entered, and Edward, whom I hadn't noticed standing at the wall, approached to pull a chair out for me at the place across from the redhead. Donovan sat next to me. His father sat again at the same time he did.

There had yet to be any introductions, yet to be any greetings at all, when the redhead—Donovan's mother—glanced up at the gold filigree clock on the wall and said, "Six thirty on the nose. Hmm."

She was clearly unhappy, though we had made it on time so I was confused as to her demeanor.

"We're here, mother," Donovan said, letting out a breath audible only to me.

"I'm simply so startled that your manners have declined to such a degree. There was a time when six thirty service meant that we were in our seats no later than six twenty. Is punctuality not that important on the other side of the world?" She leaned in toward her husband. "You've been to Japan more than I have. Is that what this is, Raymond?"

Now I understood why Donovan was so anxious to make it down here on time.

Raymond tilted his head from side to side, considering. "I imagine it's more a product of his bachelor status, Susan. They're pretty punctual there in Tokyo."

As he spoke, Edward returned from wherever he'd disappeared to after seating us carrying a bottle of wine, which he poured first into Raymond's glass.

"We are on time," Donovan said, smoothing the napkin in his lap. "We did not make it in any earlier than the designated dinner time, which is a product of traffic and weather, and has no reflection at all on my respect for punctuality. On *our* respect for punctuality," he corrected, including me the second time.

His mother sat straight-backed and silent, and I thought for a moment she might drop it.

But then she said, "You should have left earlier."

"Are you really going to be like this tonight?" Donovan asked at the same time that I said, "It's my fault. I left my luggage at my apartment and we had to make an extra stop."

Susan looked at me for maybe the first time since we'd arrived, her eyes narrowed as though she'd been approached with a puzzle that she couldn't understand.

"Leave them alone, Susan. Arguing will just delay the meal," Raymond said. His wife seemed to want to say more, but as if her husband was the final word, she pressed her lips into a tight line and didn't say another thing on the subject.

Next to me, Donovan took a long swallow of wine. Raymond signaled to Edward to serve salad plates. And I stared intently at the empty dish in front of me, unsure where to look or what to say. Donovan had told me his parents weren't friendly, but I'd expected to at least be acknowledged. I'd expected my boyfriend to point me out if they didn't.

I was jumping the gun.

Because as soon as Donovan set his glass down, he said, "Sabrina, these are my parents. Raymond and Susan." He shot his mother a daring glare. "I am instructing her to address you by your first names, Mother, so don't get your panties in a wad when she doesn't call you Ms. Kincaid like you've trained everyone else in the household."

"That was awfully presumptuous of you, Donovan. I really wish you would've asked." Susan's green eyes flared when she was angry, like her son's, I noticed.

But what a thing to be angry over.

I didn't know if I wanted to laugh or tell her off. What I did know was that we hadn't been in their presence very long, but I was already irritated that my date had allowed me to walk in so unprepared. Couldn't he have given me a heads up? Like, *hey, my mom's a crazy bitch. Ignore everything she says.*

Maybe that's what he'd wanted to say as we were walking out of our room, and given up. Well, I understood that it might be hard to speak ill about your folks, but he really should have tried harder.

"I'm happy to call you Ms. Kincaid, if that's what you prefer," I offered congenially, intending to address her as little as possible.

I could feel Donovan's displeasure with this suggestion.

Susan, however, seemed to like it very much. "Thank you,

Sabrina." To her son she said, "She has manners, Donovan, that's key in a woman."

It wasn't like *she* had any to know.

His mother returned her attention to me. "I do appreciate that offer; the gesture says everything about what type of person you are. But my son is right. A first name basis is probably more practical, especially if we are going to be seeing each other from time to time moving forward."

Seriously?

Okay, Donovan couldn't have prepared me for this. No matter what he'd said, I would not have been able to predict what kind of answer a woman like this would want from me. No wonder he hadn't tried.

I wanted to say something snide in return but her latest comments had been fairly polite, and it was perhaps best not to rock the boat.

"Wonderful, Susan," I said instead, and reached for my wine glass.

Edward had better have another bottle on hand, I thought, because this evening was going to take a lot of alcohol to get through.

"SO SABRINA, will you quit working after the wedding or will you wait until you are pregnant?"

I almost choked on my chicken roulade.

After our initial introduction, the evening had gone better. Early on, it was obvious that Raymond and Susan's only interest where I was concerned was in how well-bred I was. Or how well-bred I *wasn't*, as the case may be.

But poverty had always been my beginning, and that was unchangeable. I was used to the looks I got when people from better means heard about my upbringing. I had gotten it a lot when I had been at Harvard, in fact. And when someone like Donovan showed up with someone like me on his arm, of course his parents would want to know about my education, my current means. They probably were afraid I was after their son's money, and it was only natural to make sure that I had legitimate feelings for him.

I did my best to speak affectionately about him at every turn possible. When the time came to speak about my job, I made sure I sounded independent and secure, not reliant on Donovan for my position or his paycheck, so the Kincaids wouldn't have to worry that I was attaching myself to him for reasons other than romantic. I had thought I was easing them into our relationship.

Then Raymond completely took me off guard by asking about weddings and babies.

"We're not engaged," I said in unison with Donovan.

I was thankful he'd had the same answer. For a moment I wondered if I'd been brought here under false pretenses.

Though at the same time, I was intrigued by the idea. I almost wished I had time to consider it longer before he'd made it clear those weren't his intentions.

"Not yet, maybe," Raymond said, in between bites of his entrée. He took a swallow from his water goblet. "But why else would Donovan bring you here? He's never introduced a woman to us before."

"I knew you weren't gay," Susan said as though she had discussed it many times in the past.

Donovan blinked, shaking his head almost indiscernibly. "I'm not even acknowledging that comment."

"You've never introduced anyone to your parents before?" I patted my mouth with my napkin, trying to find a safer topic, one that might not have me on such pins and needles.

"They knew Amanda. Who else would I have brought here?"

I supposed no one. He'd told me that he hadn't had feelings for anyone since his fiancée had died so who would he have brought? It wasn't surprising that there hadn't been anyone.

Still, I was reeling from Raymond's comments. Why would he assume that engagement was inevitable when I'd only just met them?

Was it inevitable?

"You didn't answer the question," Susan prodded. She seemed to have decided to like me, but that wasn't saying a lot. I wasn't even sure she liked Donovan very much.

"What question?" The question about whether I'd quit working or not? Did she seriously expect me to answer that?

Thankfully Donovan intervened. "Sabrina worked harder than a lot of people do to get her degrees and to earn her reputation in the industry. I doubt that she will want to end her career if or when she marries, no matter how well off her husband is. She is very independent and strong-minded, and I'm certain she would enjoy contributing a paycheck almost as much as she enjoys the work itself. Not that it's any of our business what she chooses to do, since as I said, we are not betrothed."

"Right. I like working." I didn't know if I liked his answer, though. There was nothing wrong with it, and we absolutely weren't engaged, but did he have to seem so adamant about it?

Despite his son's argument to the contrary, Raymond seemed not to be the kind of guy who thought anything was out of the realm of his business. "But you will quit when you're pregnant?"

Donovan rushed to answer this as well, but this time I decided to fend for myself. "I don't see why I'd have to."

Not that I was getting pregnant. Not that I was getting married.

Raymond and Susan exchanged anxious glances.

"Oh, but dear, you can't work with a baby," she said patiently. A bit condescendingly, too.

"It's not a woman's role," Raymond agreed.

"Not in polite circles. You can volunteer for the PTA. You can head charities—that's what I do. You can still work, per se, but earning an actual paycheck is..." She searched for the word that she wanted. "Tacky. And it's not a good example for the baby."

I dropped my fork and looked at Donovan incredulously. He had his eyes closed and his jaw was working. It occurred to me that perhaps it was his parents that were the initial cause of the chronic clench of his teeth.

It sure wasn't *his* fault they were who they were.

But somehow, he was who *he* was because of them.

And so, for that reason alone, I didn't want to alienate them, no matter how archaic and idiotic their notions.

So when he began again to defend me and my future choices, I slipped my hand onto his knee under the table, letting him know I had this.

"I'll certainly consider your advice," I told them. "Of course, when the time comes to make those decisions, Donovan and I will have to seriously discuss it together."

I didn't even look to his parents for a reaction. I only looked to him. And though he didn't smile with his lips, his eyes did. Under the table, he laced his fingers through mine, and we held them together like a secret only the two of us knew for the rest of the meal.

AFTER DINNER, Susan went to bed early and Raymond asked Donovan to join him in his study for a cigar. It was clear that I was not invited, possibly because I was not his son, but I had a feeling it was because I was not a man.

It was fine. I was perfectly content to be left on my own. I went upstairs to our suite and spent an hour entering data I'd gathered on the ride up into my computer now that I had Wi-Fi. When I'd finished and Donovan still hadn't come up, I put on some slippers, stole the blanket from the bottom of the bed to wrap around me, and slipped out onto the balcony.

The night was cold and crisp, wetter and thicker than in the city. My breath was visible as I exhaled like I was smoking cigarettes. I leaned against the railing and looked out over the property and the land that stretched out beyond. It had stopped snowing and the moon was out now, and the stars. And without the lights of the city, I could see for miles—an ocean of trees and snow. Here and there a glow came from beneath the canopy, suggesting a residence underneath. But mostly there was nothing but woods. No one.

It was lonely.

As lonely as this house—this behemoth of a house that lodged two people, and perhaps an employee or two.

Donovan had told me he'd spent most of his time growing up in the city, but that his parents preferred the country home because of the space it provided them. And standing outside in the cold, alone, after the most unfriendly dinner of my life, all I could think was—how much space do three people who barely even talk need?

What a lonely way to grow up. What a lonely life Donovan had growing up.

As if summoned by my thoughts, the door behind me opened, and Donovan stepped out onto the balcony. "Two cigars and a glass of whiskey and I still didn't hear all the highlights of his stock picks this quarter." He came up next to me and held his hand out in my direction.

I looked down at his offering. A tumbler of scotch.

I accepted it and threw back a large swallow, enjoying the instant warmth that it provided.

"What are you thinking?" he asked, swirling the liquid in his own matching tumbler.

"That my amazing, loving, supportive, understanding parents both died too young. And yours are still alive. And that it's not fair." I regretted it as soon as I said it. I turned to meet his gaze. "I'm sorry. That was terrible."

"Raymond and Susan are terrible," he said, doubling down on my statement. He took a swallow from his drink and looked out over the distance. "I wish I could have met your parents."

God, I missed them. So much sometimes that my insides felt raw.

And sometimes I barely thought about them. That's how life went.

But wouldn't that have been something, for them to have met Donovan? For Donovan to have met *them*. "I don't know what would've happened if my father hadn't died—what would've happened at Harvard when I returned. But I wouldn't have made it to Harvard at all without the life insurance from my mother's death. So I suppose I can't wish that she'd never died and still have you."

He turned so that his back was to the railing, and he could face me better. "Do you still want me after tonight? After meeting them?" He nodded toward the house, as if it were a stand-in for his parents.

"I do." Maybe even more than I did before.

"You know they aren't me, don't you? I would never ask you to give up any part of who you are to fulfill some outdated societal role."

I sighed, because he couldn't understand how many times a day I was asked to do just that. How many times a day a woman in a world of men was asked to fulfill some outdated societal role —it was too many times to count, too many to know, too many to solve between the two of us and two tumblers of scotch.

"It could be kind of fun though, if you pretended that you might." I peered over at him and let him imagine the filthy kind of ways we could play 1950s housewife.

"You're such a dirty girl."

"Come on inside and let me prove it."

I put my hand in his and, together, we walked out of the lonely night.

SEVENTEEN

"DAMN. THAT'S SOME YARD." I stood with Donovan on the terrace that ran along the length of the back of the house. And I was in awe. It was the highlight of Pinnacle House—the views. No doubt about it.

Our morning had started late. We'd eaten breakfast in bed. Donovan had brought it up on a tray, egg casserole with gourmet coffee and orange juice, and a side of roasted potatoes. He hadn't said it was the reason, but I presumed we stayed in our room in order to miss his parents. Which we did.

After our meal, we dressed for the day. I bundled up in layers with a warm sweater over my T-shirt and jeans, as per Donovan's instructions. Then he gave me the tour.

We started inside, walking from one room to the next, Donovan pointing out the use and function of each. But despite the size of the house, there was nothing very remarkable about it. Most of the rooms were rarely used, but were acted as showcases instead. The second living room had a Christmas tree that had been professionally ornamented, he'd told me. The guest rooms were all decorated with impersonal taste, as though being staged for a house sale. Even a bed and breakfast had more personality. The master suite on the lower floor was closed off, so I couldn't see if it was more lived in, and Raymond had locked himself away in his study so that room was also off limits.

I did get a glimpse into Susan's life in the country house. Her personal space, as the family called it, was located on the other end of the top floor, as far from the study as possible. She'd gone to spend the day in town at some local antiques fair, so we snuck a peek into her room. It was good sized, large enough to hold a desk and sitting area as well as a bed and dresser. Like the guestrooms, it hadn't been personalized. I did notice a few items lying around that indicated an actual human spent time here—reading glasses on the desk. A glass of water on the nightstand.

"Does she sleep here?" I asked. Even if she didn't sleep with her husband, there were plenty of other rooms in the house available. She didn't have to fit her entire life at Pinnacle House into her office.

Donovan shrugged. "I'm not even sure she really sleeps."

How strange to not even wonder about the people that you live with, to share a roof and a table with walking mysteries.

Though I supposed it had been a long time since he had lived with them for real.

"What about your things?" I asked when we'd gone through the whole house and I'd seen nothing that reminded me of Donovan. "Are the remnants from your childhood stored away somewhere here?"

"Whatever I didn't take with me when I moved out, they threw away."

"Saves on storage, I suppose." Actually, I was wondering why the Kincaids even had a child. Between the lack of warmth and the erasure of his existence here, it was hard to imagine they'd really wanted him in the first place.

"I didn't have anything I wanted to keep. There wasn't

anything here that I was attached to. What I like about this house is outside."

And that is how we ended up on the terrace looking out over the endless property beyond.

The land closest to the house was tiered and landscaped. The first level had a pool that had been covered for the season. The next level appeared to be a long stretch of lawn that was now just a bed of snow. A stone wall surrounded it, and beyond were trees and hills and land. Endless, as far as the eye could see.

It was the kind of yard meant to be played in. It was the kind of yard that needed children.

"It's beautiful. Absolutely stunning." I put my gloved hand in his as we walked down the icy staircase to the lawn below. "But what did you do here? Were you one of those little boys who climbed trees? Did you capture bugs and hang them on the bulletin board in your room? Did you swim? Did you have friends around here that you met in secret forts just beyond the property line?" I tried to imagine him. He'd been on the rowing team in college, so sport wasn't completely out of the realm of possibility in his background.

He shook his head dismissively. "There are no neighbors for miles. All that land is protected. No one can ever build on it."

"Then what?"

His lip lifted into a bashful smile. "I snowshoed."

"Snowshoed?" I was taken aback. "Like those flat things that trappers used to walk on?"

"Are you making fun?"

I shook my head. "I'm just surprised. I could never have guessed that. How did you get into snowshoes? I didn't even know that was a thing people still did."

We were at the bottom of the stairs now, treading through the yard, our boots sinking into snow that had drifted two feet deep.

"Well, as you can see, the snow was very wet in Connecticut.

Not like that dry powder you have in Colorado. As a kid..." He trailed off, his jaw working as he got caught in his reminiscing. "Let's just say there wasn't much to keep me in the house. Or near it. Out there in those woods it's quiet. You can hear your own thoughts. I discovered early that I could hear myself better out there than I could in that house, silent as the house is.

"But it's not so easy to wander through the snowdrifts. You don't get very far without getting worn out." He laughed as the toe of my boot got stuck and I stumbled into him

"Yes. I see that," I laughed too, clutching onto him.

He wrapped his arms around my waist. "I would go for miles on those snowshoes. No one even noticed I was gone." He gave half a sardonic smile. "As long as I was back for dinner on time."

My chest pinched so tight. Like a fist wrapped around my heart.

He'd had so little nurturing in his life. Almost no one had modeled how to care for someone else. All the ways he'd cared for me, as misguided and inappropriate as they had been, they'd come from something truly organic. Something he'd devised completely on his own. No one had taught him how to love another person—and yet he'd still tried.

I had so little to give in return.

"If I had known you then," I offered what I had, "I like to think I would've met you in those woods."

"And if I had known *you* then, I would've schemed some way to make sure that you did."

I lifted my chin and pressed my mouth to his, hoping the heat of my body could do what the heat of his always did for me. Hoping it could erase the past and create images of a life with a vibrant house filled with warmth and love and never ever any clocks.

"YOU WERE president of your high school's campaign-finance board *and* the political action club?" I asked, reading the information from my phone.

"And the debate club," Donovan said smugly.

"And you were on the chess team. Figures."

After a walk around the property, we came inside to work. Raymond had gone into town to meet his wife for dinner, so it was just Donovan and I who'd sat at the long banquet table at six thirty precisely, eating a delicious meal of veal piccata and cranberry spinach salad.

When we finished, we poured ourselves some after-dinner drinks and headed upstairs. Earlier in the day, I'd received an email from Ferris containing the background report that Donovan had ordered on himself. I'd forgotten to cancel it in the craziness of the week. So now we were seated by the fire, Donovan in the armchair and me on the floor, while I read highlights from the report out loud.

"I didn't get this for you just so you could make fun of everything, you know," he said when I laughed about his letter in snowshoeing.

"I didn't know you could letter in snowshoe! I didn't know that was a school activity!" I was still laughing.

"It wasn't. I had to get special permission. It was taken to the school committee and there was a judicial hearing." He circled his hand in the air, signaling much to-do. "They voted in my favor."

"It was that important to you, huh?"

He shrugged. "I wanted to see if I could do it."

"Mm hm." I took a swallow from my tumbler to hide my smile. Sounded like him.

I scanned further through the document. "'Businesses identified with ownership by subject.' This is a longer list than I was aware of, Donovan." I'd known he was a wealthy man, wealthier than the investment at the advertising firm, but wow. "'Reach, Inc., Gaston's, King-Kincaid Financial.' You have ownership in your father's firm?"

He nodded. "Weston and I both have stock there."

I went back to the list. "'Ex-Ore.' That's a gas company, right?"

"Yes."

"HtoO is that water foundation... 'Lannister End?'" I looked up questioningly.

"A bed and breakfast in Connecticut. Not far from here. I'll take you some time."

"I'd like that." I scrolled past the rest of the companies he held stock in and found the list of organizations he was associated with. "Did you found all these? 'A Better Day," I read.

He seemed startled. "*That's* on there?"

"Yeah. What is it?"

"Just a charitable foundation. It's an umbrella for a bunch of other foundations." His brows were furrowed. Then he shook his head. "It's my father's organization, but he must have me listed on some of the entity papers."

"Ah." I'd moved on. "'MARCA?' What's that?"

He swirled his glass and watched the liquid dance around the bottom, as though it were more interesting than his answer. "It's, uh, it's an organization. Against rape. Men against rape culture and abuse." He let that sit, let me absorb the enormity of it.

Then he explained more. "It's geared at education. Teaching youth, especially—about consent, about women's rights."

"And you're the founder?"

"Yes."

"And you did that because of me?" I had a swell of pride and sentimentality. He was trying to be modest. I wasn't going to let him.

"Yes."

I set my phone down and stretched my feet out in front of me. The report hadn't been such a bad idea after all. I'd learned a few interesting things about him. But I'd learned just as many interesting things spending time with him this weekend.

And if I was going to learn more, I'd rather just ask.

"You graduated from Harvard with a Masters in business and stock in your father's financial firm. You already had an interest in finance and politics and ethics. You obviously felt compelled to start organizations that help people. Why did you choose to follow that by opening an advertising firm?"

He rested his elbow on the arm of the chair, his chin in his hand. "Why do *you* think I chose to open an advertising firm, Sabrina?"

"I don't want to sound narcissistic, but based on the pattern of things you've told me so far? I can't help but wonder if you chose it because *I* chose advertising as my emphasis."

"Go on."

Like I had tried to imagine him earlier in the day as a little boy, I tried now to imagine him as the young man he'd been in Cambridge. Intense and haunted. At the time, I thought he'd still been haunted by Amanda.

Now I reframed it, imagined him haunted by me—a woman he believed he shouldn't have, even when I was there in front of him. Even when I was in his arms.

"You chose advertising because that's what I chose," I said, my eyes fixed on my toes. "And you knew the irony of it because you never intended for me to work for you or with you. You just wanted to feel near me. Even when you were half a world away. Am I close?"

"It always felt like I was running away from you and running to you at the same time." His voice was low, the same timbre as the crackle of the fire behind me. "I'd lose myself in women—so many faceless women. Women who would let me treat them in terrible, terrible ways, just so I could forget you. And I never could."

I felt like he must've felt then too—like I wanted to run into what he was saying and run from it at the same time. I didn't want to know about other women. It hurt to hear it. But I wanted to hear how they would never be me.

And I also needed to know, just for my own peace of mind...

"I hate to ask this, but when you say you treated them terribly..." I trailed off, hoping he would fill in the blanks.

He did. "Most of the time I was in Tokyo, I was part of the underground BDSM scene. I never had relationships. Just sex with women who wanted to be dominated, mostly."

Now a new anxiety was building inside me. I sat up straighter. "You are a... Dominant? But we don't. I'm not." I didn't really know how to say what I was trying to say. We did some kinky stuff, but I wasn't about to be collared. "Don't you need that? I'm not a submissive. Not really, am I? Why are you laughing?"

He wasn't laughing so much as chuckling. "You are submissive enough, Sabrina. Trust me. I do need it. But it's not about the sex for me. I get what I need from you in other ways." He meant by taking care of me. By interfering and bossing and scheming to make my life the way he wanted it.

That's how he dominated me. That was what turned him on.

It was simple, and yet I had to process it. Had to let it sink in.

"Does that bother you?" he asked when I'd stayed silent for perhaps longer than he'd expected.

I tilted my head. "I'm just taking it in."

It was stirring something in me—something bigger, that I couldn't quite grasp yet.

Donovan tried to grab at the strings, tried to pull the something bigger into place. "It doesn't mean I'm not into what you need too, Sabrina."

That wasn't it. I wasn't worried about our sex life. He'd been fully present there. "I think that's been kind of obvious that you're into that."

"I'd hope so."

But that was close to it, sitting right next to the bigger thing. Because all those years that we were apart, I'd held onto Donovan through this kink that I needed. This fantasy that he would do unspeakably filthy things to me. Thinking all the time that I was crazy and sick and wrong. I'd run from those thoughts, and if he'd been in my life, I would've run from him. I *did* run from him when I first saw him again. I ran right into Weston's arms, a place I never belonged.

All the while, he held onto me through this kink that *he* needed, watching me, saving me, taking care of me. He probably thought he was crazy. I knew he thought he was sick and wrong. He tried to run from me. He hoped I'd never find out. He ran across the ocean, to a place he never belonged.

It slammed through me then, like a gale force wind, taking my breath away and taking any doubt that lingered with it.

I looked up at him sitting in the chair gazing down at me. "I love you."

He was still, silent. He blinked in natural time.

"Did you hear me?"

His lips curved up ever so slightly. "I'm just taking it in."

I abandoned my tumbler and crawled into his lap, straddling him. His arms came around my hips. "I love you," I said again.

He searched my eyes, studied my features as though he expected to see doubt etched in my expression.

My doubts were gone, and he had to already know, had to know exactly how I felt about him. He always knew everything about me before I did. Didn't he know this too?

If he didn't, I'd tell him again. As many times as it took.

I put my hand on his cheek, stroked my thumb across the

stubble, and bent down to graze my mouth against his. "I love you." A whisper this time.

I sucked his upper lip between mine then let it go.   "I. Love. You."

I couldn't tell him again in words for a long time. Because the next time I brushed over him, he snapped into action, and took over. His hand clasped behind my neck and held me tightly in place as his lips ground into mine, and his tongue thoroughly fucked my mouth.

I moaned, rocking my hips along the length of his stiffening erection.

My body ached under the weight of my clothing. Every movement with them on was like wading through a river in armor. My limbs were too heavy. There were too many layers between his skin and mine.

I tugged at his sweater and whimpered; frustrated that it wasn't already off.

He broke from my mouth with a discontented grunt, letting me know he was just as eager as I was. With frantic hands, he pulled my shirt and my sweater off over my head together and tossed them to the floor. Then he leaned down and sucked along the top of my breasts, covering every square inch of flesh with his mouth, as though I were a paint-by-body-part project, and this section of my landscape had been designated to be painted with his lips.

I arched into him as I reached behind me to undo the clasp of my bra. The cups fell down, and he pushed them away so he could take a peaked nipple between his thumb and finger while he flicked the other lightly with his tongue.

"Oh my God, I love you." I was already seeing stars. What this man could do to my breasts...

I had to have more of him. I tugged with more urgency at his sweater, and he got the hint, withdrawing from me just long enough to shed the material keeping his torso from mine. Then finally, I ran the flats of my palms along the dips and planes of his bare chest. He was so hard and solid and warm. I drew his nipple into my mouth and nipped and was rewarded with the pulse of his cock underneath me.

But that wasn't where he wanted my lips.

He gathered my hair behind my neck and pulled sharply, tilting my chin up so that he could reclaim my mouth with his. I pressed into him, rubbing against him like he was a scratching post and I was a kitten with a bad itch.

Soon he stood, lifting me with him, never breaking our kiss. I wrapped my legs around his waist and held on as he carried me to the bed. He laid me down and immediately worked on ridding me of my jeans and panties, then he pushed my thighs apart and buried his head in between.

He sucked me and fingered me, tormenting me to climax twice before he stood to remove his own pants. When he was fully naked, he stood above me and fisted his cock, heavy and thick.

"Say it." I was greedy. He'd told me he loved me more than I'd told him, told me *before* I told him, but now I decided I wanted to hear him say it again too.

I didn't know if he could guess what I wanted. Whatever he said would work. I just wanted him to talk to me. I stretched my hand out toward his hard thigh, unable to reach him. "I want you to say it."

He stroked himself. Up and down. "You are mine, Sabrina." Close enough.

He crawled between my legs, and I spread them farther to make room for him. "Because I love you," he said, dragging the head of his cock down the split of my pussy. "Because I've always loved you."

He punctuated the last line by sliding all the way inside me.

I cried out as his tip touched the deepest part of me. "I'm yours."

He lowered himself over me, holding me closer and tighter than he usually did when he fucked me. "You're mine," he repeated as he moved inside me, establishing his rhythm, steady and brisk.

"And you're mine," I said, breathless.

He slowed ever so slightly, caught by surprise. Then he nodded and picked up his swift pace. "I'm yours." He kissed me. "I'm yours."

We made love like that well into the night, holding each other, kissing, whispering words we'd never said to anyone else. We wrapped ourselves in this chrysalis; this love we'd found that would change us both. This filthy love that had reminded me what it felt like to be cared for. This rich love that taught Donovan for the first time in his life what it could feel like to belong to someone.

EIGHTEEN

"I WOULDN'T MOVE that if I were you," Donovan said as I waved my hand over my last remaining knight. "It's going to leave your queen vulnerable."

Oh, right. I could see it once he'd said that. It was Sunday afternoon, and we were sitting in the living room in front of the Christmas tree—me on the floor, him on the sofa. We'd have to leave in a few hours for the city, but first, at my request, Donovan had brought out a chessboard and was teaching me how to play more than just a basic game. I hadn't ever really attempted it seriously, but I'd thought I was better than I was. Apparently, chess is hard.

I moved my hand toward the nearby bishop, intending to pick it up, but stopped as he exclaimed, "If you touch that you have to move it."

"I want to move it." Didn't I? It was really the only move I had. He'd already captured most of my pawns. The coffee table was littered with dead white pieces, the board covered with strategic black pieces still in play.

"You might *want* to move it," he said, all smug and sexy. "But if you do, I'll have you pinned."

I looked innocently at my wrists. "You'll have me pinned? Is that a threat? Or the prize?"

He narrowed his eyes, which had gone dark with desire. "There is no place for seduction in chess, Sabrina." Despite his words, his gaze scratched down my torso, lingered at my breasts. "After, though. Definitely after."

"Then stop trying to tell me what moves to make. *After* will come a lot faster if you let me make my own mistakes." And there it was. The move I needed to make. I saw it now.

"You said you wanted me to teach you." His cell phone rang as I reached out to slide my rook.

I couldn't help it—I looked for his approval.

"Good girl," he said, looking at the screen on his phone. "It's the Tokyo office. I have to take it."

"Tokyo? What time is it there?" I didn't really expect him to answer.

But he did. "Five o'clock Monday morning." He hit the talk button and brought the phone to his ear. Then his conversation transformed into Japanese as he took his call, and I melted.

God it was hot when he talked in a foreign language.

He was hot no matter what he did. I was so completely smitten with him. So head over heels. So totally in love.

Without seeming to miss a beat in his call, he reached over the board and took the rook I'd just moved with his knight.

Fucker.

He could look that sexy, speak Japanese, and beat me at chess all at the same time. He'd better be planning to keep me. Because more and more, I wasn't sure how I could live without him. Wasn't sure how I ever had.

The nature of the phone call seemed to intensify, requiring more of Donovan's attention. He stood to pace as he talked. I made another move on the board—probably a stupid move. I couldn't tell without his discerning commentary. I spent a few minutes after that trying to imagine the next moves, the way he said good chess players did. He'd move this. I'd move that. All the way to the end of the game. But I didn't have that kind of vision. I couldn't sit with it that long. And I wasn't good at guessing what he would do.

I never had been.

I looked up at him, one hand buried in his slacks pocket as he stood, muscles tense, in front of the window. He would need me later to distract him from the dilemma happening on the other side of the world. I would soothe him with my mouth, with my pussy. Let him find release inside me in whatever way he needed.

Right now, I couldn't help him.

I stood up and stretched, and headed down the hall to find the closest bathroom. When I came out, I could still hear Donovan on the phone so I wandered towards the opposite end of the house, studying the artwork that I hadn't really looked at during our tour.

"It's you, Sabrina. I thought I heard you kids out here."

I turned around to find Raymond had stepped out of his study.

"Just me. Donovan's on the phone. Work. Of course." I peeked around him as discreetly as possible. The study was the one room I hadn't seen, and I was curious by nature.

Raymond's brows lifted. "That works out perfectly, actually. I've been meaning to talk to you. Alone. Won't you step into my office?"

Goosebumps ran down my arms despite the sweater I was wearing. Nothing good could come from a conversation that Raymond Kincaid wanted to have with me alone.

But as I said, I was curious by nature.

"Sure thing."

I stepped into the study with my back straight and my head held high. Whatever happened in here, I reminded myself, Donovan was not Raymond Kincaid. Raymond could say what he wanted. It meant nothing about my relationship with his son.

The office was impressive, but not my style. The walls and furniture were all completely done in mahogany with leather accents. His desk was oversized and ornate, gold filigree lined the scrollwork on the edges and the legs. The shelves overflowed with books that looked old and as if they'd never been cracked open. Showpieces. Probably a lot of first editions and out-of-print collector's pieces. There was a faint smell of cigars and cologne— a scent Donovan would never have worn. Too strong. Too musky. All of it was very masculine and rich. Boastful. Arrogant.

I was such a judger.

No. I wasn't judging. I was preparing.

"Have a seat. Please." Raymond gestured to the chair in front of his desk rather than the intimate seating area by the fireplace. It was a move that established authority. One that put me in my place.

Next, he'd pull out his checkbook, wave it around.

I could see his moves. Maybe I wasn't so bad at chess after all.

I took a seat, crossed my legs. But I wasn't vulnerable. He didn't have me pinned like he might've thought.

"Is this where the rich financial mogul offers the lowly girl from the wrong side of the tracks some exorbitant amount to stop seeing his son?" I said it with a smile so that we could play it off as a joke. If I needed to.

Raymond barely reacted, but he did react. I wouldn't have noticed if I wasn't watching as carefully as I was, but since I was watching him so carefully, I saw the slight jerk of his eyelid, heard the soft catch of his breath as he sat down across from me.

Then he let out a hearty laugh. "Amusing. Amusing." He straightened the calendar pad on the corner of his desk.

Everything on the desk's surface, I noticed now, was straight and tidy. In its place. I wasn't so sure he liked things clean or immaculate though, so much as he liked the look of the lines and right angles. The room was full of both.

"With Donovan just in the other room..." he said, in continued amusement.

Maybe I'd been wrong about his motives. I wouldn't be upset if that were the case.

He looked up suddenly, his brows furrowed, eyes inquisitive. "What would be an exorbitant amount? Half a million? A full million?"

My stomach sank. Even knowing this was where it had been leading, I'd hoped I was wrong. Not so much for my sake, but for Donovan's. He knew his parents were terrible, but wouldn't it be nice to find out that they weren't?

I didn't answer Raymond. I couldn't. It was too degrading.

"A full million could go a long way," he prodded. "Could pay for all of your sister's students loans. Get her set up real nice after she graduates."

He'd checked into me.

Well, I didn't have to ask where Donovan had gotten his stalking genes. I gritted my teeth and nodded as I inhaled slowly, reminding myself it wasn't cool to punch out a seventy-year-old man. If I even could—he seemed to be in pretty good shape for his age.

The shittiest part of it all? That he thought his son's happiness was only worth that much. I'd been around their kind of money long enough to know how fast a million dollars ran out. I'd felt Donovan's love long enough to know it ran deeper than money could buy.

I laughed now. It was all I could do if I wasn't going to beat him up. "I think by definition, exorbitant means there isn't an amount you could name."

Raymond studied me carefully. I could see he was forming the next bid, wondering if two million would do it. Or three. Even despite what I'd said.

Whatever he saw in my face eventually brought him to the conclusion that I was telling the truth. "I wondered as much," he said.

It felt powerful. Like I had check.

I wanted checkmate. "And even if there were an amount, you would be hard-pressed to convince your son to let me go."

Raymond nodded knowingly. "That's not surprising. Donovan likes to marry for love. Susan and I—we get along, don't get me wrong. But we both understood the reason the practice of marriage was invented. It's a social arrangement. It shouldn't be based on emotion or tied to sentimentality. It's meant to protect her assets and mine, and those of our heirs. You can understand why I would therefore be concerned about you. You would be the mother of our grandchildren. While I would prefer a more suitable wife for him, we certainly cannot dictate whom he spends his life with. It didn't hurt to try."

"Wait—that's it?" I was reeling, disoriented like a fish pulled fresh from water. I couldn't keep up my own reactions to his revelations. First, that he and his wife had a loveless relationship—which I could've guessed—but for him to admit it was something else entirely. Then, to hear his outdated stance on marriage, and finally to arrive at the conclusion: 'oh well' he'd tried?

And Donovan and I weren't even engaged!

"I'll certainly recommend that Donovan choose otherwise if he asks. But he won't. A decade ago, I'd have told him there is nothing wrong with having a marriage for propriety and a mistress on the side. Prince Charles did it. Now even *he* is married to his mistress." He might as well have said, 'what is the world coming to?' The subtext was evident.

"Yeah, no. I could not stand to be a mistress." This was the oddest conversation to be having with my boyfriend's father. "And Donovan wouldn't stand for that either," I added with certainty. "And we are not –" *engaged*.

I stood up and rubbed my sweaty palms along my leggings. I didn't want to talk about this anymore with him. After this weekend, I actually could begin to see a future with Donovan. Long reaching winters, and summers, and chess games, and children.

But those were conversations to have with him. Not his father. Not because it was best for the future of the family name.

"You're welcome to leave anytime," Raymond said, rising to his feet. "I've said my piece."

And I'd said mine. I nodded, unwilling to say thank you for whatever this had been.

As I turned to go, my eye was caught by a series of plaques on the wall by the door. They were honorary plaques that had been given over several years to an organization I recognized—A Brighter Day. I stepped closer to examine one.

"This is from the president," I said in awe.

Raymond came up behind me. "Ah, yes. We are very proud of what we've done with A Brighter Day. Donovan has been very involved since high school."

"You must be. What kind of organization is it exactly?" I was only interested because Donovan's name had been attached to it. And obviously the organization was a big fucking deal. Plus, the man really needed to brag more, assert his authority.

"It's a series of foundations," Raymond explained. "They address a variety of different issues, each one tailored to a specific need. There is one that helps children prone to asthma that live or go to school in areas near freeways, which studies have shown can increase asthma attacks. Another provides free education to coal miners who are searching for another line of work."

So Raymond wasn't completely terrible after all. No one ever really was, I was learning.

"Another provides scholarships to kids with exceptional IQs, particularly those who have graduated early, and are seeking help to bridge the gap to Ivy League schools since those universities don't generally provide full rides. Another—"

The hair on the back of my neck stood up. "That one," I interrupted. "What's the name of the scholarship foundation?"

I already knew the answer. I could already see this move. It was a move I should've seen so long ago.

"The MADAR Foundation."

NINETEEN

THE WORDS WERE STILL THROBBING in my ears, still pulsing in my veins, still vibrating in my body when a different voice piped in from behind me.

"I can explain."

I shifted to see Donovan at the door, panic clearly written all over his expression.

"Sabrina. Come with me, I'll tell you everything." His hand reached out, beckoning, his voice pleading. His eyes pierced through me, but I couldn't see him the way I had previously. He seemed blank to me, or my eyes were too glazed. If there had been a piece of art there, I'd no longer see it.

Raymond clapped his hands suddenly. "That's why I know your name!" he exclaimed. "You were one of the scholarship girls. I'm not very good with names, especially out of context, but I should have put that together sooner."

Me too, Raymond. I should have put it together sooner, too.

Though now he wasn't so sure. He squinted, trying to recall. "That *was* you, wasn't it? What happened? You dropped out of school."

"Let's talk about this on—"

I put my finger up to hush Donovan. He'd had his chance to talk. He'd had weeks, months, *years* to tell me the truth.

I turned instead to Raymond. "My father had a heart attack. And I missed the end of the semester to go home to watch him die." My throat was tight as the rage from all those years ago returned like bile. "My scholarship was pulled because I missed finals, and when I appealed..."

I turned my focus on the younger Kincaid; there was venom in my stare. Just like before when my past had been reformed in my mind when Donovan had shown where he had been the puppet master behind the scenes, it was being re-created again now. The anger and hostility I had felt for a decade had been toward some vague corporate charitable foundation. Now there was a face to hate.

But which one?

I spun back toward Raymond. "Who decided?" I was desperate for the answer. Desperate for the answer to be different than the one I knew it was. "Who decided to deny my appeal? Did you even read over my case or was the decision all in Donovan's hands?" My elbows were tight at my sides, my hands in fists, and I was shaking. Shaking from rage that made my breathing shudder.

Raymond lifted one brow and turned his stare toward his son, understanding lighting his gaze. "You already tried to give her up," he said pointing a finger in Donovan's direction. "That's why you didn't want her back at Harvard." It was clear he was just putting pieces together himself.

He hadn't been part of this.

It had all been Donovan.

And I'd been such a fool.

I needed some space to breathe. Needed to be away from the two pairs of eyes staring me down, watching my every reaction. I wanted off their chessboard. I brushed past Donovan, running from the room, no destination in mind except to get away.

He was right behind me, on my heels, as he always was.

"Don't listen to my father. Let's talk about this. Let me explain. It was better if you weren't there, Sabrina."

We were in the middle of the house when I whirled around to face him. "Better for *who*? For *you*?"

"For *you*. Always for you." His voice was thick with agony.

But his misery couldn't dare to compare with mine. His was a lie. A boldfaced lie.

"Better for me because I wouldn't ever have to face your family? Because you'd never have to bring home a scholarship girl to meet your folks? Because you thought I'd be ashamed to stand in the presence of the almighty Raymond Kincaid?" I'd believed him when he'd said he wanted me away from him because he was afraid he would love me too much.

Stupid, stupid me.

He wasn't afraid of loving me too much. He was afraid his parents would hate me too much.

"No, it's not true. What he said is not true. He's guessing. He thinks I give a shit about their opinion, and I don't. I never cared about that."

I rocked back and forth on the balls of my feet. I wanted to believe him. It could be so easy to let him take care of this—of me —like always.

Down the hall, Raymond stepped out of his study to watch us, and I knew I had to ignore "easy." He was a visual reminder that he'd had Donovan first. I couldn't dispute that he was at Donovan's roots any more than I could dispute that my parents, and Audrey, were at mine.

I shook my head. "I'm finding it hard to believe you right now."

Before he could argue again, I turned away and ran upstairs to the room we'd been sharing and slammed the doors behind me.

He followed. I knew he would.

"What about trust?" he said, bursting through the doors. "You said we should trust each other."

I bent to pull the cord of my charger from the wall by the bed, then dropped it into my purse along with my cell phone. "Well, that was stupid. I was stupid to believe that someone like you could ever learn anything about trust."

"Don't say that. I've shown you parts of me that no one else has ever seen." He stood at the foot of the bed, his fist anchored on his hip as if that was the only way to keep it from reaching out to me.

"You mean I saw you vulnerable?" I spat. "So fucking sad. I'm sure it doesn't even compare to the parts that you saw of me."

"I was only ever trying to protect you."

"Bullshit. I am tired of the fucking bullshit. Just tell me the goddamn truth!"

"This is the truth," he yelled.

I tilted my chin up defiantly. "Okay. If it's all true, why didn't you tell me that day in the office? Why didn't you tell me when I asked you if there was 'anything else?' Why didn't you confess this when we decided no more secrets? What about that?"

His lids shut halfway, as though the things I said were too heavy and hard to bear. When he opened them again fully, they were glossy and deep green.

"Because I knew this would hurt you," he said softly. "And I was done hurting you. I didn't want to hurt you anymore."

"You didn't want to hurt me. Of course." My tone was thick with sarcasm. "Let me guess—you 'didn't want to hurt me' is the reason you snapped away my scholarship too. Just like the reason you didn't want a relationship with me. *You didn't want to hurt me*. It's the reason you always run. The reason you always fucking end up hurting me."

"It's not that simple." His body was tense with how complicated it was.

"It never is," I laughed sardonically, spotting a stray earring I'd left on the nightstand. I grabbed it and stuck it in my purse.

Donovan took two steps towards me but didn't go farther when I put my hand up in protest.

"If you had been with me, I would have destroyed you," he said emphatically. More emphatically than he would have if he were closer. "Look how close I came to destroying you while you were at school. Look what I did to you with my jealousy over Weston. With your grades. I couldn't have you at Harvard. You were better off away from me."

And there it was, spelled out. Finally. His reasoning. His confession. His truth. No better than the excuses Raymond gave.

"Do you have any idea how nearly you destroyed me by taking that away from me?" My voice was as unsteady as my hands. School had been the only thing I thought I had left to live for after my father's death, besides Audrey. "Harvard was supposed to have been our way out. It was going to be the future for my sister and me. And you took it away because you couldn't handle yourself around me?"

His shoulders sagged with the weight of this truth. "I took care of you. I tried to make it up."

I blinked back tears, but it was useless. They were coming anyway. Angry and hot. "Did you ever even really love me? Or was the decade that followed just a way to assuage your guilt?"

"How can you even ask that?" Deep in his throat, his voice broke. "I love you, Sabrina. All this time, I have loved you."

I bit my lip and tugged my purse up on my shoulder, hugging my arms around myself. "I don't think you know what love is."

With tears streaming down my face, I strolled past him out

the doors. His mother had come out of her room at the other end of the hall, but she didn't try to talk to me. Just watched. A family of watchers and stalkers—none of them knew how to connect with people. None of them knew how to love.

I'd feel sad for them all if I wasn't so busy feeling sad for myself.

I trotted back down the stairs. My luggage was already by the door, waiting for our trip back home. I waited in the foyer for Donovan to arrive, because of course he would.

And he did.

"You're wrong," he said, as he walked toward me. "I might not love you in the pretty traditional way that you're looking for, like some *hero*, like Weston might. But I do love you. Everything I did —everything I *do*—is because I love you."

I ached for him.

Every limb, every joint, every cell ached with the pain of his words. Because I loved the way he loved me. I preferred the way he loved me a million times to the way a man like Weston could— or *any other man* could even dare to try.

But I couldn't heal his hurt.

Because I hurt too much right then too. I hurt with my own pain, pain that he had inflicted with his lies and deceit and betrayal. Maybe he wasn't lying about why he sent me away, why he took away my scholarship. But at the very least he had lied by keeping the secret since we decided to be together.

He should have told me.

I couldn't say whether I would've forgiven him or not.

But he should have fucking told me.

"I'm going to call a cab," I said, not looking at him directly. "I can't be in a car with you."

"Don't be ridiculous."

I spoke right on top of him. "I'm not being ridiculous. I don't want to be in a car with you for two hours. I can't stand to look at you. I can't stand to hear you breathe. I can't be near you."

His nostrils flared. He opened his mouth, his expression saying he was about to argue more.

But then I added, "I'm too hurt." And if he couldn't see how wounded I was, how absolutely heartbroken, then he was blind.

He looked at me a moment, and his shoulders sagged. "Fine. John can take you. I'll take one of my father's cars."

Good. It was what I had wanted.

And not what I wanted too. Part of me wished he'd have put his foot down and said he was coming with me. Wished he would prove to me the truth he wanted me to know. Everything hurt and I wanted it to stop. I wanted to bury my face in his sweater and sob. I wanted him to make it better like he always did in his crazy Donovan ways.

How ironic that I still wanted that? That the cause of my pain and the source of my balm could be one and the same?

But we were done talking. No more words were exchanged, none with meaning anyway. There could be no comfort. There could be no balm. He didn't try very hard, and I couldn't let him give it to me.

I refused his help in putting on my coat. I turned away from him as I waited for the car to pull up. But while John put my bag in the trunk, I snuck a peek in Donovan's direction and caught his eye accidentally.

Immediately, I turned my head away, but he'd already seen me.

He took that look as an invitation, and rushed to get my door.

"This isn't over, Sabrina," he said holding it open for me. "You can take whatever time you need to be angry with me. We can fight. We can be silent. But you and I are not over. I think we can agree that I've already proven myself a patient man."

I pursed my lips together, unwilling to give him anything—

not a scowl, not a pout. Definitely not hope. I climbed into the back seat and refused to watch out the window as he became a tiny figure in the distance.

DONOVAN'S DRIVER WAS A PROFESSIONAL. He was trained not to react to what happened in the backseat of the car, whether it was sex or a woman crying her eyes out all the way from Washington, Connecticut to Hell's Kitchen.

I was thankful for that. It gave me the quiet I needed to think. To mourn.

Maybe mourn was dramatic. But was it?

I wasn't a teenager involved in my first real relationship. I didn't assume that the first fight equaled the end. I was mature enough to understand that even the most aggrieved wrongdoings could be forgiven. That even the most horrendous betrayals could be overcome.

But this thing with Donovan was so complicated and multifaceted. It wasn't just about whether or not I could forgive him. It was also about whether or not we could move on from this. Whether there was a decent enough foundation.

And one thing I did know about relationships was that people never changed. How could I ask him to be a different person? Someone who understood how to really love someone else. Someone who could truly put my needs and wants before his own self-defeating behavior. Was it even possible?

I couldn't think about any of it right now. I couldn't even think about talking to him. I was in too much pain. Too heartbroken. And too angry.

I got to my apartment building around eight thirty that night, exhausted and worn down. John offered to help with my bag, but

I insisted I'd take it myself. It wasn't heavy and I didn't want to deal with a hassle.

I was alone on the elevator, and when I got off, the hall was quiet except for a deliveryman standing at my neighbor's closed door. His ski hat was pulled low, his head bent and hidden by the white paper sack filled with something that smelled like curry. I trudged past him to my door with my suitcase and fished in my purse for my keys.

I must've been too distracted by my thoughts, by the avalanche of emotions that had buried me, because I didn't notice the deliveryman slip up behind me as I slid the key into the lock.

I didn't notice him until his hand was on my hip and the knife was at my throat and his mouth was at my ear.

"Hello again, Sabrina," Theo Sheridan said. "Did you miss me?"

TWENTY

I DIDN'T SCREAM. Because of the knife at my throat. But I made a shuddering noise as I inhaled, as close to a wail as I dared without risking my life, and the blade trembled against my skin, my heart pounding underneath it.

I might've thought this was a dream, that I'd fallen asleep on the ride home and this was yet another one of the frequent nightmares I'd had over the years about Theodore Sheridan coming after me. I'd had so many.

As real as those had felt in the moment, when I woke with sweat pouring from my skin, my heart pounding against my rib cage, the hair raised on the back of my neck, I could see now how very different reality was from the nightmare. I could see how it really felt to have a predator at your back, threatening, in control. I *remembered* now. Remembered how much more terrible the real thing was.

"Careful," Theo warned, pressing the metal against my jugular. "You won't make another sound now, will you." It wasn't a question. It was a command. It was a directive.

"No." But that was a sound, so I shook my head carefully,

quickly, both erasing the word uttered and acknowledging that I would do as he said. The feel of the blade against my neck as I made the movement was nearly paralyzing. But I couldn't let it be. I had to do what he said.

Because if I didn't...

I couldn't think about what would happen if I didn't do what he wanted. I couldn't think about what would happen period.

"Good girl." Those familiar words, a phrase I loved to hear from Donovan, now made my stomach turn, and I had to fight not to throw up. He eased the knife away. "Now put the key back in the lock and let us in."

Sound rushed in my ears like I was in a wind tunnel. The hallway felt like it was closing in around me. Like soon there wouldn't even be enough room to take a full breath. I knew if I went into that apartment with him, alone, my chances of walking away unharmed decreased exponentially.

Yet there wasn't a single alternative action I could think to take. A dozen self-defense classes over a decade and I was stumped. Any move I made, he'd have that knife on me. He'd cut me where it hurt.

I had no chance. No choice.

I nodded and lifted my trembling hand back to the lock. Though I intended to keep silent, a long whimpering sound came from my mouth as I tried to align the key. What was he doing here? Why was he out of jail? I sent up a quick furtive prayer to whoever would listen that someone would walk down the hall and discover us. Maybe if I took my time...

The metal of the blade scraped my skin again and I jolted.

"Hurry it up, Sabrina," he warned. "I'm telling you right now, I'm not putting up with any games from you."

I hurried, got the key in the lock, turned it, heard it click. I moved my hand to the knob and opened the door.

I didn't move until Theo nudged me with his knee. I couldn't bring myself to enter my dungeon so willingly. That's what it would be now. A place I couldn't escape. A place that was no longer safe.

I choked back a sob as I started across the threshold.

"Take your suitcase," he said when I'd made to leave it in the hall. "Grab the delivery bag, too."

He moved away from me so that I could grab the items and I wondered if this was my chance to escape, but I couldn't think fast enough. He was too big. And I was too scared.

And now he had me at another disadvantage—when I walked into the apartment, my hands were full. My purse was on one shoulder, my hand clasped the suitcase handle, and the other arm held the delivery bag. I stood frozen, unmoving, waiting for his next order.

Theo shut the door behind me and locked it, not bothering with the deadbolt. The sound the lock made was a simple click, but in my ears, it clanged like the closing of a cell. He flipped on a couple of lights, then scanned the interior of my apartment, looking at *my* things. At my *life*. At pieces of me he had no right to look at.

How had this happened? How had he gotten past my doorman?

The overwhelming scent of curry coming from the bag I held gave a clue. "Is this how you got in here?" I asked.

"Yeah." He was visibly proud of himself. "I hung around until someone else was walking in. Then slipped in with them. No one shuts the door on food delivery."

He'd planned this. It wasn't just a whim. He'd carefully planned this.

Theo took the bag from my arms and laid it on the ground. "Drop the suitcase. Where's your phone?"

I blinked. The question was easy, thinking was not. "My purse. It's in my purse." My phone was in my purse! I was so close to a way of communication. It felt like I was handcuffed, having it so near and not being able to use it.

"Hand it over." He held his palm out, waiting.

Slowly, I dragged the strap from my shoulder and looked inside. I was still shaking, but I made more of the production, going slower than I needed to. If I could find it, if I could call Donovan with a swipe of my thumb...

"What's taking so long?" He was too smart. He pointed the knife at me like a gun.

I stayed focused on my goal, peering into my bag, doing my best to ignore the weapon aimed at me. "I have a lot of stuff in here. I'm looking." I already had it in my grasp. Just couldn't get it unlocked.

"Give it to me." He yanked the purse from me and the phone dropped into the belly of the bag. He found it easily and swiped at the screen. "What's the code?"

I hung my head, defeated. My defeat was in losing the phone, not in surrendering the code to get into it. I didn't really have anything in there that I was afraid of Theo finding. What I feared was already standing right in front of me. "1123."

He punched the numbers in and smiled when he got access. "Sit on the couch," he said without looking at me, distracted by the contents of my cell.

I shuffled to do his bidding, but was this my chance while he was distracted? I looked around the room for an opportunity, for something that could be used as a weapon against his knife. The lamp next to the couch—was it too heavy? The fire poker—was it too far?

A rustling of paper caught my attention. Theo had reached into the delivery bag and pulled out a bottle of beer. He snapped off the bottle top and took a swig as he came around the couch.

The beer was in one hand, my phone in his other. Then where was the knife?

I quickly searched down his body, my eyes landing on the sheath fastened at his hip.

"Don't even think about it, Bri." He caught me looking. "I'm a fast draw. And I'm not too bad at improvising, either."

His expression said he wouldn't mind if I tested him. I had a feeling he enjoyed the idea of improvising. I was sure I wouldn't.

So I wouldn't cause trouble right now. Not until I was sure it was trouble I could get away with, or at least trouble that had a chance.

"When did you get out of jail?" I didn't want to talk to him, but just like the delivery question, I wanted to know. I needed to know how all of the things that had been set up to keep me safe had failed. It was a less terrible form of torture than imagining the things he was about to do to me, and anytime I stopped thinking about the *how's*, my mind immediately went to the *what's next's*.

"So you knew about that? I wondered." He paced a couple steps in front of me. "Was that your idea? Sending me away in the first place."

He said it casually, but the subtext was undeniably filled with vengeance.

Oh shit.

Was that why he was here? Revenge?

"I didn't know anything about that until just recently. I promise." I sounded desperate for him to believe me. I *was* desperate.

I pulled my coat tighter around me. It was warm in the apartment, and I didn't need it, but it was a barrier between him and me. Small, but I'd take any barrier I could get.

"Doesn't really matter." He shrugged. "See, I know it was Kincaid who put me in a jail cell."

"No. It was you. You put yourself in that jail cell when you raped that woman." I regretted the words as soon as I said them, true as they were. It wasn't a good idea to provoke him.

Yet, here he was provoked. He slid my phone into his back

pocket, and stared at me hard with greedy eyes. "What's with the coat? Hiding something?"

"Just..." *myself.* "Cold."

"I don't like it. Take it off. Make yourself comfortable. We're going to be together a while." He set his beer bottle on the coffee table.

I trembled so much it was hard to slip the buttons through the holes as I removed my coat like he'd asked. I kept my focus on my task, but I knew he watched me the whole time. I could feel the weight of his disgusting, captivated gaze. When it was off and bunched up around me where I sat, I felt naked, even though I was still completely dressed in my leggings and the thin nylon sweater I'd been wearing all day. I suddenly wished I'd worn something heavier. Something not so light. Something that didn't show my form or the line of my breasts. Something much more difficult to remove.

I forced myself to look at him, and my vulnerable feelings only intensified. His expression, though still dark, was now also terrifyingly excited.

"Much better." His smile was gleeful as he pulled out his knife and came around the coffee table to bend down in front of me.

I cowered back involuntarily.

He grabbed my sweater and fisted the material in his hand. Then pressed the knife down at the V of my neckline.

There was nowhere to go, but I tried, I really tried to press myself into that couch, to make myself smaller as he cut down the center of my sweater with his knife. To make myself not exist. To make myself nothing because if I was nothing I couldn't feel this or know this or ever remember what it was like to feel a madman breathing over me, sawing through my clothing with the blade. It was a really sharp blade I discovered. He nicked me a couple of times with the tip.

Because he wasn't careful.

Because he didn't care.

Because he wanted me to know just how sharp the blade was.

When the entire front of my sweater hung open, he leaned back to look at his work. "I think I'd like it better if you didn't have the bra." He looked at me expectantly, as if waiting for me to do something.

I was already trying to be someplace else. Where did I want to be? Anywhere was better than here. But if I could find the perfect place, I could lose myself completely, and not be here at all.

After I didn't move, he said, "Are you going to take it off, or am I?"

I shook myself from the daze. He wanted me to do something. Something gross and terrible and I couldn't do it, but I couldn't let him do it more. "Just take off the bra?" I asked.

"Stop procrastinating. Take it off or I will."

I reached behind my back and somehow managed to undo the clasp. Then I slid the straps down one sleeve of my sweater and pulled the whole thing out of the other sleeve.

Theo bent forward toward me, and I shrunk away.

"Stay fucking still." He flashed the knife, and now I had to do his bidding. My face crumpled, but I didn't move this time when he leaned in and arranged my clothing, pulling the sweater open wide enough that the inside curves of my breasts could be seen.

I felt disgusting. Like trash. Used, and he hadn't even used me yet.

Yet.

I sat silent for him, but inside I was screaming.

He sat back on the coffee table, and studied me appraisingly. His eyes darkened. "That's really nice."

I tried to imagine what he liked most about what he saw. The damaged clothing that proved non-consent? The blood trickling down my skin? The hint of flesh that he would soon take as he willed?

I had to lose myself. Where could I go? I could be in the cold, in the snowdrifts of Washington, Connecticut, holding onto Donovan, letting him kiss me warm.

"I would've gotten off," Theo said, turning back to the earlier conversation. "I had the better lawyers. That woman couldn't afford shit for lawyers. And that's what really matters in these cases."

Jesus, he was such a sick fuck.

I wanted to ignore him, and I tried, tried to live in Donovan's arms, in the cold, in the snow. But I could still hear Theo's voice penetrating my fantasy.

"Then Donovan Kincaid shows up with his million-dollar law team and suddenly the trial goes an entirely different direction. That is not how that should've gone down. What the fuck was with that? Why did Donovan care about *me*? It didn't make any sense." He was angry and animated.

He paused to pull on his beer bottle before going on. "So I've been in jail. And I've had time to think about it. You have a lot of time to think in there. I thought about you—about that night outside The Keep clear back at Harvard. I have to admit I couldn't remember your name for a while. I wasn't sure that you were the connection, even with that history."

He set the bottle down, and leaned forward again, his elbows on his thighs. "But then two things happened." With one hand he held up a single finger. "First, I was told I was getting early parole at the end of the week." He held up a second finger. "Second, the day after I came home, my brother said he'd been at a wedding with Donovan, and his girlfriend was some chick named Sabrina Lind."

I'd been scared about how he'd violate my body since the

minute he'd shown up in the hallway. Now I was terrified that wasn't all he had in mind.

"Yeah," Theo said registering my fear with a new gleam in his eye. "All the pieces fell together for me." He stretched forward and set one finger at the base of my throat, right where my pulse was. My heart was pounding, and now he could feel it. He could actually feel my fear.

I didn't move.

I didn't breathe.

I tried to will my heart not to beat.

After a few seconds, he trailed his finger downward, between my breasts where sweat had gathered, through the blood that stained my skin. "Kincaid put me in jail as some sort of revenge for you. Which is bullshit." His volume increased sharply on the word bullshit, making me jump.

He sat back again and brought his finger to his mouth to suck on. Calmer, he said, "I never even got to fuck you. There was no reason for revenge."

I was shaking again, or shaking *more*; I'd never really stopped.

How could I get out of this? How could I possibly get out of this?

"You don't want to do anything to me. You just got out of jail. You don't want to go back." Jesus, I was begging. Did begging even work with predators? I couldn't remember what I'd read over the years.

"Why not? Did you know I have to register as a sex offender for the rest of my life? No one's going to give me a job on Wall Street. I'll never get to work with money with a prison history. I really don't have much to look forward to, Sabrina, besides this." His eyes narrowed into slits as he hissed, "Nothing's fucking taking it away from me."

He had nothing to lose. That made him more dangerous now than he'd been a decade ago.

I sucked my lower lip under my teeth, and tried not to cry.

He retrieved my phone from his pocket. "What was the code again?"

I told him, and he entered it into the screen.

"This wasn't me though," I said, trying to find a way to reason with him. "I wasn't the one who stopped you that night, even. And I had nothing to do with Donovan getting involved in your case." It was all true, but I felt like the most terrible person in the world to pretend I hadn't wanted Donovan to save me. To pretend I wasn't proud of the actions he'd taken against Theodore.

But this was about survival. Whatever I needed to do to get out of this. Whatever I needed to say, I'd say it.

"That doesn't really matter, like I said. This is about what will hurt Kincaid." He glanced at me. "I'm pretty sure hurting you is going to hurt him more than anything else I could do to him. Plus, this is going to be pretty damn fun for me. I haven't been able to play in a long, long time."

He slipped my phone back into his pocket. "You and Kincaid don't text much, huh? Was sure a sweet shot of your pussy you sent him, though. Makes me nice and hard." He rubbed a hand over his erection.

Bile crept into the back of my throat. I swallowed it down.

I'd only sent one picture in all the time I'd been with Donovan. The picture with his initials drawn on my skin in an intimate region. It was probably the only naughty picture on my phone. Of course that's what Theo would find.

I started rocking back and forth now, hugging myself. And the whimper I'd been trying to hold down returned.

"What are you going to do to me?" I knew already. He'd basically already said. But I didn't know the details, and maybe if I knew them, maybe if I heard him say the words, I could better prepare myself for what was coming.

Who was I fooling? There was nothing that would prepare me for this. Tears streamed down my face.

Theo cocked his head. "I haven't decided yet."

"Really?" I could hear the stupid waver of hope in my voice.

He laughed, a big hearty laugh. "Oh, I'm going to fuck you. I just haven't decided how I'm going to like it most."

I pressed my thighs together instinctively.

And then, when I saw how much my fear and panic turned him on, I jumped and ran, darting for my bedroom. It was automatic. Spontaneous. I didn't think; I just did. It wasn't like the bedroom was any safer. It was simply... away.

I didn't make it very far before he grabbed me. Wrapping his arms around my waist, he lifted me off the ground in a horrible parody of the scene with Donovan at Weston's wedding. I kicked and screamed, which earned me his hand on my throat. My scream transformed into a choked gurgle.

"I told you to shut the fuck up." He dumped me face down on the couch, and held me with one hand at my neck, while the other pinned one of my arms at the small of my back.

I managed to turn my face so I could breathe, so I could see the room. He had knocked over the beer bottle when he bolted after me. It lay only a couple of feet from me now, the remains spilled but unbroken. I watched it roll towards the fireplace and wondered if that would be my focal point while this asshole raped me.

And I was mad at myself now, too. By running, I'd made it more fun for Theo. He might've waited a while before deciding he was ready.

Not that waiting would've mattered. He would've raped me eventually, and this time I didn't have Donovan watching from above.

Or did I?

A new flame of hope kindled inside me. *There are cameras in my bedroom.* I didn't know if they were in the main part of my apartment. I'd made Donovan promise not to watch me on them anymore. But I'd learned tonight that he'd broken promises before —and wouldn't he be more likely to want to watch me when it was the only way he had access to me? When we were fighting, and I wasn't answering his calls?

If I could get Theo to the bedroom, maybe I would have a chance. It was a small chance, but a chance.

"I'm sorry," I said, trying my best to feign obedience. I gave him my other trembling hand voluntarily to demonstrate how sorry I was. "I was just thinking you might like it better in the bedroom."

"I like it better when you don't do any thinking," Theo responded gruffly.

Right. I knew that.

"I meant," oh God, oh God, it was so hard not to sob as I said it, "I thought you'd like it better if you had to chase me."

He had moved his hand from my throat so he could hold my wrists while he undid his jeans. At least, I was guessing that's what he was doing from the sound of the belt and the zipper—I couldn't see him from this position. But at my words, he stilled.

"Sabrina," he said, a note of awe in his tone. "If we play chase, you're likely going to get hurt."

As if I wasn't going to get hurt anyway.

"I'm not advocating against it. I'm just telling you how the game works." He pressed against me, and even though I still had my leggings on, I could feel he was bare. His naked penis rubbed up and down along the crevice of my ass. He felt thick and gross.

I started crying harder. He was going to put that inside me. I didn't even know *where* he was going to put it inside me. He could put it in so many places. He was going to hurt me. He was going to violate me.

And I had to fight.

He let go of my hands, to maneuver my pants, and with everything I had I pushed up off the sofa, shoving him backward and off of me.

He was slightly surprised, but he knew I was his captive. And he enjoyed the chase. So he was more amused than upset.

Like before, I made a beeline for the bedroom. If I could just get in there, if Donovan could see us, he would call the cops or the doorman—someone who could get here immediately. I believed it. I had to believe it.

But Theo jumped in front of me, cutting off my pathway to the door.

Fuck, fuck, fuck.

I pivoted and ran in the other direction. Acting as much on instinct as anything else, I bent down as I ran past the fireplace, grabbing the beer bottle that had rolled over there, then circled around the sofa with the item behind my back. Suddenly, I could see his moves in my head. Theo would double back and head me off. I had him pinned, and he didn't know it.

He did exactly as I'd guessed. He doubled back.

And when I came face-to-face with him, I pulled the bottle from behind my back and swung with all my might, hitting him across the face.

Check.

He stumbled backwards, cursing incomprehensibly.

Just then my front door burst open and Donovan stood there. "Get the fuck away from her, Sheridan," he shouted.

Checkmate.

TWENTY-ONE

"DONOVAN!" I cried. Dropping the beer bottle, I rushed for him.

I could feel a tug on the back of my sweater, but I didn't give into and I made it safely into Donovan's arms. When I did, I turned back and saw Theo was wielding his knife again. If he'd managed to grab me—if I'd given into that tug—the blade would be in my throat by now, and it wouldn't matter that Donovan was here.

I'd been aware of the danger I was in all night, but now that it was nearly over, it consumed me. I burst into sobs and buried my face in Donovan's chest. He held me tight against his side, angling me so that I was away from my predator.

"Let me out the door," Theo said, as if he had room to bargain now, "and we can forget all of this, Kincaid."

"You're not fucking walking out this door. You're lucky I'm letting you live right now." I'd never heard Donovan so riled.

"I don't think you're in the position to bargain. I'm the one with the weapon." He waved it around a few times, proving he knew how to use the blade. "Let me go. We can forget your mistakes. Forget everything you've done to me."

"Done to you? That's a laugh. But you're right. I've made two mistakes. Not persuading Sabrina to prosecute you the first time and deciding that jail was good enough for you the second time."

Theo grinned, as though Donovan's "mistakes" were his war trophies. "I guess I'll have to go through you. The only question is whether or not I take Sabrina with me when I do."

I started to scream.

Just then, a voice from behind us shouted, "Drop the weapon!"

I peered around Donovan and found a handful of police officers at the door, guns pointing at Theo. He had no chance, and he knew it. He dropped his knife and fell to his knees, immediately placing his hands behind his head. The officers ran to attend to him. Though he'd surrendered, Theo struggled and spat in the face of an officer as another one placed him in handcuffs.

"Careful, boys," one of the officers said after reading his rights. "He's trying to provoke us so he can sue the department." He addressed Theo directly. "We know your type, and it ain't gonna work. My men don't play your games. We're the good guys here."

It was satisfying to see Theo deflated, though I personally wouldn't have minded seeing him roughed up a bit.

Actually, I didn't want to look at him at all.

I turned away from Theo and the police and into Donovan who was waiting for me when I did.

He tilted my chin up and searched my face. "Are you all right? Tell me you're all right. Tell me I got here in time."

I didn't know how to answer. I wasn't all right, and I was. I would never be all right again, yet he hadn't gotten to me like he had before. Maybe the question was wrong. Maybe the answer wasn't important.

"He didn't hurt me," I managed, a compromise on a thousand different levels.

Donovan was inspecting me anyway. His face went white when he reached the bare skin of my torso. "There's blood..."

I looked down at my wounds. I'd barely felt them; I'd been too afraid of the real damage that could be done with the blade. "They're scratches," I assured him. "They don't hurt."

"Where did he touch you?" The question sounded almost caught in the back of his throat, forced out by mere will.

"He didn't. I'm fine." I was obviously not fine. Tears kept streaming down my face and I kept shaking even though I felt feverish.

Donovan scraped my cheek with his knuckles, gathering my tears, and then looked at me as if it were a challenge to tell him yet again that I was fine.

I crumpled. "I was so scared. I thought he was going to..." I couldn't even say what I thought he was going to do. "I tried to get him into the bedroom because I knew there were cameras there. I thought maybe if you were watching, you would see us and you'd get help."

He caressed my jaw, his other arm pinned firmly around my waist. "There are cameras everywhere. When you didn't lock the deadbolt..." He took a deep breath as if recalling what he'd imagined, as if it had been the worst. And then when he'd looked, he'd actually been *faced* with the worst.

"It's tied into the security system," he explained after a minute. "It sends me a message. You *always* slide that bolt when you're home." The pain in his expression was unbearable. "Forgive me. I worried."

It was almost laughable. He was apologizing because his over-protective obsessing had saved me from sexual assault and possibly saved my life? How could he be sorry for that? I was fucking out of my mind with gratitude. I was hysterical with relief.

And then I remembered how I'd left him last.

It was a gut punch in slow motion. I could feel every part of the blow. The renewed awareness that we were in a fight. That he'd betrayed me. That years ago he'd stolen my dream in order to make his life more comfortable. That what he'd ministered as love for a decade had merely been retribution for what he'd taken from me.

I felt like a stone sinking slowly through the mud. My mind was sludge. I'd been in danger and all I wanted was Donovan, all I thought about was him. I'd turned to thoughts of him for safety, and he'd been the one to save me in the end. If he didn't really love me, would he have looked at those screens? If he didn't really love me would he have even cared about that years-long retribution at all?

I wasn't sure.

But he was here, holding me when I wanted him to hold me. That seemed bigger than anything else happening between us at the moment, and to be honest, if being here when I needed him wasn't the very definition of love, I didn't know what was.

"Thank you," I hiccupped. "For worrying."

We stared at each other, our eyes locked. He swiped at my tears again with his thumb. I grabbed his hand and brought it back to my face, pressing my cheek into his palm. I was never not going to love him, I realized. No matter what happened between us from here on out—I was never not going to love him.

And maybe I could survive that. With him at my side.

Perhaps he felt the weight of the moment too. The lines at his eyes pulled down and the creases by his mouth tightened. "Sabrina, I—"

He was cut off by the bustling of the officers escorting Theo out of the apartment. I refused to look as he was taken out. I kept my face buried in Donovan's shoulder until he was gone, concentrating only on the feel of Donovan's hand as it rubbed smooth concentric circles over my back.

Once the perpetrator had left, all the attention shifted to me. An officer came over to speak to me about what had happened, along with a paramedic, to determine that I was indeed unharmed. Donovan was taken a few steps away to be interviewed as well, and while I wanted to hear him, to listen only to him, my attention was mainly on the questions being asked of me —Does it hurt here? Have you had a tetanus shot?

I didn't miss hearing the policeman though, when he asked Donovan about the cameras, and when he did, I stopped listening to the people talking to me and focused only on that.

"I'm not clear on why you have surveillance on Ms. Lind in the first place," the officer said.

"I own the building," Donovan said, clearly trying to dance around the answer.

"It's consensual," I called from where I sat on the couch being treated. Both Donovan and the officer turned toward me. "It's complicated and private," I went on, "but all that should matter to you is that it's consensual. And it is."

I caught the exchange of glances between the officer and his partner that clearly said they thought we were into some kinky shit—which, I supposed, we were. Under her breath, the paramedic whispered, "Hot."

"Damn straight," I said with a smile. I snuck another glance at Donovan and my smile settled into something more somber when I found him already watching me. I really did love this about him too. I really did love all of the parts of him. I really did accept all of it as *us*.

I would forgive him for what he'd done all those years ago. There would be scar tissue, but we'd work through it. Because this thing we had, whatever it was, it was stronger.

Then why did I still feel like there was such a chasm between us?

Probably because there were so many people in the room, and still so many loose ends to tie up before they left. I was worked up and fragile. A million people kept asking what I needed. What I needed was to be alone with Donovan. He was the only one who could fix this restlessness inside me.

It took hours, literal hours, to go through everything with the police, but finally sometime after midnight they had everything they needed and were ready to go.

"Are you going to be okay staying here tonight?" one of the officers asked before he left.

I hadn't thought about it before then. I looked at the room, testing how badly it might haunt me later. I couldn't deny that my stomach tied up in knots just thinking of being alone in my living room, sitting on my couch. Would I have to move? That was silly. Or it wasn't. I didn't want to decide tonight.

I turned to Donovan, seeking guidance.

"I can take you to my place. Or a hotel." He was gentle and concerned. "Or I can stay here with you. I can sleep in the guest room or on the couch."

My brow rose at the suggestion that he wouldn't sleep with me. Did he really think I was still angry with him after all of this? Or maybe he was being respectful of how I'd feel after a near rape. I'd fix that when we were alone.

"Would you stay here?" It felt weird to ask him outright, even when he'd just offered.

"Of course."

I told the policeman I'd be okay, and after they left, Donovan watched while I triple checked the deadbolt.

Then they were gone, and my apartment was empty of everyone but us and my ghosts. Donovan leaned against the back of the couch and studied me intently. "What do you need?

A drink? Something to eat? Would you like a change of clothes?"

I tightened the belt of the robe I was wearing. The officers had taken the damaged sweater as evidence, and Donovan had thoughtfully brought my robe from the bathroom when they had.

I didn't want any of the things he'd mentioned though. I didn't know what I wanted, exactly. I felt restless still, and irritated that he didn't know what I needed. He *always* knew what I needed.

And why was he so far from me? Physically. Emotionally. Why was he so distant?

"You're blaming yourself," I said, suddenly. It was a guess. A blind shot in the dark and it might be so far off that he'd laugh, but that would be better than this weird tension.

But he didn't laugh.

And he didn't say anything, and he didn't move closer. He just stood there.

I'd hit the nail on the head.

I sighed, walking toward him. "You can't blame yourself for this," I said gently. "I'm okay. I didn't get hurt."

"You could have."

"And I didn't because you got here in time."

"I wouldn't have *had* to get here in time if I had handled him differently."

I was face to face with him, my hands curled up in fists at my side so that I wouldn't be tempted to touch him before he was ready to be touched. I wasn't going to coddle him.

I also wasn't going to let him play the martyr. "How differently could you have handled him? *Not* sent him to jail? He *belonged* in jail! That was a good thing you did when you helped Liz Stein send him away. Think of all the other women you saved from him."

"There were other ways I could have gotten rid of him." He

was dark and dangerous as he held my eyes. His stare, piercing and void, let me know he meant murder.

I slapped him. Because that was dumb. Because I didn't want him to be a murderer. Because I was wound up with energy and adrenaline and anger—at him and Theo and everyone—and I needed to hit someone.

Then, with my palm still burning, I wrapped my hand around his neck, dug my nails into his skin, and kissed him.

His mouth responded, but I was the one driving the kiss, raging and greedy. I bit his tongue and clawed at his skin. I pressed my body against him, writhing like a feral cat.

Despite his responsiveness, it wasn't long before he put his hands on my hips and pushed me away.

My rage flamed higher, and I slapped him again. And again. He grabbed my wrist the third time so I beat at his chest with my other fist, fighting him much like I did that day he took my virginity in his office.

He seized this wrist too, circled them both with his large palms and stared sternly into my face.

"Is this what you need?" He twisted my arms behind my back and pulled me against him where I could feel he was hard. My heart rate spiked, my mouth watered. "Is it?"

Yes, I screamed silently. Didn't I always? I needed Donovan to erase everything that had happened earlier. I needed him to re-create it with his face and his body and his mouth and his words, so that when the nightmares came—which they would because they always did—I would have better memories to replace them with.

That was how we did it. That was how he saved me from this darkness. Every time.

I didn't need to tell him, though. He'd already gotten into character. His eyes had clouded and now he was hungrily studying the bare skin at the neckline of my robe.

"Where did he touch you?"

I swallowed back a sudden surge of shame and tugged my arm where he had my hands bound. He got the hint and brought one around between us so I could show rather than tell. Guiding our hands to his mouth, I put one of his fingers and one of mine between his lips. He sucked on them, getting them nice and wet.

"Undo my robe," I told him.

He tugged the knot free then I laced my hand back in his and brought his wet finger to my chest. Together, we traced the path that Theo had drawn along my torso.

I watched Donovan's eyes as he drew along my skin, saw the weight of his lids as he fought to keep them open, as though it was unbearable knowing that Theo had seen this part of me, had touched me like this.

"And the blood?" It was almost a whisper.

"He nicked me when he cut my sweater open." But I didn't want sympathy. I didn't want that pitying look in his eyes. It wasn't what I needed right now. "Believe me, I'd rather have had the knife than his slimy-ass fingers."

Donovan's jaw twitched, his expression hardening. He wrenched my arm behind my back again, and spun me so that I was backed up against the couch. He needed this too. I could feel it in the way he kicked my legs apart, making room for himself between my thighs. I could feel it in the steel of his erection pressed up against my belly.

"Where else did he touch you?" he asked with a growl. He let go of my hands and pushed tighter against me so they were trapped between my ass and the couch. "Here?"

He opened my robe more and groped my breast, squeezing it until I whimpered.

I shook my head.

He lowered his touch past the waistband of my pants and reached inside my panties to finger my hole. I was tight and mostly dry, but I grew wet immediately. "Did he fucking dare to touch you here?"

"No." My knees buckled from the sudden wave of pleasure. "No," I said more forcefully, twisting my hips to push away his hand because that was the game, but also because the sensation was already too much. "He didn't touch me anywhere else."

"Good. Because you aren't his to touch."

Warmth shot through my body, electric pulses ran down to my pussy like lights along a runway triggered by his possessive words. Roughly, he pulled my robe from my shoulders, down my arms, and flipped me around so that I was facing the sofa. He gathered the silk material at my wrists and twisted it until my hands were trapped inside the bundle.

Then he pulled my leggings and panties down together. I struggled as he did, instinctively, because that was also the game. His knuckles knocked against me and into me as he maneuvered my clothes down my legs. There would be marks tomorrow — marks I could focus on instead of the ones that Theo had left. I'd wear them like badges. I hoped they were dark.

I struggled more to make sure they were.

I'd never taken off my boots and Donovan didn't now, so my pants stayed chained around my ankles. With one hand pressing on my restrained wrists at my lower back, he used his other hand to work on getting his cock out. I could hear the zip of his slacks, the familiar rustle of his clothing as he fought for freedom.

I wanted to watch, but I didn't look back. The angle was too awkward. Instead, I closed my eyes and pictured him undoing his slacks, tugging down his boxer briefs just far enough to release his erection, then fisting his hot throbbing cock before notching his firm crown at my pussy and shoving inside.

My eyes flew open, and I screamed at the delicious invasion. He'd gone in to the hilt then pulled out right away to the tip, not giving me any time to adjust or stretch. He plowed in again at full force. It was uncomfortable and painful, and incredibly amazing all at once. There was anger in his thrusts. There was cruelty. As though he were mad at me for what had happened tonight. As though he were taking his anger at Theo out on me, and this, *this* was what I needed. This scouring. This primal fucking. This savage violation. This exorcism. It declared me as his, and his alone. It left absolutely no room for anyone else to possess me.

There was also pleasure. He always made sure that I felt the beauty in our filthiness, and this time was no different. He wrapped his arm around my hip and massaged my clit in progressively aggressive strokes, the approach so deliberate and contrary to the frenetic tempo of his fucking.

I was mindless, able to only concentrate on the space between this thrust and the next. I focused on what was ahead of me. The fireplace, the place I'd stared at while Theo had me pinned on the couch earlier in the night.

Then a sudden flashback burst into my head, like lightning, striking me just as forcefully. I was sitting—my sweater open, my skin exposed—and Theo's hand was at my throat, pressing into my pulse point.

"My neck," I said breathlessly. "Put your hand on my neck."

And the thing about Donovan? The thing that made him fit me so perfectly? Was that a demand like that from me never made him ask *why*. He just did it and he understood without an explanation.

He circled his palm around my thin neck and squeezed, ever so lightly.

Though it wasn't exactly the same way Theo had touched me, the pressure was similar, and it was just the push I needed to fall over the edge. I lost myself, spinning in a rush of euphoria and joy. I gasped, lifting my chin up as I went rigid, a flower turning up into the sun after a devastating rain.

I felt good. Unbelievably good. So good and wanted and

loved, and after the shitty way that Theo had made me feel, I was desperate to hold onto it for as long as possible.

Too soon, it was over. My vision cleared and my muscles relaxed. The dizziness was fading, and I realized I was now empty—literally empty. Donovan hadn't released and was no longer inside of me.

I bolted upright and found him standing to the side, already tucked away.

"Uh-uh," I said, trying to twist my way out of the makeshift shackles. "I know what you're doing and I'm not letting you do it."

"Really. What is it I'm doing then?"

The robe dropped to the floor and I hurriedly pulled up my pants so that I wouldn't trip on them as I walked over to him. "You're still trying to play the martyr," I said as I drew near to him. "But it's coming off as playing the asshole." I reached for his zipper.

He shoved my hand away. "I could have gotten you killed!"

I jumped at his sudden volume, but was undeterred. His passion only made me more resolved to show him this wasn't his fault. That I didn't blame him.

"You're right—I could have died." I backed him up against the wall by the kitchen. "But I didn't. You saved me. And we're in this together." I had his zipper down and his cock in my hand now. It was still stone hard and wet from being inside me.

Damn, he made my legs tremble every time I touched him.

And I needed him to feel good and release as desperately as I had needed it for myself. I pumped him with my fist and wrapped my other hand around his neck to bring his mouth down to mine.

He resisted at first, but I refused to give up. Because I couldn't have if I'd wanted to. His taste was the best drug, his lips so firm and familiar, it was like going to church. I suckled on him, savored him as I stroked him, molded his mouth until it became pliable against mine.

And then he was desperate too—lifting me up, carrying me to the kitchen table. He shoved a chair aside so he could set me down and it toppled to the floor. With my ankles wrapped around his waist, I hoisted my hips so he could pull my pants down enough to get inside me. He rocked against me, gently but eagerly, searching for my entrance, and when he slid in, we sighed in unified relief.

"I fucking love you so much," I whispered against his lips. "My dark warrior."

He kissed me brutally, then pressed his forehead against mine. "I'm so weak when it comes to you." He cupped his hands around my chin. "So fucking weak. You make me lose my head. I make bad decisions around you, Sabrina." Then his mouth was too busy kissing me to say anything else.

I relished everything he said, every second, every glorious sensation as he rode me harder and faster to his release. I tried to memorize all of it. Tried to take it all in, because while this was the closest to heaven I'd ever been, the knot in my stomach wouldn't go away. Because I could see the board. I could see his next play, and I prayed to God I was being paranoid, that he wasn't already distancing himself. That fucking me against the table wasn't his way of saying goodbye.

When he came, he let out a long guttural groan. He looked into my eyes and clutched onto me, his fingers dug into my skin so deeply it was like he'd never let me go.

But he did.

He picked me up off the table, set me on the floor, and helped me readjust my clothing. The tenderness wasn't gone, but he was reserved, as if we'd just shared an elevator and not our hearts.

"Don't do this." I reached for him, but he stepped back.

To his credit, he didn't deny it. He looked me dead in the eye when he made his move.

"I don't deserve you," he said plainly. Matter of fact. Like the simple slide of a bishop along the diagonal spaces of a chessboard, knocking out the pawn at the end.

My throat suddenly felt tight, and I couldn't swallow past whatever was stuck there. "And that's going to be your excuse?"

"It's not an excuse. It's—"

I cut him off. "It's bullshit!" He jerked at my exclamation, but didn't defend himself. "And what? You'll go back to hiring private detectives to follow me around everywhere? Watching from a distance? 'Loving' me from afar?" I'd have to move now. It would be bad enough working with him. Living in his building with his cameras on me knowing I'd never get to see into his life again— that would kill me.

What was I thinking? Being without him at all would kill me.

"It's better for you this way, Sabrina." There was no energy behind this breakup. That's how pathetic it was. He'd just decided that it was the right thing to do, the virtuous and noble thing, and even though he didn't *want* to give me up, he was going to do it because this was one thing he knew how to commit to.

Donovan Kincaid knew how to run away.

Well, fuck him.

"Fuck you." I crossed my hands over my chest, hiding myself, as if I could un-bare what I'd bared to him. As if I could cover myself up when he'd already seen all of me. "You don't deserve me? You're right. You don't. Maybe you don't know how to love someone, and it's not your fault that you didn't learn before. But you're a grown up, and you're old enough to start trying. Your parents are hard; I'll admit that. But I don't see you even trying to love them. And now you're not trying to love me. And I deserve someone who will try."

I was crying now, tears fully streaming down my face, but

despite the display, I felt a burst of strength. "Love doesn't have to be perfect or traditional, Donovan. I can put up with a lot of mistakes, and the way I'm loved doesn't have to look like the way anyone has ever loved me before. It doesn't have to look like the way anyone has ever loved anyone else in the world. And that will be enough as long as someone tries."

I wiped my cheeks with the butt of my palm. "But running away every time there's a problem isn't trying. And peering in on my life and nudging now and then like you would on the paddles of a pinball machine isn't trying either. Which is a real shame, because I really did try with you. I really did fall in love with you."

"Sabrina..." He trailed off, and I waited for him to say more but more never came.

He didn't even know how to try to console me.

I swallowed another threatening sob. "I'm going to bed. Stay if you need to, but I'm going to be just fine if you go."

I didn't look at him again. I swept back to the sofa and picked up my robe, determined to leave as little of myself with him as possible. And then I headed straight to my bedroom, shut the door behind me, and immediately sank to the floor, my back pressed against the wood, and silently sobbed while pretending I hadn't just told the biggest lie of my life.

TWENTY-TWO

I KNEW my apartment was empty when I woke up the next morning. In my mind, he'd left during the night. I was sure of it before I opened my eyes. But my heart held hope that he'd stayed, and so the first thing I did after I found my living room empty was to check the guestroom to see if the bed had been slept in. I stared at the pillows. Had they been rearranged? The comforter certainly looked unruffled.

He'd really left.

Not just politely given me my space. And the only way he would've really left, after the horrors of last night, was if he was really *gone*.

I would grieve this more when I let myself feel it. Right now, I was numb.

I shuffled into the bathroom and faced myself in the mirror. I'd slept in, but my reflection's puffy face and eyes indicated I needed at least another two hours of sleep. I called my secretary and told her I would be in later in the day then asked her to transfer me to Weston's assistant since I was still filling in for him.

"Mr. Kincaid said not to expect you at all," Roxie said when I informed her of my plans for the day.

I pricked at his name, like it was a thorn I'd stumbled upon unexpectedly. And then I hated myself when I looked for the rose attached. "Really? What did he say?"

"That you had a rough night. You sick?"

I deflated. I didn't know what I was expecting. That he would've left some clue that he was still thinking about me with an administrative assistant at our company? Of course not. He was simply thinking of the business. And himself. Explaining my absence beforehand so that no one would come looking to ask him later if I didn't show up.

"Yeah. I'm not feeling too hot." It wasn't a lie.

I took three Advil and laid back down, barely resisting the urge to give the middle finger to the empty space of my bedroom, in case he was watching.

Honestly, I was afraid he wasn't.

Mostly I was afraid he never would again.

"I DIDN'T EXPECT to see you in the office today," Nathan Sinclair said, leaning back in his red modern high-back swivel chair, his hands laced behind his head.

I sat down on the white faux leather chair opposite him. Nate's workspace was the most artistic of the men, fitting for the creative director of the agency. He did have a desk, but it was a standing desk and he never conducted meetings across it. If he wanted to have a conversation with someone, he would most likely have him or her seated where we were now.

I rarely came to this corner of the floor, but since I was coming into work nearly three hours late, I figured I should check in with one of my superiors, and I was not voluntarily going to Donovan.

"I live to exceed expectations. What can I say?" It was my attempt to be cute, but without any "cute" behind it, the attempt failed miserably.

"You sure you want to be here? You don't have to stay."

"I'm sure." I pulled my hair over my shoulder and tugged at the end, letting my answer sit to be sure I was sure. Luckily Nate was good with silence.

I'd napped fitfully. While I'd slept dream-free the night before, my morning rest had been filled with nightmares of a faceless man standing behind me, his hand on my throat. I'd awoken wanting Donovan with an intensity that I couldn't begin to examine. Not just because he'd always been my go-to balm for these situations, but also because I hadn't begun to truly imagine that we were over. It hadn't settled in the deepest parts of me, the parts of me that seemed to need him most.

"If you're trying to prove something to him, I think he already knows."

I pulled my gaze from the silver and blue metal floor sculpture that I'd been absentmindedly staring at.

"What did Donovan tell you?" I was surprised he'd said anything. Donovan never talked to the guys about his personal life, it seemed. And Nate rarely butted in, though I had a feeling he was aware of much more than he let on.

He dropped his arms and looked out the window instead of at me. "Not a lot, but enough. I hope it doesn't embarrass you. He told me there was an assault attempt. That the man's in custody. That you had a frightening encounter."

That hadn't been what I'd been expecting either.

Why I thought Donovan might've talked about *us* instead of my near rape, I had no idea.

"It was pretty terrible. But, horrible as this is to say, it's not my first rodeo." I already knew from experience that what had happened with Theo would take a long time to deal with. I didn't know how long it would take to deal with what happened with Donovan.

I wasn't sure it was possible to fully recover from either.

It was a terrible thing to say though, to Nate. Most people had a hard time knowing what to say in times like this. I didn't need to make it harder for him.

"Does that make this time better or worse?" He surprised me by appearing truly interested in my response.

I didn't have to think about it. "It just makes this time the next time."

He nodded without judgment, without opinion. As though he understood that there were things that happened in the world and some of them were fine and some of them were not fine, and living was what happened in between.

"Last time I *did* stay home all day," I admitted, remembering how I'd stayed in bed for two whole days after Theo's first assault. "And this time I wanted to try out the distraction of work."

"Work is good for getting your mind off... a lot of things." His pause was loaded with baggage, and for the first time since I'd entered his office, I thought to look beyond my own burdens and notice someone else's. Nate had circles under his own eyes and worry lines in his forehead. He had something on his mind too.

"Why, Nate Sinclair. You sound like a man who has a woman under his skin." It was strange how discovering someone else's romantic woes could suddenly lighten your own.

He rubbed his hand over his face. "Is that why I can never really get her out of my mind? Because she's under my skin?"

I totally knew how he felt.

"For me, he's in my veins." I didn't need to say his name for us to know who *he* was. "So it doesn't matter what I'm thinking about, because he's still coursing through my blood. Even when he thinks he's walked away."

Nate stretched his legs out in front of him and crossed his arms over his chest. He understood me. Better than he should, maybe. "I thought you and Donovan were making it work together."

"I thought so too."

"Well, aren't we a sad mopey pair?"

I narrowed my eyes. With Nate's David Beckham looks and his broody artist personality, I had a feeling he was a chick magnet. No one complained about men like him being mopey.

Women in my position, on the other hand, were supposed to be strong and steel. Bitches.

I was feeling bitchy, but not strong. Not steel. "I imagine I'm pretty impossible to be around right now."

"I don't know. You seem like good company to me."

I laughed, which was nice. It felt good to laugh. "You're a fellow moper, though. I don't think you are a good judge of company right now."

"Perhaps not." He drew his legs in and sat forward. "But I'll tell you what—I haven't given up. And neither have you."

My burst of humor was short-lived. I was somber again. I wasn't sure what *he* had to not give up on, but I knew about myself. "Actually, I think maybe I have this time."

"Nope," he insisted. "Want to know how I know?"

"Sure." I was humoring him.

"You came into work today."

I THOUGHT about what Nate said for the rest of the day. Maybe he was talking broader than I'd thought. Maybe he didn't mean I hadn't given up on Donovan. Maybe he meant I hadn't given up on life, and that's why I got out of bed and faced the world.

But even if that wasn't what he meant, he'd put the thought in my mind that he was talking about Donovan. And then I wondered if that was really why I'd forced myself to come in. Because I wanted to see him. Or be near him. Or just feel his presence. And every time someone came to my door, every time there was motion outside the glass, I sat up, hopeful.

But Donovan never came down the hall. He never called or passed by, and eventually I darkened the glass so I could focus on my tasks instead of wondering whether or not my ex-boyfriend meant it when he said it was over.

By the end of the day, I'd given up on him altogether.

It was quiet, and employees left me alone until Roxie came in and said goodbye at five. She made me promise not to stay too late, and I vowed that I would finish what I was working on and then close down for the night. She'd been my only interruption all afternoon, so when there was another knock right after on the doorframe, I expected she'd forgotten something.

But when I looked up, it was *him*.

I wasn't prepared.

I was never prepared, and seeing him at my door—at *Weston's* door—asking for entrance, something so out of character, was like seeing him for the first time after a decade all over again. It felt like he was trying to prove we couldn't possibly have a personal relationship, one that would allow him to make assumptions or just walk in. Jesus, he couldn't even allow himself to be my boss. Couldn't exert authority over me. He had to knock like we had nothing between us.

Yet we had *something*.

The mere sight of him sparked a chain reaction of the things he did to the inside of me—the stomach drop, the heart race, the butterflies. *Ah, the butterflies.* Those reactions were strong and sudden and dramatic—the kind of intense reactions expected after being apart from someone you love for several years, and not several hours.

Did I not spark anything similar in him?

"Can I come in?" he asked, and if he were a vampire I still would've said yes knowingly.

But I couldn't look directly at him as he walked past me to stare out the windows. Not until he was behind me, facing away, could I look. He had his hands in his pockets and his stance was wide. He wore my favorite three-piece bespoke gray suit. It fit him like he'd been sewn into it. The fantasies I'd had with him wearing that suit. With him taking off that suit...

Would I ever stop being turned on by this man?

Would it ever stop hurting to be near him?

"I meant it when I said you look good in this office," he said his back still to me. "I can go back to Tokyo and you could have mine. Operations isn't your thing, I know. Weston isn't attached to marketing, though. You could shuffle duties between you."

My heart had already been broken. Now he was just stomping on the pieces.

I wouldn't cry. I refused. "Is that what you're planning to do?" Somehow I managed to sound ambivalent.

He turned to look directly at me. "No. I'm not."

And now I didn't know what to feel. Was he playing games? And if he was, why on earth was I surprised? He'd always been good at that, slinging me back and forth and back and forth.

I opened my mouth to scream or yell or tell him to stop once and for all, goddammit. Tell him to go to fucking Tokyo at this point. I'd hurt less without him here to yank me around.

But he cut me off before I even started, his own anger more impossible to contain than mine. "Do you know why I waited to come out and help you that first night?"

"At The Keep?"

"Yes. Then."

He'd taken his time before rescuing me from Theo. Long enough to notice what was happening and then fully lace up his boots. I'd always figured he couldn't decide if he really wanted to get involved. Theo, nasty as he was, still had a better pedigree than I did. He was the "right" kind of person, and Donovan had no loyalty to me. I had always understood Donovan's hesitation.

Now he was suggesting there was more reason than that?

I shook my head.

"Because you were the one who was supposed to save *me*." He let that settle on me like a heavy chain around my neck. "Don't you get it? I was never good enough for you. All the days I spent in that classroom with you, you never saw me, and I just knew that if you did, you'd be able to fix everything that was wrong inside me. But you never looked up.

"And then there you were outside my door. Then outside my window. And it was *you* who needed someone. You who needed help, and I knew that once I played that role for you, there would be no turning back. You would never see me any other way, so I waited before coming down there. Waited for someone else to help you. Waited until it was almost too late."

He paused, making sure I understood exactly how he'd struggled.

And I did. Somehow, I did.

"You saw me then," he went on. "But it wasn't how I'd wanted to be seen. I wasn't a hero. I didn't want to be your demon, but that was more accurate. The way you looked at me after that night—like you didn't know if you wanted me to fuck you or forget you—I didn't know what to do with that. What could I do with that?"

His voice was harsh and raw and his words impassioned, and I had no answer for him. Nothing to give him for this burden he'd been carrying for so long, nothing to offer in exchange for this weight that he was finally laying in front of me except to listen.

He crossed in front of the desk, his hands still safely in his pockets. "So I tried to be your hero, Sabrina. I tried to give you everything you needed. Tried to take care of you. I wanted to keep you from everyone I thought would do you harm, and that included *me*. Because I knew I could hurt you. I wanted to, even. You can't imagine the contradiction of wanting to hurt you and wanting to save you at the same time. Rescuing you from the frying pan meant throwing you into the fire. From Theo to me. But I was never supposed to save you, Sabrina. It's your name that means 'savior.' *You* were supposed to save *me*."

He suddenly became clear, like the signal from a radio station when the interference was removed. I could see him, and he was in focus and I understood him and I understood everything that had happened between us. He'd been so alone and desperate after Amanda's death, and he'd found me. And all I'd seen was the sun. All I'd seen was Weston, while Donovan had waited for me to find him in the dark. Waited for me to save him.

And, man, did I know what that was like, because when I finally saw Donovan, I thought he was the one who could save *me*.

And then he did.

And wasn't that what people did for each other?

I had a feeling Donovan's intent with his confession was to make me see how impossible everything was between us. But it did just the opposite.

"I guess I thought we could save each other," I told him.

His eyes widened, like he hadn't been expecting that. Like I'd caught him off-guard, which was hard to do with him.

He chuckled even—he was so surprised. "You always were smarter than me."

I would have made a big deal about his compliment because

he rarely gave me credit for my brains, but I didn't give a flying fuck about what he thought about my IQ at the moment.

I *did* care about what it meant that he'd said it, and I sat up, wary. Hopeful.

"I don't want to love you from afar, Sabrina." He stood in front of me, naked, vulnerable, and I was already lost to him. "I've done that already, and it's not enough anymore. And I've fucked up. But no one else can love you like I can up close. No one."

Of all the things he'd ever offered me, it was the first time he'd only offered himself. It was the only thing I'd ever wanted from him, really.

"I know," I said, and my voice caught.

"You do?"

"Of course I do." I pushed aside my laptop and climbed across the desk because it was the fastest way to him. "Who else is going to love me like you do?" I rubbed the palm of my hand across the scruff of his cheek, and he closed his eyes, sighing into my touch. "This isn't how everyone wants to be loved. But it's how I want to be loved. I love the way you love me."

He opened his eyes and brushed a strand of hair out of my face before planting his hand on the side of my neck. "The way I love you brought a rapist into your house," he said, with both worry and apology.

"And the way you love me brought you there to save me in time. Both last night and ten years ago."

His mouth opened slightly, and I brought my thumb up to trace along his lower lip, silencing whatever regret he meant to share next.

"We can't look back and say 'what if this happened' or 'what if this didn't,'" I said. "We've both lived long enough to know that sometimes the good is anchored to the bad, and if we changed a single detail, who knows if we'd be here now? I want to be here. Now."

"I tossed and turned on the sofa last night." *So he* had *stayed.* I should have known he wouldn't leave me alone. "Knowing you were just in the other room, wishing I knew how to say exactly that."

"You don't have to *know.* That was my point. You just have to *try.*" My knees were going numb from kneeling on the hardwood of the desk, but I didn't care.

"This is me trying." He brushed his knuckles across my cheekbone, and when he did, his fingers were trembling. "I'm going to fuck it up sometimes."

"Just fuck it up *with* me, not on your own anymore." But I didn't want to talk about failures, because we were always going to fail. That was a given. And maybe—together—we wouldn't fail sometimes too.

"I can do that." His mouth hovered over mine, but he had yet to kiss me.

"I love you so much I don't know how to keep it all inside of me."

"Even though I'm controlling and interfering and frequently cross boundaries?" His lips grazed mine, and I wondered how he'd ever managed not to light me on fire with his kisses before this. I was kerosene. I was waiting to be destroyed.

"Do you even know the *meaning* of the word boundaries?" I teased.

The smile he gave seemed almost like a shrug. "You're moving in with me. I decided already." He wrapped his arm around my ass and pulled me tighter against his body. "I can't stand thinking about you in another building after last night. I need you close to me, where I can keep you safe." Finally, he kissed me, likely trying to stifle any objection I might have.

I didn't actually have any objections. Mostly because I was still stunned by the declaration in the first place.

I pushed off him gently. "Are you...serious?"

"Completely. Except that wasn't exactly the whole truth." He paused, watching for my reaction. "I want you with me to keep you safe, yes, but also because I want you in every part of my world. I want it to be *our* world."

"I always wanted to be in your world," I said, nodding. I was saying yes.

"Sabrina, you *are* my world." He studied my face, his hazel eyes warmer than I'd ever seen them.

He kissed me again, tender and brief, but it was powerful in its simplicity, like the single square a pawn moved when it finished its journey across the board and was crowned queen.

"Come on. Let's get out of here before I'm tempted to give Weston another show." He lifted me off the desk and set me on the floor. "The movers should be at my place with your things soon anyway."

"Movers? At your place?" I smoothed my skirt as I sorted out his words in my dizzy love-struck head.

Wait.

I froze, comprehension settling in. "Did you already have movers packing up my apartment?"

He looked mildly guilty. "Is there a wrong answer here?"

I'd just told him I would accept him and how he did things. But surely he hadn't moved me in with him without my permission. Had he?

Wasn't I kind of hoping that he had?

"The only wrong answer is an untrue one," I said honestly.

"Then, yes. I've had movers packing since shortly after you left to come to work. I didn't tell you until now in case you were planning to argue about it. I thought it was better the office was empty for that so we could have proper makeup sex when you were done." He gave me his best devilish grin, and if it wasn't a *purposeful* test, it was a test all the same.

And it wasn't even hard to pass. Because I was only a little bit irritated, and even that was only because I thought I should be.

Mostly I was happy. Completely, overwhelmingly happy.

"You were that sure you were going to win me over?" I asked, teasing him. I reached behind me to shut my laptop, and turned back to where he was waiting.

"If I didn't, I was going to kidnap you."

Damn, he'd make a sexy kidnapper. There would be ropes and blindfolds. I could imagine all the ways he'd violate me...

"Can we pretend that's what happened?"

"You're such a dirty girl." His tone was filled with mischief. He reached his hand out toward me.

"And you're such a filthy man." I put my hand in his, and it fit, exactly. "I guess we're perfect together."

EPILOGUE

NINE MONTHS LATER

SHE'S tight as my finger pushes inside her. Tight and hot and soaking wet.

"Donovan," she scolds, pressing her thighs together, as if that will keep me out. Her cheeks flush and beneath the thin cotton of her sundress, her nipples turn into hard beads. She glances up at our driver in the front seat, but I think she'd rather find he's looking than that he's not.

Her pink tongue flicks along her bottom lip and her lids have fluttered closed as I rub against the wall of her pussy.

Fuck, I want to suck on that tongue. Then I want to wrench her hands behind her back and shove her to her knees in front of me and make her use that tongue on my cock.

"How am I supposed to finish looking over Tom's report when you distract me like this?" Her hands are shaking as they continue to try to hold the tablet up.

"Do you want me to stop?" I *should* stop. We only have ten minutes or so before we'll arrive at Pinnacle House, which is not nearly enough time to satiate either of our needs. I shouldn't have even started this. But I'm antsy. Eager. And it's always hard to keep my hands off her.

"No!" She grows more coy. "I mean, your hand is already down there." She spreads her thighs, making room for me to explore, sighing as I do.

"Put down the iPad," I coax, nibbling along her jawline. "We're on vacation now. Tom has things covered at the office."

She mumbles something that I assume is acquiescence since she drops the tablet and succumbs to my ministrations.

It's different to love her like this.

Near her. In her space.

It's not harder, but it's not easier. It's different.

I can no longer move pieces on a board without feeling the consequence of their shift. Before, I could send her to LA. I could give her a new job. I could deliver her an opportunity. And then I could sit back in my chair with a cigar and a drink and feel good about the decisions I had made. For her.

There was no living in those moments with her. I was an emperor who ruled her, and though I was pleased when she yielded, though it fulfilled me, my love for her wasn't directly attached to her.

But now, there are times she sits next to me, and I can feel her breathe. Or when she's trying to work out a problem, she gets moody and short and her words are brusque and I feel the brunt of her agitation. I never felt those details when I loved her from afar. Then when she figures out her solution, her glow is nuclear. She could solve a small country's energy crisis with that fucking smile.

These are all details I never got to know before. They are precious. The touch of her hair, the smell of her, the feel of her skin. How her body feels when it bucks against mine. The sounds she makes when she laughs, when she cries, when she's mad. When she comes. Her heartbeat as it drums against my fingers when I run them along her neck. The weight of her in my arms. The taste of her mouth, of her cunt. The way she's sometimes fragile and sometimes strong and sometimes both at once.

She rarely surprises me. I learned her in that decade, like a man studying for the final exam that comes before a dream job. She is my dream, and now I'm living. *With* her.

Which is somehow a whole hell of a lot better than living *for* her, and that was pretty incredible already.

I manage to bring her to climax just as we turn down the driveway of my parents' country house. Good. She's relaxed. Soft and affectionate. I adore her like this. She always seems so pure and vulnerable when she's just come, and it makes me want to treat her very, very badly. I want to fuck her in fifty filthy ways.

I'm uncomfortably hard thinking about it.

But it will have to wait.

We've visited my parents a few times in the nine months since our first visit together here. She was right when she said I'd never tried with them. Nothing can make up for the relationship we had when I was growing up, but I'm an adult now. I can accept responsibility for my part going forward. I can't say that we've grown close, but we're definitely closer. We talk about mundane things—business, the weather. Scientific advancements. Safe topics. My mother, it turns out, is very fond of Italy, and enjoys talking to Sabrina about her heritage. It's not much. But it's a start.

They are roots that Sabrina and I have begun to plant. It's exciting. Different. Not what I ever imagined for us, but I'm only looking forward now.

Especially after today.

Today.

I can't believe it's happening.

I'm suddenly nervous as the car stops in front of the house. My knee bounces with wound-up energy, and Sabrina notices.

"Make a beeline for the bedroom, and I'll take care of you," she whispers as we climb out of the car, thinking my agitation is due to my raging hard-on.

"Let's go into the front room," I say, trying to remain vague so I don't give any of my plans away.

"Oooh. This sounds exciting." The blush in her cheeks says she's thinking I have something dirty in mind.

She's going to be surprised. Pleasantly surprised, I hope.

She walks into the house ahead of me, greeting Edward as she enters, then strolls into the front room. I don't have to wait for her to notice the crowd outside. The windows are large and the back-yard is the main focal point. They're impossible to miss as they mill about drinking champagne and punch, and talking in the late summer afternoon sun.

"Is there a party going on?" she asks innocently. She scans the scene more closely as I walk up tentatively behind her, and I can feel it when she realizes. Her breath catches audibly. It's obvious. The chairs are set up in rows facing an archway decorated in flowers. All our friends are in the yard—Weston and Elizabeth, Nathan and his girlfriend, Trish. Some employees from work have been invited. Roxie is here with Frank and Tom Burns has brought his wife. Dylan flew in from London, but, since he's such a Scrooge about love, and because he can't stop sneaking glances at Audrey, I gather she's the real reason he's here.

And if nothing else gives it away, it's her presence that must. Sabrina's sister wouldn't be here if this was anything else.

My girl—the love of my life—turns to me, visibly trembling. "Donovan...?" Even her voice is shaking.

I've already pulled the ring out of my pocket where it's been burning against my hip the whole ride up. "I'm not asking you," I say, stepping toward her. "That's not how we do things."

Her eyes are tearing up despite the smile that won't budge from her gorgeous lips. "That's okay. I have a safe word."

She does. And that's why I knew I could do this—could pull off a surprise wedding without ever having talked about marriage and know it wasn't a huge mistake.

Still, I'll give her the chance to call this off. "Are you going to use it?"

I hold my breath even as I begin to slip the platinum diamond ring on her finger. I'm not wrong about thinking she wants this—I know I'm not—but I've been wrong before.

"No," she says softly, and I can tell she's too choked up to say anything else.

"Most men want to hear the word 'yes' when they're slipping a ring on a woman's finger." I slide the band past her knuckle and into place, and then bring her hand up my mouth to kiss her palm.

A tear falls down her cheek. "Thank God you aren't most men."

"Thank fucking God." I pull her to me and kiss the hell out of her. There's a hair technician and a makeup artist waiting upstairs for her as well as several wedding dresses for her to choose from. Audrey will come in to help her sister get ready. Weston brought a tux for me and I'll need to change as well. Our guests haven't been waiting long, but they'll grow antsy soon, so we need to get hustling.

But not right now.

Right now, I'm kissing her. I'm holding her. I'm loving her. These aren't moments to be rushed. These are the moments I want to live in.

WESTON AND ELIZABETH have a story of their own. Book one in their duet, Dirty Sexy Player, is available for preorder now.

FIXED FOREVER

FIXED #5

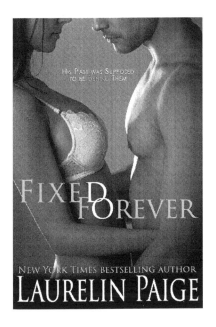

His past was supposed to be behind them.

June 25, 2018

Preorder now

DID YOU KNOW...

This book is available in both paperback and audiobook editions at all major online retailers! Links are on my website, laurelin-paige.com.

If you'd like to order a paperback with a cover that looks like the ebook version you've just read, my signed paperback store is open several times a year on my website as well.

ALSO BY LAURELIN PAIGE

First and Last

First Touch

Last Kiss

Written with Kayti McGee under the name Laurelin McGee

Hot Alphas

Miss Match

Love Struck

Written with Sierra Simone

Porn Star

Hot Cop

ABOUT LAURELIN PAIGE

With over 1 million books sold, Laurelin Paige is the NY Times, Wall Street Journal, and USA Today Bestselling Author of the Fixed Trilogy. She's a sucker for a good romance and gets giddy anytime there's kissing, much to the embarrassment of her three daughters. Her husband doesn't seem to complain, however. When she isn't reading or writing sexy stories, she's probably singing, watching Game of Thrones and the Walking Dead, or dreaming of Michael Fassbender. She's also a proud member of Mensa International though she doesn't do anything with the organization except use it as material for her bio.

www.laurelinpaige.com
laurelinpaigeauthor@gmail.com

ACKNOWLEDGMENTS

Many books are hard to birth for different reasons. Dirty Filthy Rich Love was not hard because the story blocked me in any way, but because my body did. First, emergency gallbladder surgery then a broken arm, both causing major delays in the writing of this book. Eventually, I had to learn a completely new way to get my words down on screen, and now I can say I have discovered the world of dictation—a world that has literally changed my writing life.

So my first thank you have to go to everyone who helped me through this learning curve (more like baptism through fire)—Anthony Colletti, Lauren Blakely, Nana Malone, Dragon Rider's group, and most of all, Kayti McGee. If it weren't for Kayti, who read through each of my dictated words and turned all the fake words into real words, I'd still be curled up in my bed crying right now. Thank you to each of you who helped me learn Dragon. Without you, Donovan and Sabrina would not have an ending.

Next to my earliest readers and my support team, Sierra Simone, Roxie Madar, Ashley Lindemann, Candi Kane and Melissa Gaston. Each of you were personal cheerleaders and moral support at a very painfully depressing time. As well as reading my words, you listened to me moan and kvetch and pretended the world revolved around me. I leaned on you know so very, very much. You can't know how much you were my life-lines. (Ashley—Scorpio J forever.)

To Liz Berry for reading and encouraging me and for the best conversations of the summer and the softest blanket I've ever owned. The healing angel you sent is not quite as lovely as you, but I feel your love when I look at her.

To my Snatches and the best retreat—Camp Snatch. Melanie Harlow your lake is magic. I see why you've set so many stories there. I hope you know we're coming back every year.

To Rebecca Friedman my agent and best friend who lives too far away. To Flavia Viotti and Meire Dias for being the best foreign agents and the best women in the industry.

To Andi Arndt for producing such amazing audio recordings. I could listen to your Sabrina all day long. Sigh. I'm so glad we're working together!

To Christine Reiss who came to (not) see the eclipse with me —you're just fucking amazing and I never get tired of your brain.

To Jenn Watson my ever-friend. I will never not love talking shop with you.

To the Fab Four and the ShopTalkers and The Order— women might not rule the world, but they rule MY world. You're all the best people to know, and I know you. Lucky me.

To my LARCs—God, you guys are amazing!—and the Sky Launchers. You're all the best readers a girl could ask for. And to the bloggers and the readers who love these books and share them with others—I'm amazed by you and grateful every day.

To my family who saves me from this world and to my God who saves me from myself. You're beautiful. You make me beautiful. We're going to be just fine.

23858602R00167

Printed in Great Britain
by Amazon